KING CAL

By Peter McDade

TROUSER PRESS BOOKS

King Cal © 2025 Peter McDade

All rights reserved. No part of this book may be reproduced or stored in a retrieval system or transmitted in any form or by any means — electronic, mechanical, photocopying, recording or otherwise — without the express written permission of the publisher.

Cover and interiors designed by Kristina Juzaitis / February First Design

ISBN 979-8-9898283-7-1
Library of Congress Control Number 2024950355

Published by Trouser Press Books
Brooklyn, New York
First printing March 2025

AM 2

www.trouserpressbooks.com
facebook.com/trouserpressbooks
E-mail: books@trouserpress.com
www.trouserpress.com

Clarissa spent most of her life thinking about some one thing or another.
—Virginia Woolf, *Mrs. Dalloway*

THURSDAY, JUNE 15
12:35 a.m.

Calvin stands in the parking lot behind the Variety Playhouse, watching Melli's car drive away. Aside from some scattered trash and the lingering odor of stale beer in the air, he is all alone.

He remains standing in place even after she is out of sight, hoping her Honda will magically reappear. In the movies, just when all hope seems lost for our hero, the fates intervene and reward him with a happy ending. But Calvin's life is not a movie. She really left without him. He wonders if this means she broke up with him. As impossible as that is to imagine, as much as his brain cannot even begin to think about the end of his first real romantic relationship, he has a more immediate problem. He doesn't have any other ride home, the buses have stopped running, he's broke and he used the last of his Uber gift card to get here.

The world is suddenly very quiet. After the noise of the show and the crowded dressing room and all the talking afterward, it feels weird to be standing in so much silence.

He takes out his phone. No notifications from Melli or Grady. Just missed messages from his brother Alex and the time in big, unrelenting numbers: 12:39. He has to be at work in less than five hours, a realization that makes him suddenly desperate to sit down. In one night he's managed to lose his band and his girlfriend, and it turns out fighting with people you love drains you emotionally and physically.

The coffee shop next to the Variety Playhouse has outdoor furniture, so he heads there. Everything is tied down with heavy-duty chains, but he can still squeeze onto a wobbly metal chair. It feels right to be chained in place. Looking for someone to blame for the sudden implosion of his two most important relationships, he settles on his parents. To say that he and Alex never had role models for How to Be a Couple is to say that potato chips are addictive, that dropping acid and heading to Six Flags in July is a bad idea. Twenty-two, and he can't remember ever seeing either of his parents look happy when they were in the same room. What he *can* remember is Alex asking — the two of them on the couch eating frozen dinners at five o'clock — why Mom and Dad couldn't be more like Bert and Ernie. "Good question" was the best answer he could think of. Maybe he shouldn't be surprised Melli broke up with him after a year; maybe he *should* be surprised that he managed to keep the relationship alive for that long.

He stares onto Euclid Avenue. Across the street, a drunk couple loudly debates whether to go back to the Yacht Club. He wants to go home but she wants just one more and doesn't want to fucking leave. They keep taking a few steps in each direction and backtracking, repeating the same angry phrases. Calvin places his phone on the table and then leans his head down as well, ignoring the sticky spot that greets his hair. All he wants to do now is not move for a few minutes. Or forever.

WEDNESDAY, JUNE 14
6:00 a.m.

There's always one waiting. Lights on, engine idling. Sometimes ten minutes early, sometimes five. Calvin studies this morning's first car through the closed-circuit monitor above the register, wondering what the driver is thinking about: trying to understand how their life has gotten to the point of being willing to waste some of their finite time sitting in a car, waiting for the Burger Buddies reader board to light up? Or are they really just thinking they're hungry, and this is the first place they found open, a modern hunter-gatherer waiting for a rabbit to hop into view? Even if he is ready early, Cal refuses to take that first order until the computer clock hits 6:00. There are rules in this universe that cannot be ignored. "WelcometoBurger-BuddiesmayItakeyourorder."

It used to be two sentences, or at least a long sentence with a comma in the middle, but it now comes out as a single word. In theory it's a question, but Calvin stopped bothering to phrase it like that a long time ago. The people in their cars never listen anyway; on days when he was feeling especially rebellious, he spoke in gibberish, and the unseen customer always responded as if nothing was wrong. Everyone knows their role at the drive-thru, and everyone wants to think as little as possible while playing that role.

KING CAL

Today's first order comes through slurred and rushed. Maybe because it's six a.m., or maybe the guy is stoned or drunk, or maybe Calvin is so tired everything is going to sound fuzzy all day. After two-plus years and thousands of orders his brain can still understand just fine: "Sausagebiscuitnomakeittwoandacokeabigcoke."

(Thousands of orders? Really? The accusatory inner voice that has haunted him since puberty, ready to pounce on any possible misstatement, lives on inside his head. But yes, after more than two years of working here full-time, it has to be thousands. That makes taking orders at Burger Buddies one of the things he has done the most in life, up there with days wasted in school and hours playing piano.)

Calvin gives the total and walks to the drink station. Pulls a large cup out of the dispenser on the wall, fills it with Coke, sets it on the counter and slides open the window. A red Volvo erratically stop-starts its way down the lane. When it finally arrives, window open and Pearl Jam blaring, the driver appears to be softly crying. Middle-aged; Buddy Holly glasses too small for his head; rumpled button-down shirt hanging loosely off his skinny frame. Oh, Sad Pearl Jam fan. You relate that much to poor Jeremy, or you just having a crappy day already? Two sausage biscuits are gonna make things better? A thousand calories gonna straighten things out for you?

Calvin hands Pearl Jam his Coke, takes a credit card, swipes and returns it, avoiding eye contact the whole time — not out of politeness, just a desire to not start the day by watching a stranger cry for any longer than he must. At least it's something else he can add to his list of Things Seen in the Drive-Thru: couples fighting; couples making out; several men without pants; naked babies; more Confederate flags than he would have expected, even in Stone Mountain; more joints and open bottles than he could count. This is the fifth or sixth person he's seen crying, but the first adult man.

Calvin's been working the morning shift for over a year, opening up with Little Ron and Annie. Breakfast is slow enough that the three of them can manage until more people start clocking in at ten, though sometimes there's a rush of customers that requires Big Ron, the morning manager, to reluctantly emerge from the safety of the back office. Annie, who runs the dining room register, has to be pushing fifty but her husband left her for their oldest daughter's best friend, so she's probably stuck at the job until she can retire — which seems like it's never going to happen. Calvin's done the math: how much money Annie could possibly be saving towards what she would need to survive, even in some tiny crappy apartment, divided by how many more years she's likely to live. Little Ron looks to be around the same age, and while Calvin would never put up with being called "Little," Ron seems like someone who spends his life avoiding any potential conflict.

He pops open a paper bag and heads down to the breakfast board to wait for Little Ron to make Sad Volvo's biscuits. *Crying alone in my Volvo, crying in front of someone I don't know.* The lines slide into his head; he puts them on repeat in his brain, slowing down and speeding up the syllables to see if the idea might fit on top of the music he wrote last night. *How did I wind up here?* Luckily, the music playing in the background at Burger Buddies does not interfere with the music in his head. It's the kind of generic classic stuff usually heard in elevators, aside from one terrible month when they tried Top 40. Sales went down, and bland strings, easily ignored, returned.

"Sausage biscuits ready to roll," Little Ron calls out, much too enthusiastically for six a.m. "That's how you do it!"

Calvin wants to lean in close to Ron at moments like this, close enough to tell him, in a whisper no one else can hear, how ridiculous it is for a middle-aged man to be that self-satisfied at his ability to slice open two biscuits, stick a piece of sausage in the middle of each, and wrap them both up in thirty seconds. Instead, he says "Thank you" loudly, as if he means it, because the only thing worse than over-excited Little Ron is the Little Ron who gets sad because he feels unappreciated.

Calvin stuffs a napkin in the bag and hands it through the window. Sad Volvo, who has stopped crying at least, takes the bag and then just stares at it. Calvin has a flash of fear, imagining the guy turning to tell him some awful secret (my wife left me my mom died my kids hate me I don't like who I am). But, after a moment, Sad Volvo shakes his head as if to wake himself, tosses the Burger Buddies bag onto the passenger seat — already cluttered with bags from Hardee's and Wendy's and who knows where else — and loudly sucks some snot up into his nose before pulling away.

The drive-thru timer indicates the car sat at the window for fifty-seven seconds.

The time on the register: 6:02.

Only seven hours and fifty-eight minutes left until he clocks out.

Crying alone in my Volvo, even sadder because you'll never know. My wife left me, my kids hate me, and I can't remember who I am.

As is often the case, there's a gap between that first order of the morning and the next, giving Calvin time to pour himself another cup of coffee. He should be able to use hours of sleep last night less than the recommended eight (five) and multiply it by some variable x to figure out how much coffee he will need to make it until two o'clock. If only he'd paid attention in math class. Then again, he clocked in at 5:30 and this is already his second cup, so he doesn't need algebra to know the amount will be large today.

This is one of those days where he doesn't mind feeling tired, though. If the exhaustion is because he was up late working on music and the results were satisfying, a pleasant buzz carries him the next morning. When a song comes to him like it did last night, determined to push its way out of his brain and into the world, he has to follow whatever path it creates. Even an idea for the vocal melody fell into place, and it usually takes a few days of living with the music for that to happen.

And now there's an MP3 waiting on his phone, so he's got some-

6:00 AM

thing to look forward to. Having some music he is working on to listen to on his break can make the morning almost—

"WelcometoBurgerBuddiesmayItakeyourorder."

The screaming toddler should make it impossible to hear, but Calvin can filter the sound out; it's just like mixing one track lower than another to bury it in the background of a song. Taking the frazzled mother's order as he moves imaginary faders in his brain, he decides to add "Tune out crying babies" to his growing list of Things He Never Imagined Learning How to Do:

1. Hold conversations with two different customers at the same time: one idling at the drive-thru window, making some complaint or asking for seventeen packets of ketchup or deciding at the last minute that, well, actually, they wanted bacon instead of sausage on that biscuit; the other in his headphones, slowly reading every item on the menu board aloud, as if this is the first time they've ever even seen a Burger Buddies. "Double Buddy? Is that, like, two little sandwiches on top of each other?"

2. Tell when the hash browns are ready to come out of the fryer from the change in the sound of the bubbling oil.

3. Show up on time. He learned early on that the best way to survive a crappy job is to do it well enough that you set the terms of engagement. Consistently showing up when he was supposed to moved him into the top ten percent of employees.

(Not that it came easily. The first nineteen years of his life he'd been late for everything, from school to important family gatherings. It drove his father crazy — he never forgave Calvin for being born at 12:02 a.m. on January 1. Three minutes earlier, and he'd have been a tax write-off for the previous year. Whenever he was late, his father would sigh, shake his head and lament the way his son was never on time for anything, even his own life.)

4. Embrace routine. Accept and appreciate the way routine makes survival possible.

(Not everywhere, but certainly at work. It probably would have

KING CAL

helped him get through school, too, if he'd been smart enough to figure it out. Doing the same thing every day allowed him to let his brain think about anything but where he was.)

    5. Tune out crying babies.

6:45 a.m.

Not long after Minivan With Screaming Brat, there's one of those unexpected customer surges. It's normally closer to 7:30 before the big morning rush, so no one is quite ready to kick into a higher gear. Little Ron keeps dropping biscuits and saying, "Hello, Wednesday! Hello, Wednesday!" and even Annie looks flustered by the steady stream of dining room customers.

Big Ron finally comes out of the office to see what is happening. As usual, management attempts to solve problems wind up creating more of them. He should go to the sandwich board and help Little Ron, who has trouble keeping up even with a small rush, but instead he tries to fill orders for Annie and Calvin. Orders can't be filled faster than the food is made, but managers will do anything they can to avoid actually touching the food, much preferring to just demand the employees somehow break the laws of physics and make sandwiches instantly appear. Calvin has a soft spot for Big Ron, though, this pear-shaped man who only seems at peace when watching video clips on ESPN.

Calvin suspects he's the only employee happy to see all these customers. The more tired he is, the more helpful it is for the restaurant to be busy; the soundtrack in his head shifts from ambient Brian

KING CAL

Eno to early Clash. Taking one order as he's bagging another speeds up time, and the clock hand moves from seven to eight much faster than it would have otherwise.

Mixed in with the morning rush there's a handful of regulars. Calvin assigned a couple of these business dudes their own numbers so they wouldn't have to repeat the same order; he had no idea how funny they would find it. The large guy in a tiny red Kia was especially pleased, and at 7:45 — same as every weekday, plus or minus five minutes — he shouts "Number 4" into the speaker, giggling. Calvin can never decide if Red Kia is the kind of guy who takes joy in everything, or if he leads such an uneventful life that being given a number by the drive-thru cashier is a cause for celebration.

"My man." Red Kia passes his credit card. "How's it going?"

"Hey hey, another day in paradise," Calvin says.

"What's up with all these other cars?"

"Right? I tried to clear them out before you arrived." He swipes the card and hands it back, unable to avoid a large yawn, a sudden wave of exhaustion washing through his body.

"Late night, huh?" Red Kia says with a knowing grin. "Believe it or not, I remember being young enough to stay up partying and still get to work."

Calvin nods, one young party animal to another, instead of explaining that he was alone in his room all night writing a song. It's much easier this way, and it helps him maintain a clear line between Real Calvin, who will someday only play music full-time, and Burger Buddies Calvin, who wears a ridiculous outfit and stands at a little window passing out bags of—

"Ham egg and cheese up! Take that, Wednesday!"

—ridiculous food.

He hands Kia his croissant, accepts the traditional fist bump and returns to that list of Things He Never Imagined Learning How to Do.

6. Bond with lonely businessmen.

7. Pretend to take ketchup seriously, even though he still thinks it insane, the time and energy spent talking about something he finds inedible: complaints about the number of packets received, instructions about the amount that should top a burger, sober edicts from management about when it should be given out (only upon request, one per each item that could possibly use ketchup. Kendall had fun with that last one: "I do like it on my pie, sir. Can I give a packet for each pie ordered?")

8. Speaking of Kendall: Become good friends with a Black guy from a small town in Alabama.

("I'm your first Black friend, right?"

"Wait, we're friends?"

"Fuck you. Just say I'm your first." Hand held up to cut off objection. "And no, Sly Stone, Hendrix, Prince — they don't count."

"So, they weren't my friends?")

The phone in his pocket buzzes during the rush, but even when he has time to check, he doesn't. His brother doesn't message this early in the day, so it's probably Melli, and he likes to save her messages for his break, a reward for having made it through the first half of his shift. It could also be Grady. It was early for someone in a touring band to be awake, but maybe he'd been up all night, playing video games and watching movies the way bands did when they had enough fans to travel on a bus. Four weeks, Grady had promised. He would go on tour with One Four Three, a local jam band that was having some inexplicable success, for a month. Make some money, make some connections, then come home so he and Calvin could get back to working on their own music.

That was four months ago.

Tonight will be the first time Calvin has seen Grady since he left, so they can finally talk in person, instead of by text, and work out a timeline—

"WelcometoBurgerBuddiesmayItakeyourorder."

—for getting back to The Plan.

The Plan had been one of Calvin's greatest achievements, one of the few things in his life that worked exactly the way he wanted it to. It had been put on pause when Grady took the gig with One Four Three, but hopefully that will be over soon.

They met in eighth grade. Calvin's parents both moved after the divorce, dumping him into a new middle school. It was actually a relief, to start over. No one knew about the countless mistakes he'd made in gym class that cost his team a victory that, for some reason, mattered to the other kids, or the way he preferred to stay inside during recess to read and talk with his teachers.

The new school was bigger, allowing Clean Slate Calvin to disappear into the throngs of teens crowding the hallways, and that was fine by him. The less he spoke, the lower the odds of saying the wrong thing. The back-and-forth of conversation baffled him; it seemed like some skill everyone else must have learned while he was daydreaming. How did people know when it was their turn to say something? When was it OK to interrupt someone, and when was it not? He eventually figured out that he needed to listen to people talk for a while before he had a sense of their individual rhythm, which told him when he could answer.

That's why he'd first noticed Grady: Grady seemed to know how to talk to anyone.

One day at recess, not long after Christmas break, he was standing close enough to Grady and his usual posse of four or five other mid-level dudes to hear them talking about forming a band. Music was one thing that did make sense to Calvin, the only thing that made living in either his mother's or father's place bearable — listening to it loud, in his headphones, and, for the last three years, making it himself. He was amazed in fifth grade when his parents did exactly what he wanted them to, combining their Christmas and birthday spending to get him a keyboard. Even got him the exact one he asked for. "Not paying for any lessons," his father added, but Calvin hadn't wanted any lessons. He had more fun watching YouTube tutorials and figuring things out on his own.

So, when he heard Grady pointing to people and asking what they'd play, he wandered closer to their circle. Too close. This time he was noticed.

"What about you?" Grady asked, looking at Calvin.

"Who the fuck is that?" asked someone else.

"It's Kevin. He's in my homeroom."

Later, Calvin would be proud of himself for not walking away after receiving so much attention. Not only did he stay, he corrected Grady. "Calvin."

Grady shot Calvin a look he would see a lot over the years — that stare that let you know he heard what you said but was still convinced he was right. "Calvin? You sure?"

"Uh, yeah, man. I've known myself my whole life. My name is Calvin."

Grady laughed. "I guess that's fair enough. So?"

"So what?"

"What does Kevin-Calvin play?"

"Keyboards," he said. "What about you?"

"Guitar."

Calvin nodded. They were talking about music, so he felt less stressed than he normally would talking to someone he didn't know. He decided to risk bantering. "And do you, like, really play? Or just say you play because you want to?"

"Kevin-Calvin with the tough questions," Grady said, nodding as if in appreciation. "Not for long, but I really play."

"So, you own a guitar?"

"Of course. I mean, my brother does." He shrugged. "What about you? Do you actually own a keyboard?"

The two of them spent the rest of recess talking about music they were into and what kind of band they'd want to create. The other guys Grady had been talking to slowly drifted away, and it turned out none of them owned any of the instruments they said they "played." Grady seemed bummed when he found out, but none of them had talked about music the way Calvin and Grady did, so Calvin suspected they were all bluffing. A big band could have been a cool thing, but also would have meant more people to deal with, and Calvin was worried enough about dealing with one. By the time the day ended, he'd become so excited by the idea of actually having someone else to make music with that he worked up the nerve to track down Grady in the hallway after school.

"There are lots of bands with just two people," he'd said, as if their previous conversation had never stopped. Grady had proclaimed that bands couldn't work with just two people, and Calvin had spent the rest of the day working up a counterargument. "White Stripes, Black Keys, Twenty One Pilots—"

"Yeah, but those are all guitar and drums. Guitar and keyboards is pretty impossible to make work."

"Nah." Calvin worked hard to mimic the chill tone he heard so many of Grady's friends use, trying not to make it obvious how much this meant to him. A day earlier he hadn't imagined ever being in a band, ever, but once the possibility emerged, however faint, he suddenly couldn't bear any more time passing without making it happen. "I can create plenty of loops to play along with. I mean, Twenty One Pilots have layers and layers of loops and shit. And, hey," he continued, thinking of an indie band his younger sister had just played for him, "the Generationals? That's just two guys with keyboards and guitar."

"The who?"

"Generationals. From New Orleans."

Grady pulled out his phone, pulled up Spotify and searched for them. "I'll check them out," he said, moving toward the buses. Calvin turned in the other direction, since he walked home, and cued up some Generationals himself. It was the first time he'd suggested music to anyone besides his sister Alice and he suddenly worried that he'd made a terrible mistake. If talking to other people meant you doubted yourself so much your stomach hurt, he wondered if it was worth it.

The next morning put that fear to the rest. Grady found him before school even started, wanting to talk about particular tracks he liked and to get Calvin's phone number so they could set up a time for their first practice. "I wanted to text you about this last night, but, like, no one I asked had your info. You some sort of narc or something?"

"I prefer the term 'undercover operative,'" Calvin said, texting Grady his info. "If you share this with anyone, you know, I'll have to kill you."

After a few weeks of sending each other songs that might work, Grady showed up one Saturday with his guitar. Calvin would have preferred to go to Grady's house, which he imagined was more normal than his mother and stepfather's Lysoled prison. He couldn't think of how to get there, though — it was too far to bike, especially with his keyboard and amp, and he couldn't imagine any of the four "adults" in his life being willing to drive him. So, he picked a day when his mother and stepfather would both be at work and prayed one of them didn't get home early and scare Grady off.

Alice, who hadn't yet asked Calvin to call her Alex, could not hide her disbelief when Grady walked through the front door. "Wait, you're here to see Calvin? My Calvin?"

"Yeah, of course. You must be Alice."

"And he even told you I exist?" She stared at Grady skeptically. "You sure? That would mean you're almost, like, friends or something."

"Goodbye, Alice," Calvin said, quickly steering Grady toward his room. He was hyper-aware of how nervous he was as they set up, his voice cracking more than once as he talked too much and too quickly. He had spent hours learning the songs they'd planned for this practice — one pick each — but was still worried Grady would think he wasn't good enough.

Grady's choice was "Karma Police." Calvin loved Radiohead and had figured that one out on his own months ago. After a lot of internal debate about whether to play it safe and choose an early Beatles song or another Britpop classic, maybe something by Blur, Calvin ambitiously picked "Blank Space." It was a song he'd studied closely, a mechanic looking under the hood to see how something could sound so smooth and perfectly arranged. Grady groaned at the idea of Taylor Swift, but after he'd listened to it, he conceded it was indeed a great pop song. Calvin's biggest worry, as they tested the vocal mic and edged closer to actually starting to play, was that they wouldn't be able to pull it off. Or, more specifically, that *he* wouldn't.

"Do you mind if I take a crack at singing first?" Grady asked.

Calvin shrugged. "Sure." The truth was that was just what he had hoped Grady would say. It had always made more sense to Calvin for Grady to sing. Lead singers needed to have that strut of confidence. The moment Chrissie Hynde, Prince or Taylor Swift came on stage, everyone in the building knew exactly who was in charge.

He was hoping they'd begin with "Karma," but Grady was adamant that they begin their musical career with Taylor: "It'll be a much better story, years from now, when people ask what our first song was." As soon as Calvin hit play on the drum loop he'd programmed, Grady clapped in delight. Calvin immediately relaxed. Unlike school, it turned out music was something he was good at. By the second time they ran through "Blank Space," it sounded like a Taylor Swift song but also like something new. Grady's voice was strong, with a unique tone that caught Calvin by surprise, in a good way. He helped Grady through some of the tricky spots and tried not to look surprised when Grady asked if something should be slower or faster, or if his guitar tone was correct. This must be what it's like, he realized, for those smart kids to walk into a class and ace a test.

The hardest part for Calvin, that first practice, was the non-playing time. When Grady suggested they take a break and get a drink, Calvin turned into the sweaty, nervous kid in some bad movie with no idea what to do. But Grady just wandered into the kitchen, chatted with Alice and settled for an apple when they explained about their stepfather's ban on all salty snacks.

The summer before high school started, Grady was over once or twice a week and, much to Calvin's surprise, he started to enjoy the breaks — the bullshitting between songs, even the hanging out with Alice — almost as much as playing music.

9:00 a.m.

When the crush of cars slows down the adrenaline burst that had kept Calvin going fades away. He drinks another large coffee while taking care of the odd mix of late-morning customers: stray moms stealing a secret snack, college kids smelling of weed grabbing hash browns on their way to class, pain-in-the-ass construction workers needing a half-dozen sugars for their coffees and extra salt packets for everything.

All alone in my Volvo, nothing outside my window.

He stares out the drive-thru window. The contrast between the clear blue sky and the landscape of fast-food places and strip malls stretching out as far as he can see feels especially stark this morning. Who would have guessed that, after all those days spent driving around after school with Grady and his older brother Ken, complaining about their small town and dreaming of a closer place to get a burger and fries, he would wind up surrounded by fast food and end each work day shrink-wrapped in the smell of grease?

All alone in my Volvo, where did all my words go?

"WelcometoBurgerBuddiesmayItakeyourorder."

"Large coffee, two creams, please."

"You got it," he says. The woman's specificity pleases him; if only

9:00 AM

everyone would just tell him exactly what they need instead of just asking for "some" of something and being unhappy with the amount he gives them.

Calvin is working on a list of other parts of life that would benefit from people being more specific — teachers and parents, for example, in terms of expectations; friends who clearly define what they need and when they need it, instead of trying to make you guess — when a yellow Beetle pulls up to the window. A smiling, older woman is behind the wheel, three enormous baskets of flowers on the passenger seat. Is she on her way to a wedding? Some sort of Uber for flowers? The woman stretches her arm out toward him, far enough so that he doesn't have to strain to take the credit card. After he returns it and hands her the coffee, he flashes a thumbs-up.

"I'm awarding you customer of the day," he says. "Bonus points for clear language and not making me climb out the window to reach you."

Flower Lady winks at him and gives a little honk as she drives away. The whole exchange took less than thirty seconds, and she never said a word. Everything is so much easier when people just do what they're supposed to do.

All alone with what I don't know, wondering what to do / I wish someone would just let me know / How to get back to you.

None of the lyrics he worked on this morning sound particularly great, but playing with the words helps calm his other thoughts. He takes out a washcloth and starts to slow-walk wiping down the counter, trying different combinations of syllables and sounds, hoping to look just busy enough no one asks him to do anything else.

It used to exhaust him, spending so much time with the overactive thoughts that bounced around inside his head. In eleventh grade he started writing his own music, though, and could distract himself by trying to organize the chaos into lyrics.

When he and Grady first began playing together, they had focused on copying the songs they covered, getting as close as they could with just a keyboard, guitar and programmed drums. Once they developed a system to do that, they started trying to screw up the originals, so they would sound like different songs. Then that started to get dull, so Calvin decided to figure out how to start a song from scratch.

He quickly learned that he could not just sit down at the piano and piss out cool melodies. Finding a starting point was the hardest part — his fingers would hover over the keyboard, unable to decide which notes to strike. It worked better for him to make a drum loop first. The ideal pattern was one complicated enough to create a foundation he could build on, but not so busy that it was hard to find guitar or keyboard parts that worked. When he could just feel the rhythm of the loop, imagine it running musical circles in the background, he would start to play something on top of it. Sometimes a riff, sometimes chords. Sometimes he kept the initial drum loop, but sometimes he swapped out that first drum machine pattern for a new one or programmed something more complicated. Or just took out the drums altogether — sometimes the answer was found in empty space.

It would cause him literal pain to ever admit it out loud, but that stage of the process reminded him of Phil, the awful high school football coach his mother married. One Saturday, when Phil was hanging shelves in their garage and Calvin was trying to sleep, he'd insisted Calvin help him, because at twelve it was "time a boy start to do a man's work." Calvin wanted to make a joke about watching too many old movies when he heard the phrase, but he shuffled out to the garage anyway, knowing Phil would take it out on his mother if Calvin resisted. Phil never hit her, but he shouted at everyone as if they were teenage football players.

Why had his mother married another shouter, anyway?

That day in the garage, Phil made a big deal of how you needed to take your time, measure the spots on the wall where the hooks for the shelving would go and mark them with a pencil. Calvin was so clueless about anything handyman-related he was surprised a neat freak like Phil — the kind of guy who went around and straightened the silverware after Calvin set the table — would write on his precious walls. But when the shelves were up, the marks disappeared.

That's how it was sometimes with loops. They helped Calvin to know where to hang shit, then they disappeared.

Once he had a final piece of music he liked — a chord sequence over the original loop, maybe with a riff, maybe a longer sequence of chords and riffs that had moved far away from the original drum pattern — he'd save the file and start the process all over again. He stockpiled these fragments, which ranged from fifteen seconds to a minute, and gave them names to help him remember what they sounded like: "Slow circus thing," or "Vegas Ramones," or "Drunk Wilco."

Eventually he would assemble songs from those files. He would find a few with similar tempos and place them in different sequences, adjust tempos so they matched, see what the combination sounded like, shift some of the pieces around. Repeat. It could take hours of arranging and rearranging. Sometimes all that work revealed a new section of music that needed to be written and recorded, or drum loops that needed to be changed. Other times the map of the song revealed itself quickly, as if it had always existed and just needed to be heard.

He explained the method to Grady after school one day, when he'd finally written something worth sharing. He thought about just sending the MP3 to avoid being in the same room as Grady listened, but then he couldn't bear how hard it would be to wait to hear back. And, knowing Grady, it could be a while before he remembered to open the file, never mind listen to it.

Calvin picked a day that he was at his mother's to play him the song. She and Phil both had jobs that would keep them out until eight or nine, which meant Calvin and Grady could split a joint before listening. Grady was less manic when he was stoned, and, if he didn't like it, Calvin could just blame bad weed.

"So, I've been writing some songs," he said casually, when they'd burned through their joint.

"No shit," Grady said, opening a bag of Lay's. "Since when?"

"Couple of months." Calvin grabbed a handful of chips and explained the way he did it, with the loops and piecing together of files. He didn't think Grady would care all that much about the process, but it was one way to stall.

"That sounds complicated, man. Doesn't it take, like, forever?"

"Sometimes. Sometimes a little less than forever."

"But you can barely sit through class without going nuts."

"That's different. That's school. This is. . . " He shrugged, unable to explain any further. "This is just what I do. What I want to do."

"Well, OK, Calvin with the secret superpower. Play me one."

Calvin set up some headphones with the splitter they used to listen to music together loudly without making his mom or Phil angry. As soon as the song started, two things allowed him to exhale. First, Grady was the perfect audience — he and Calvin had been listening to the same stuff for years, and even if they didn't agree on everything, each could usually see the value in something the other liked. Second, the song was good. Maybe even really good.

When it ended, Grady just smiled and hit play again, not saying anything until after the second listen.

"I can't believe you wrote that. Like, just made that shit up."

Calvin raised his eyebrows. Now that it seemed Grady at least liked the song, he could banter again. "Doubted my abilities?"

"No, but for just starting to do this? I didn't think it would sound so, like, finished." Grady paused to eat some chips. "It's got some of that Radiohead beepy stuff, but the groove feels less . . . tense. Like, if someone less weird than Radiohead was playing it. Does that make sense?"

"Yeah," said Calvin, trying to be casual about how happy that description made him.

9:00 AM

"And I love that little keyboard lick between the verses."

"Thanks." Calvin had hoped Grady would notice that part.

"There are no vocals, though."

"Not yet. I mean, you're the singer, right?"

Grady smiled. "Yeah, but what am I going to sing? Have you figured out a vocal melody yet? Written the words?"

Calvin had thought about trying, but the house was so small, there was no way for him to be sure no one would hear him. And he would have to know what to sing. "I don't think I can do that part."

"Why not?"

"I don't know. Whenever I tried to imagine a vocal line, it seems like it would get in the way, or something. And you know words aren't exactly my thing."

"Why don't I try?"

Calvin nodded. From Zeppelin to Radiohead, lead singers had usually written most of the lyrics. He sat on his bed and pretended to do homework while Grady sprawled out on the floor and started jotting down some words. After an hour of listening to the song on repeat, Grady groaned and threw the pen across the room. "This is a lot harder than writing a term paper."

Calvin tried not to look too disappointed. "It's not like it needs to be written right now. Sometimes it takes a while to hear the right part."

"Oh, I hear the part," Grady said. "I know what the words should sound like. I just have no idea what they should be."

"What do you mean?"

"Like, I can hear the sound and rhythm of the words. I can hear the notes they should be. But not the words."

"Huh. OK." Calvin had learned it sometimes took a while for the music to come into focus, so he suggested Grady just sing some "bas" and "dahs" for the melody. "You know, like David Byrne talks about doing. Worry about the specific words later."

That worked. An hour later Grady had recorded two melodies,

and after he left Calvin mixed the best parts of each together. Grady kept texting to see if he was done, and offered to do Calvin's math homework so he could finish the song. The result was even better than Calvin had expected — Grady's voice seemed to know just when to shadow the melody lines of the keyboard or guitar, and just when to go off in its own direction. He made a new mix and sent it to Grady, who responded with the kind of excited emojis and exclamation points that he mocked others for using.

we have a fkn song but it needs some fkn wordzzzz!!, he texted.
so write em
no good i tried
ur the one always fkn talking
just do this first one so we can finish!

Calvin knew Grady well enough to see this was one of those times he was going to be stubborn. He was also excited to hear the song finished, so he decided to give it a shot, and only tell Grady if he found something that worked.

He paced his room with his headphones on, listening four or five times before he decided to start typing in his Notes app. Halfway through the first chorus he hit stop, and started matching syllables to sounds, not letting himself think about it too much. "Open me up," Calvin wrote, Grady's melody in his head, "and look inside of me." He cued up the start of the chorus again, and after being happy with the first half, he listened to the second. The words suddenly sounded like they'd been there the whole time but hiding. "I want to know what is inside of me." Walking in a circle, ignoring the dirty socks and empty chip bags he was stepping on, he edited the phrases as they repeated in his head. Saying "inside" twice didn't really work, having "is" right before "inside" could be hard to sing, and "want" didn't feel desperate enough. "Open me up and tell me what you see," he mumbled, when he felt like he was closer. "I need to know what's left inside of me."

Once he had the chorus, the verses came pretty easily. He liked the way Grady's melody moved between shorter and longer lines, and he was surprised at how satisfied he was when he was done. When he wrote the words out, he put in a few timestamps to show how everything fit together, but Grady was able to sing along the first time they played it back, pacing Calvin's room and grinning.

"I knew you could do it," Grady said. "Never any doubt."

"Oh, plenty of doubt. But I just, like, listened to your melody and stopped thinking. And that worked."

"Good plan. Thinking sucks."

"Tell me about it." Calvin paused. "So, the lyrics are OK?"

"Dude, they're perfect. Even if I don't know what they mean."

"You don't know what they mean?"

"Nope. 'Open me up and tell me what you see / I need to know what's left inside of me'? What's up with that?"

Calvin opened his mouth to answer, then he realized he wasn't sure, either. He laughed, feeling like he was stoned. "I'm not even sure. It's just, like. . ." He paused. "It's like, it's hard to find the other words to explain what the words mean? If that makes sense?"

"Sort of? But remember, I couldn't find any words to work. You did."

"Only after you found the melody."

Grady stared at the lyric sheet. "But it has a mood, right? I should know what the mood is when I record it, I think."

"Fair, fair." Calvin closed his eyes, trying to remember what writing the words had felt like. "I guess the verses," he started, "are almost a little, like, sad, that something is gone?"

"I can see that. The verses seem like they could be about you and Alice. Maybe?"

"Huh." Calvin opened his eyes. That hadn't occurred to him, but it made sense.

"But the choruses are more, like angry? Sort of Calvin pissed off at the world?"

"I think you got it," Calvin said, learning a key lesson about song-

KING CAL

writing. He would try to trust himself, trust there were meanings buried in a song that even the writer might not see at first.

Grady nailed it in two takes. With a finished vocal track, "Open Me Up," the first official Lords of the Living original, was complete. Grady was tired of it by the time they moved to Atlanta, but Calvin liked to have it in the set and usually lobbied to open with it. It was the song that showed they were both needed for the band, that they both had roles to play, and that together they could make powerful new sounds appear.

9:30 a.m.

At 9:30 Little Ron takes his break, marking the start of what is usually the slowest part of Calvin's shift. As nice as it is to have fewer customers to deal with, time stops moving when things are too quiet and that gives his body a chance to complain. Standing on this hard floor makes his knees ache, it feels like he fucked up some muscle in his neck last night while he slept and four hours into his shift the polyester shirt clings to his back, glued in place by the grease that moves from the air to his clothes. It's a perfect time to practice the art of cleaning slowly, to spend long minutes wiping down the counter displays, those cartoon drawings of a burger and a bag of fries, each with creepy arms and legs, hand in hand and skipping through the air. *We Make Good Food & We Make Good Friends!*

Remembering how ridiculous this universe is keeps him from taking it too seriously.

Ideally, Calvin would luxuriate in this stretch of silence, carefully cataloging his aches and dreaming of a long, hot shower after work, but Annie loves to chat when things slow down, talking nonstop while they deal with occasional orders and stock up for the lunch rush. Her questions used to make Calvin nervous: where was he from and why did he move to Stone Mountain and really, a musician? that's interesting what does he play and does he have a girlfriend and why not with those pretty green eyes and how did he wind up at a Burger Buddies of all places? Over time, he came to understand that Annie just wanted to know everything about everyone; after he heard about her husband running away with one of her daughter's friends, it made sense. Maybe she wished she'd asked more questions before. Maybe she was worried she was missing other things she should know about.

Or it's less complicated than that, and Annie is just lonely. She must miss her own kid, who, rumor has it, sided with the asshole father. Calvin tells Annie as little about his own family as he can, though. Talking about his parents or step-parents honestly would just inspire pity, and how depressing would that be? He could talk about Alex, but if he slipped and referred to an old memory of Alice, the conversation would get complicated. It's hard for him to know if Annie would shrug it off or be freaked out, but, more importantly, he doesn't think Alex would like Calvin talking about something so personal with this woman at Burger Buddies he doesn't even know. It's much easier to talk about *Jeopardy!* or *Wheel of Fortune*, two shows Annie watches every night.

"Those 'Before and After' puzzles on *Wheel*, they drive you as crazy as they drive me?"

All alone in my Volvo, don't know how to get home.

"I mean, it's better than the 'Thing' category, right? I mean, that could literally be, like, anything?"

"Which show would you rather be a contestant on?" she asks, helping him stock up napkins and straws. "Gotta be *Wheel*, right? Those questions on *Jeopardy*? I swear, how's a body supposed to keep all that information in their head?"

"My father loved *Jeopardy!*, though," says Calvin.

"Ah, so you wanna go on and make him proud?" Annie smiles. "That is sweet."

"Not really," Calvin says, smooshing the napkins to squeeze a few more into the holder. As full as it is, it will still need be reloaded halfway through the lunch rush. "I wanna go and do well and prove he was wrong about me." He's answering without any filter, something he is prone to do when tired, but he's glad he said it — it's not like his father has earned any protection from the truth.

"Oh, you," Annie says after a brief pause. She looks into the dining room, where a woman and two grumpy-looking toddlers are walking in. She needs to get back to the sandwich board. "I can never tell when you're joking and when you're being serious! You had me for a minute there."

It felt good to be honest with Annie, but he didn't need to tell her any more — didn't need to talk about the volume his father could generate when angry, the way the sound, as deep as any bass track, still rumbles in Calvin's head or the way his mother would taunt his father, trying to get more of that anger out, a trebly tease: "Oh, come on, you can do better than that, can't you? Louder? Can't you break something at least, you piece of shit?"

He and Alice had always seemed to be some sort of annoyance to his parents, pawns on the chessboard to be sacrificed quickly so the adults could take out their frustrations on each other. More than once he wondered, as he listened to his mother and father debate just whose turn it was to tend to toddler Alice, why they'd had a second kid at all. It didn't take Alice long to figure out she should just go to Calvin for whatever she wanted, and he learned that meeting the relatively easy needs of the very young can be rewarding. Find her a snack, hand her the iPad, fix whatever doll had been twisted in some unnatural fashion, and she looked at him like he had grabbed hold of the sun with his bare hands. When he tried to look for upsides to his childhood, he listed that as one: His parents were so uninterested in raising their kids that he and Alice wound up being very close.

His mother and father finally worked up the energy to get a divorce when he was twelve and Alice was six. After spending years fighting over who would have to deal with the kids, his parents immediately launched a nuclear war over who "got to have" them at what times, with charts and calendars and days broken into hours, to make sure everything was split evenly: weeks during the school year, summer vacation, holidays. Calvin couldn't believe what he was hearing, listening to the two of them talk about how important family time was.

The school therapist he was forced to see tried her best to pitch it as a good thing. "Both your parents want you," she said, working on her Soft and Caring Eyes schtick from behind her thick glasses. "Isn't that great?"

He shrugged, then offered a half-hearted, "Sure." He knew that was bullshit, but he just wanted the sessions to end as soon as possible. The real reason both parents wanted time with them was just the same old competition. Instead of fighting over whose turn it was to get stuck with the kids, they started fighting over who got more hours each week.

Calvin and Alice never stopped moving. They left for school from their father's on Wednesdays but went home to their mother's. Sunday morning, back to their father's. For parents who paid their lawyers a lot of money to make the schedule, neither one seemed all that happy to see Alice and Calvin. Their mother usually hadn't bothered to wash the sheets or stock up on food, though things improved when Phil moved in. Their father was inevitably still sleeping when they showed up, but he usually remembered to leave the apartment door unlocked, and sometimes even had cereal for them. He married Dottie less than a year after the divorce, and she would be waiting for them. Although they worked up some cruel impersonations of her eagerness ("Look who's heeeeeeere"), Calvin secretly thought it was nice to have someone notice they had arrived.

Two homes, two groups of neighborhood kids to try and figure out. Well, one and a half groups of kids — his mother's neighborhood was either older women or families with babies who couldn't even

9:30 AM

walk yet, and she didn't care if they ever went outside. Meanwhile, their father complained about how child support payments had forced him to move into an apartment. He usually ended those rants with an order that Calvin take his sister to get some fresh air.

The first time that he and Alice went outside, it only took a few seconds for a half-dozen kids to surround them on the street. The leader, who was old enough to harbor a ridiculous fauxstache under his nose, acted like he had superpowers. As Calvin tried to act like he didn't give a shit, he took one look at them and grinned. "Mom's place or Dad's?"

"Dad's."

Stache nodded. "Week at a time?"

"Switch on Wednesday and Sunday."

A small girl from the back said, "Tuesday and Saturday here. Sucks balls."

"But hey, two rooms, right?" Stache said. "Twice the shit!"

Two rooms, two rooms: everyone always talked like that was a great thing, but Calvin hated it. He wanted one room. One room that was his, where everything he wanted would be, so he wouldn't forget where he'd put that book he was supposed to read for English, where he wouldn't have to be constantly adjusting to different pillows. Instead, he had two rooms, neither of which ever felt right.

Stache and the gang rode away, probably having figured out that Calvin and Alice were not eager to join in the random bike and scooter riding that passed for entertainment on Willow Lane. So, when their father kicked them outside, Calvin would walk Alice down to the Quiki Mart two blocks away. They had to pass houses with broken windows and the sketchy laundromat full of people who never seemed to be washing clothes. He'd distract her with impersonations of his teachers, hoping she wouldn't see how nervous he was and use money he'd saved from not always buying lunch to get them a candy bar and a drink to split. Then they'd walk to the bench that used to serve as a bus stop but now seemed to be a bed for one of the homeless guys and play "Better or Worse."

"French toast versus waffles?"

"Better."

"French toast versus pancakes?"

"Worse."

"PE versus Art."

"Come on. PE versus anything is worse."

"Mom's versus Dad's."

"Better."

"Agreed," Alice would say. "She doesn't make us go outside."

Stache's real name was Jim. He never became anything like a friend, but he did become Calvin's best weed connection in high school. And, when he was stoned, Calvin could run the table in many a *Jeopardy!* category.

10:00 a.m.

Kendall clocks in at ten o'clock sharp and walks over to Calvin. "You've earned a break, amigo," he says, putting on his headset. "Go get yourself some of this high-class cuisine."

Calvin had planned to avoid becoming friends with any of his co-workers, another way to protect Real Calvin from the grease-soaked walls of Burger Buddies. Thank God, Kendall had somehow ruined that plan. He must have decided his job description included talking to everyone, even the weird white kid who never said much. He may have been the only employee shorter and skinnier than Calvin, but his confidence was impossible to miss.

Kendall had started with the worst job in the restaurant, same as everyone else. Working the broiler meant standing in front of an invisible wall of greasy heat, placing frozen burgers on a conveyor belt that rolled the patties over a steady flame. The smell of cooked beef saturated your polyester uniform, where it would live until you washed your uniform — and sometimes even that was not enough. The sweating began immediately, and if the heat didn't drive you crazy and you didn't burn your hands on the bursts of fire generated by the droplets of fat, then the timing would get you. It was impossible for whoever was running the broiler to avoid getting berated at least once a shift. When things were slow, you got yelled at if you cooked too many patties ahead of time. When the lunch rush arrived, there was no way to keep up with the demand, since the machine only moved so fast, so you got yelled at for that.

On his third day of long broiler shifts, Kendall came to grab a drink from the drive-thru fountain. Hair damp from the steam and smelling of grease, Kendall looked around Calvin's lair, with its open window and relative isolation, and grinned. "I think I need to come help you here," he said. "This is clearly the place to be."

They'd only exchanged a few words, but he'd heard Kendall's nice Marvin Gaye echo when Little Ron shouted "What's going on?" one day, which seemed like an encouraging sign. "Plenty of room," Calvin had answered.

Kendall took a swig of Coke, topped off his cup and nodded firmly, as if concluding complicated negotiations. "Give me a few days, and we'll start running this show together."

Calvin smiled but also thought that unlikely. He'd been there long enough to notice Black male workers rarely got moved to the front of the restaurant. It wasn't right, but Calvin didn't know what he could do to fix it. Speak up and risk being sent back to the broiler himself? His strategy was to keep his head low, cash his check and stay liked enough to get nights and weekends off, which was crucial for the band.

But when Kendall clocked in that next Monday, he headed to the drive-thru, held his hand out so Calvin could give him five and then pointed to the order ticket Calvin was holding. "So, you keep a copy, and then give me a copy, right?"

"Right," Calvin said, handing Kendall the yellow slip. "But first you have to tell me how you pulled this off."

"Oh, Big Ron has a big crush on me," Kendall said with a smile.

"Really?" Calvin has never imagined Big Ron having any sort of romantic feelings for anyone. Ever. Even for the wife he occasionally mentioned.

"What, I'm not crushable?"

"No." As would often be the case, Calvin felt like he was moving at a slower conversational pace than Kendall. Was Kendall gay, or just pretending to be, so he could get ahead at work? Was Big Ron gay? "It's just. I mean, he's married, right? To a woman?"

"Uh, yeah. So that's why he wants a piece of this."

"Has he ever—"

"No, no. I wouldn't put up with that. It's all in his eyes, 'cause it's all in his head. That's what makes it harmless." Kendall grinned. "But it did come in handy when I mentioned, you know, being curious in how things worked up front. And let him know the broiler steam was messing with my complexion."

"Oh."

Calvin's tone must have given away how confusing he found that strategy. Kendall shot him a look of disbelief. "How small was this town in Florida, anyway?"

"So small there's only one supermarket," he said. "Though, like a lot more bars than that. Maybe a thousand people actually live there?"

"A thousand? That's smaller than my high school."

"And that's why I had to get out of there." He wondered what Kendall would think of Mayo, named after a Confederate general. If Kendall had been born there, they probably would not have become friends. The racism wasn't as open as it must have been fifty years ago, but it was still thick in the air — sort of like the way the grease floated through the air in Burger Buddies.

Later on, Calvin would learn just how very straight Kendall was, thanks to lots of stories about multiple girlfriends, all of whom he seemed to tire of quickly. Kendall and his stories became a crucial part of the routine that got Calvin through the day. Those stories, most of which were about his crazy, younger siblings and his loving, if intense, parents, helped the slow stretches move more quickly, even as they also made it clear the two of them did not have much in common. After Kendall clocked out, he went home, changed and spent several hours Ubering. He used the same car his father drove during the day, his income crucial to keeping the family he clearly adored afloat. What the two of them did have in common, besides being around the same age, was a love of music. A pop-culture obsessive, Kendall clued Calvin in to a few musicians he'd never have heard of otherwise and soaked up hearing about the "dead white rockers" and "emo dudes making music with their laptops" that Calvin liked. They even exchanged numbers, so they could send each other flares if they had a musical tip to share.

It turned out to be helpful to have one person who also saw things as they were, another inmate who understood that screaming about french fries or the amount of ice in cups of soda was something to quietly laugh about, not something to get stressed about. Like Calvin, Kendall combined a perfectly caustic attitude about all things Burger Buddies with efficiency. Don't take the job seriously, ever, but also do it well enough that no one hassles you. Because the only thing worse than working at Burger Buddies is working at Burger Buddies and having to listen to lectures about how you could be a better worker.

10:03 a.m.

"Go on, get the hell out of here," Kendall says, shooing Calvin away. "So you can come back with that refreshed glow."

Calvin realizes he's been standing at the register, just staring into space. "Is it a refreshed glow? Or is it just, like, the oil seeping out through my pores?"

"Is there a difference?"

He makes himself an egg biscuit, fills a cup with Coke and goes out to the parking lot. It's been his break routine since day one. Thirty minutes in his car — away from the smell of grease, away from the sound of his co-workers — makes surviving the rest of the day possible. It's also the perfect time to listen to whatever he'd recorded or mixed the night before.

When Calvin gets out to his car, he connects his phone to the stereo and cues up the rough mix of the song he worked on last night. The dominant sound so far is the acoustic guitar; when he finally went to sleep he planned on adding keyboards, but listening now, tuning out as much of the rest of the world as he can, he thinks it should just be acoustic for the whole first verse. Maybe some weird synth stuff in the second verse, gradually building up the layers? He's just humming a version of the vocal melody, and while his voice sounds uncertain and tired, he can hear how well it might work.

He sets the song to play on loop and starts eating his "food." Nothing from Burger Buddies has any taste for him anymore, which at least makes it easier to swallow. He thinks of it like astronaut food, eaten to keep people alive in space — not for taste.

Space/Taste: an interesting rhyme. *There is no space for taste.* Awful as a lyric, but maybe a slogan for a new, much more honest Burger Buddies ad campaign.

Calvin shuts his eyes and leans back in the car seat, trying to keep the wall between what he wants to ignore and what he can't stop thinking from crumbling under the weight of exhaustion. He tries distracting himself with the Sad Pearl Jam Fan lyrics, but he's not sure there's anything there beyond a funny title. The song he wrote last night needs words, though, so he tries hitting a reset button so his thoughts can follow a new trail. There are so many trails that he has trouble focusing.

There's too much in my head today, too much for my words to say.

Not bad, maybe even an OK start, but it makes him think of an old Kinks song. At least he's stealing from a good writer. That's something Grady was always telling him, that everyone steals ideas from everyone else. The best artists steal from people worth stealing from. Maybe switch the order? *My words don't know what to say / there's too much in my head today.* Still close to that Kinks line, but better.

Too many words running in my head / Hiding so they'll stay unsaid.

As much as he resisted writing words for Grady's melodies at first, he's glad Grady never asked to take that role on, because converting some of the crowded thoughts in his head into lyrics relieves some of the pressure. Having a reason to focus all those jumbled words into shorter phrases is good for Calvin. Maybe Grady somehow sensed that. Grady read people much better than Calvin could, and after all their years hanging out, Grady could read Calvin very well. More than once he did something Calvin didn't want him to do, but it usually turned out to be something that helped Calvin.

And if Grady hadn't played their songs for his brother, even though Calvin had told him not to, they might not have made it to Atlanta at all.

He and Grady started hanging out with Grady's older brother Ken when they were freshmen and he was a junior. He would be the first person, besides Grady, to make Calvin believe he should spend his life writing music.

They caught rides with Ken to Gainesville. It was an hour away but had a great used record store. They'd hunt for vinyl and get music tips from Ken, who had been playing guitar since he could walk. When Grady and Calvin started writing their own songs, Grady kept asking to play them for Ken, but Calvin kept saying they weren't "ready" yet. In truth, he was so impressed by Ken's musical knowledge he was terrified about what Ken would think.

So, of course, Grady played stuff for Ken, anyway. Calvin found out after one of their record store runs. He'd helped Ken hunt for Stevie Wonder on vinyl; when he found a copy of *Innervisions* misfiled (under S for Stevie — *really*?), Ken was so grateful he bought Calvin the record just behind Stevie's, an album by someone named Elliott Smith that Ken was sure Calvin would love. They decided to celebrate by going back to Grady and Ken's house to listen, while enjoying some especially good weed Ken had been saving for a special occasion.

By the time they were halfway through Side Two, Grady was asleep, which was not unusual when he got stoned. It was weird for Calvin to be basically alone with Ken, but having Stevie on in the background helped. Ken also tended to ramble when he was stoned, and he had a lot to say about the last two songs on *Innervisions*, and the way they interacted, and the pros and cons of ending an album with a song that fades out.

Ken stood up when the record ended, and carefully slid the vinyl back in its sleeve. Then he pointed to the Elliott Smith record on the ground next to Calvin. "Let's play that one now."

"Yeah, great," Calvin said, handing it to him. "Thanks again for getting it for me, man."

Ken was in full music professor mode. "This might sound like kind of a weird move at first, from Stevie to Elliott, but they actually have a lot in common," he said. "The singer-songwriter thing, yeah, but these are also two guys who played just about everything on the record."

"Everything? That was Stevie on drums?"

"Stevie on drums, man. I love his weird-ass drumming." Ken carefully lowered the needle, then sat down again, holding his finger up for silence. "We have to shut up for this first one, cause it's—"

He stopped talking as the song began, a quiet acoustic guitar being plucked. The vocal melody was nice, but as much as Calvin trusted Ken's musical tastes, he wondered if the song was a little... sleepier than he would normally listen to? As if reading Calvin's mind, Ken looked over and pointed at Calvin. The drums crashed in, and the second half of the song built on that quiet opening, with new instruments taking turns holding the melody. The volume and intensity rose and fell more in the last minute and a half of that song than Calvin would ever have imagined trying. When it was over, he turned to Ken and grinned. "That was all one guy?"

"Yep. I mean, there are some strings and some other people playing an instrument here and there, but, like, ninety percent of it is Elliott."

The next song started with another quiet acoustic. Calvin was just beginning to focus on it when Ken started talking again.

"So. Lords of the Living."

They had only recently named their band, and Calvin still wasn't sure it was right. "Uh, yeah. I mean, names are hard."

"Sure. But if the band's good, no one gives a shit about the name. If the band sucks, no one gives a shit, period."

10:03 AM

Calvin's whole body relaxed—not only because Ken didn't voice disapproval, but because he was right.

"The name's not what matters, now. What matters is, you guys could be great. I mean, do you know how good those songs are?"

They had been smoking strong weed for a while, so he had to replay Ken's words in his head, slowing them down, like he'd listen to a recording at half speed to look for a weird noise. "Those songs? What songs?"

"Your songs, dickweed."

As his brain tried to accept that Ken was really referring to the stuff Calvin and Grady had written, the next song on the Elliott Smith record was beginning. It started with a simple 3/4 beat — kick, snare, snare, kick, snare, snare — but something about the way the guitar was strummed on top of that just made it feel like more. Which must be a lesson about writing. "Our songs?"

"Yeah." Ken took a hit, inhaling slowly. "Grady played some for me. Said I wasn't supposed to let you know, because you told him not to." He exhaled, his eyes tracking the smoke as it drifted away. "'Cut me open, tell me what you see / I need to know what lives inside of me.'"

Hearing a line of his come out of Ken's mouth was so jarring he coughed.

"You should know by now Grady and I both have a hard time doing what we're told to do." He passed Calvin the joint. "Or not doing what we're told not to do."

Calvin wanted to be angry at Grady for playing Ken their songs, but he was too happy that Ken had liked them. "Thanks," he said. "I'm glad I didn't know he played them for you. I'd have been too fucking nervous to breathe."

"Need to relax, amigo. The songs are good."

Calvin took another hit, then studied the joint. "This thing is like some Jesus loaf," he said. "It never gets any smaller."

Ken took the joint from Calvin and examined it, as if looking for signs of a miracle. "All praise thee, Jesus loaf."

"All praise," Calvin repeated, in a voice so solemn that he and Ken both laughed.

"OK." Ken turned to look at Calvin, after he stopped laughing. "So, what are you going to do?"

"What do you mean?"

"I mean, what are you going to do?" Ken repeated, this time adding an extra layer of bass to the word "do."

No one had ever asked him that before. Lots of people asked what he had done, usually in angry tones, but what he was going to do? Never. "What do you mean?"

"I mean, you can write a good fucking song, and you must have good ears, because the production is already decent, too, considering the limited gear you probably have. And you're still in high school. You guys could have, like, a future."

No one had ever complimented him like that. Grady liked the songs, but Grady was Calvin's best friend and bandmate — he had to think the songs were good. And Calvin was blown away by the idea that Ken liked the way the songs sounded, too, because he felt like he was stumbling around in the dark still, when it came to mixing their music. "Thanks. But, I mean, you're the one with the future. Like, you're the best guitarist I've ever seen play, like, in person. In the real world."

"Sure, I can play OK and move my fingers fast and I'm getting a handle on my tone. But I can't write music. I've tried and tried, but I can't. You can write. You write actual songs, and they're good. That's a golden ticket, man."

"Oh." Calvin wondered if his face was really fiery red or just felt that way. "Thanks."

"And it turns out my brother can even sing," Ken added, nodding at Grady, who was still asleep.

"He can," Calvin agreed quietly. He didn't know if it was the weed, or having Ken say good things about his music, or being grateful for the existence of people as talented as Elliott Smith — talented people he didn't even know existed yet, making music he would someday have the thrill of hearing for the first time; how many more were out there? — but suddenly he was overwhelmed with gratitude for Grady, and the way he'd helped bring the songs to life.

"But what are you going to do about it? You guys need a plan."

"A plan?"

"If you don't make one, man, someone else will make it for you."

He must mean what they'd do after school. But why would Ken be talking about that already? "But we're stuck in high school for a long time."

"Not that much longer. And I guarantee your parents are already thinking about ways to plan your life. I know ours are, for Grady."

"My parents don't give a shit what I do."

Ken thought about that for a minute before nodding and laughing. "Yeah, well, you may be right there. Your parents are not like our parents."

"Lucky you."

"Yes and no, no and yes. There's something to be said for having parents who ignore you. It'll be easier for you to do your own thing — but you better know what you want that to be or the moment will be wasted. And you better help Grady come up with his plan, because my folks will certainly have ideas about what he should do."

"But we're only—"

"Sophomores, yeah. But remember, I just went through all this. Junior year is when SATs and all that shit start to happen. And my mom and dad are for sure gonna start mapping out Grady's next moves, the same way they had a list of places for me to apply. I never had any ideas of my own." He paused, shrugged. "So, it looks like I'm probably gonna wind up in Iowa or Nebraska or someplace, majoring in business."

Ken had to go pick up his girlfriend, so after he flipped the album over Calvin was alone with Side Two, depressing thoughts of Ken studying business somewhere and a sleeping Grady. The songs were just as good as they'd been on Side One, but it wasn't just the melodies that excited him — it was all the layers that had been created by just one musician. Staring at the back of the cover as he listened, he was surprised to see it was recorded before he was even born. How great would it be to make something that could last for so long? Smith would never know how much the album meant to Calvin, but all that mattered was that the music still existed. The music would always exist.

Calvin would remember a handful of moments after they finally left Florida, and this was one of them. It was the moment when he figured out what he wanted to do: make one record, just one, that would sound as good, twenty-plus years after he made it, as *XO*. And who knows, maybe something that could last as long as *Innervisions*? Even as he made that vow to himself, though, he could hear Ken's voice, warning him that if they didn't figure out what to do, someone else would figure it out for them. Now that he knew what he wanted to do, it was time to figure out how to make it happen.

The album ended with an *a cappella* song, of all things. After all the careful layers and production, the pure vocals and melody somehow sounded even more haunting, and powerful. He woke Grady up, telling him they needed to find potato chips, and then they needed to make a Plan.

10:15 a.m.

Fifteen minutes left on his break. "Food" gone.

Buzz.

Calvin adds his lunch trash to the collection on the backseat floor and swipes open his phone to check the morning's messages. Once he's done eating and erased all traces of Burger Buddies from his life for the moment, he gets to connect with his real life. He has seven messages; five are from Melli:

hey
how r u
how did u sleep
I need more ketchup man
brk? msg when u can

The other two are from Grady:

Gig was good but Florida is still so fucking Florida u never need to go back again
Load in 4 soundcheck 5 c u there

Calvin doesn't have the time for a long text thread with Grady, so he writes an answer that wraps things up for now.

Thx for the advice never going back :) c u tonite

Hits send, closes the thread, clicks on Melli's name and starts typing a response.

Didnt sleep much and work sucks but hey its halfway over.

He hits send and leaves the window open this time, hoping she'll write back quickly.

Still on break? Talk?

Calvin checks the time: 10:23. Seven minutes until he has to clock back in, but her voice will make him feel better. He pauses the music and hits call.

"Hey, you."

"Hey," he says, closing his eyes.

"Egg biscuit?"

"I've become predictable."

"That place just might make you a vegetarian yet."

"Do vegetarians eat eggs?"

"Sure. Why not?"

"Um, I hate to break this to you, but those eggs are really—"

"La la la," she says, cutting him off.

"Well, I'm not convinced we use real meat here. So, vegetarians might be OK."

Pause. "You ready for tonight?"

"It's gonna be great to see Grady, but I wish we didn't actually have to, like, see the show," Calvin says. "Watching Roddy soak in all that applause is not gonna be easy."

"We'll sit in the back and make fun of everyone, like the cool kids in high school."

"I finally get to be a cool kid."

"You've always been cool," she says. "You just needed someone cool enough to see it. Luckily, you found me."

He had found her at the first show Calvin and Grady played in Atlanta. Six months in town and they hadn't had any luck with drummers, bass players or finding a gig as a duo. One of their housemates, though, had some rich friends having a house party in Buckhead. "That's where the old money lives, boys," Downy had explained, wriggling his fingers as if in anticipation of an imminent treat. "Buckhead's got the kind of money that's got roots and branches, branches where new money starts growing just to show off."

Downy's friend wanted a live band but didn't want a "whole bunch of smelly musicians," so two guys with a keyboard and a guitar was perfect. He'd pay them two hundred bucks and as many tapas as they could eat. Downy was pretty sure there would also be plenty of booze and weed. Calvin was hesitant, since they had less than a week to work up two sets of music, but Grady convinced him it was the perfect way to launch their Atlanta career. "It's like practice but we get paid."

As soon as they started playing their first song, a cover of "West End Girls" intended to win everyone over, Calvin had to admit that, once again, his friend was right. After dealing with the chaos and stress of finding a place to live and getting jobs and trying to make recordings good enough to post online, playing to drunk gay guys who danced badly and whooped a lot felt like playing Madison Square Garden. They'd only done two other shows — a Battle of the Bands senior year, when they'd lost to a Duran Duran cover band, and a party Grady's friends threw before they left Mayo. This was their first show in Atlanta and the first time they would actually make money. Even though it was just someone's garage — albeit a fancy, three-car garage — it felt like the start of their career.

There weren't many women at the party, and most of the ones who were there were old enough to be their mothers. Melli was their age, though, with this wide-open smile, huge brown eyes and brown hair that draped over her shoulders. Even more than her natural beauty and this inner glow she seemed to have, Calvin was struck by the way she moved. She danced around the large garage with ease, arms drifting through space so gracefully that she appeared to be floating. And while she looked like she was by herself, it also looked like she was dancing with everyone else, all at once. Calvin couldn't remember being that comfortable anywhere, besides hiding behind his keyboard.

He spent the first set trying to watch Melli without it being too obvious, wishing she would come over and talk to him and Grady during the break. He was thrilled when she did and surprised to see that she was shorter than him. She had looked taller, somehow, when she was dancing. He was terrified, trying to think about what he would possibly say to her, then disappointed, if completely unsurprised and maybe even a little relieved, when she went straight for Grady.

"So that last song," she said. "How long have you had this thing with mayonnaise?"

Grady flicked his bangs out of his eyes and smiled. He'd just started letting his brown hair trail its way down his forehead, and he said he liked the way it made his eyes look even bluer. "Nah, I don't have a thing with mayonnaise," he said. "Unless you do, in which case I totally have a thing for it."

"'I'm drowning in mayo'?" she asked, repeating the key line of the chorus.

"That's our hometown," Grady said. "Mayo, Florida."

"Really? Like, named after the goopy white stuff?"

"Even better," Calvin said, forcing himself to say something. "Named after a Confederate general."

Melli looked at him for the first time. The moment seared into the back of Calvin's eyes, an image he can shift his focus to linger on when he needs a little reassurance that life really can sometimes feel like a perfectly executed magic trick. "Who's the quiet guy in the back?"

"Calvin," he said.

She nodded, as if deciding that name was acceptable. "OK, Calvin with the nice green eyes. Thanks for the clarification." She looked back to Grady. "So. Two white dudes from a town in Florida named after some racist general. How fast should I be running?"

"Ah, nothing to be afraid of," Grady said. "We already did the running, as far from that place as we could get with, like, no money. That's what the song is all about, right — how we had to get out of there before we drowned."

Calvin wanted to say something that casually made it clear they had written the song together, but before he could find the right words, Melli and Grady had moved on to the flirting stage.

"So, you're safe, then?"

"Oh, I didn't say that." As he spoke, Grady flipped his hair again, this time with an even bigger smile. Calvin knew any battle for Melli was over before it even began.

Calvin was used to being Just Friends with pretty girls, so when playing that role seemed like his best chance to spend time with Melli, he knew what to do. They started hanging out once or twice a week, when she came over before Grady got home from his job at Office Depot. She'd knock on the bedroom door and poke her head in, saying, "OK if I come in? I just needed to get out of my house." Then she'd sit next to Calvin and surf her phone while they talked. He'd pretend he was still focused on what he'd been doing, which was usually playing the keyboard, hunting for patterns and melodies. When she was around, it was a good way to keep his hands and mind busy.

The first couple of times it was just the two of them were a little awkward for him. He was always worried he wasn't talking enough, that she must be bored and regretting even showing up. And even though he only allowed himself quick glimpses of her face, watching her eyes as they followed whatever she was scrolling on her phone, he always worried that his look lingered too long. Her eyes were such a perfect dark brown that he had trouble keeping his own eyes from glancing at them. Plus, the sound of her breath did weird things to his sense of time. It was hard for him to know, when he was with her, how long a silence had lasted or how long her right leg had been casually pressed against his left.

He loved their time together, but he was also confused by her visits and kept trying to figure out why she wanted to talk to him at all. It was easier to listen to Melli than share his own thoughts, so maybe it was that simple — she just needed someone to talk to? He learned about her mother and father, both children of Cuban immigrants who settled in Miami by way of Mexico City, carrying nothing but the clothes on their back and a fanatical Catholic faith. When her father got into Georgia Tech, they moved to Atlanta, and a year later her mother also got accepted. Evidently both parents came very close to dying multiple times when their only child announced she did not want to become an engineer or a doctor. The only known remedy for that was marriage to an engineer or a doctor. She'd graduated from the University of Georgia, but did an English degree even count? She'd used the state scholarship for her undergrad, so her parents had money set aside for grad school. They wanted her to start right away, but she was enjoying having a low-pressure job at Abbadabba's, a hipster shoe and clothing store in Little Five Points. She worked with her best friend, Diane, and was having fun making money and not worrying about living up to academic expectations for the first time in her life. "That night I met you guys? Diane's brother was going to the party, and I went because I'd had a huge fight with my parents."

Calvin tried to respond just enough to keep Melli talking, so he wouldn't have to say too much. "What did you fight about?"

"Grad school. They think I should get an MBA, but I wanna talk about books and get an MA in Lit." She must have figured out what he was doing, and started asking direct questions to make him talk more. "You ever fight with your parents?"

"All. The. Time."

"They must have flipped when you said you were going to skip college, move to Atlanta, play music, all that?"

Calvin stopped playing, shrugged. "Not really."

She stared at him for a moment, then shook her head, put her phone down. "Nope."

The answer made so little sense he needed to make sure he'd heard her correctly. "Nope?"

"Nope."

"What does that mean?"

"Means I'm not buying it. It means you listen real well, but you don't ever tell me anything."

"Not much to say."

"Nope."

"Again with the nope?" When he thinks back to this conversation, which he does a lot, he remembers being nervous at being called out, but also feeling kind of excited, to think that she cared enough to call him out.

"I see you, Calvin."

"You see me?"

She smiled. "All Mr. Cool and Quiet, watching the rest of us."

"You see me watching, huh?"

"Of course." Pause. "Come on. You've listened to me complain about my family I don't know how many times, and you've never said a word about yours."

"Not much to say. College was never in the cards for me. I think everyone in Mayo was surprised I graduated high school."

"But you don't miss them? Your parents?"

Her tone made it clear he should answer "Yes," because of course everyone missed their parents, at least all normal humans did. He had started to figure her out by then, too, and knew if he lied she would be able to tell. She might get angry, and maybe stop looking for him to talk to. "Nope."

Her eyes widened. "Not at all? I mean, my parents can drive me nuts, but I'll miss them when I move out. I'll even miss the wall of Popes."

"Uh, wall of Popes?"

Melli nodded. "Framed photos, lined up in the hallway into the kitchen."

"Wow."

"They can really make a guilty teenager feel like shit." She gave his shoulder a gentle push. "Come on, there must be stuff like that? Stuff that drove you crazy at the time, but you sort of miss now?"

She looked so genuinely confused by the idea that he didn't miss his parents that he almost said he was just kidding, of course he missed them every day. He even tried to invent a fake memory he could share, his own Wall of Popes. Instead, he told her the truth. Looked at her, right at her, instead of only half at her the way he often did because he was too nervous to make steady eye contact. "Nope. They're just fuck-ups. They fucked up their marriage to each other and then got remarried and fucked those up but were too embarrassed to do anything about it. Like, neither one wants to look like they lost some sort of second marriage contest to the other."

Melli watched him closely but didn't say anything, so he continued. "My sister and I spent years bouncing from one weird and stressed house to another, watching four fucked-up people use us to take out their frustrations on each other. I got out of there as quickly as possible and don't see any need to look back."

"Wow." Melli stared at him for a second, then said, softly, "That sucks."

Calvin nodded. "And," he continued, because after doing his best to avoid the topic, it felt good to let it all out, "they don't seem to miss me at all. I get a random e-mail from my stepmom every now and then, but that's it. I think as long as I never bother them for money, they'll never need to talk to me again." His fingers started moving again but were no longer nervously roaming the keys; they moved with more of a purpose, hunting for the melody he could hear forming off in the distance. When he looked back at Melli, he didn't know if he'd zoned out for a few seconds or a few minutes.

"You went somewhere else, huh?"

"Yeah, sorry," he said. He started playing again, still hunting for the sound. He could feel her watching, but did not mind. "Just heard something."

"You always wanted to play?"

"Always."

"You think the kind of family we have determines the things we wind up wanting to do?"

He smiled at that, letting part of his brain continue working on the new melody while the rest of his brain worked on an answer. "You mean, do I love music because my parents sucked?" He'd never thought about any sort of cause and effect between having crappy parents and writing songs. If he really played because of his parents, that would almost make having put up with them worth it. "I don't think so? Because I don't think they have anything to do with my life." He meant to just say "no" and leave it at that, but the words just kept coming out. "Just some fluke mixture of genetics and bad luck that led to me being here. And I can't, I can't imagine some version of Calvin that doesn't love music."

"I'm sorry," she said after a short pause.

"Don't be sorry. Loving music saved my life."

She smacked his arm lightly. "You know what I meant. I meant sorry about your parents."

"Oh. That." Repeating the last chord pattern, he shrugged. Of course, he knew what she meant, but slipping in a joke might inspire a playful smack, and he was happy for any kind of physical contact with Melli. "Not your fault."

"I know. But I'm still sorry that you didn't get to have good parents."

"Are your parents good parents?"

"Yeah. I think so? I mean, the pressure and the guilt can be a lot. And knowing that they're always there can, you know, be a lot? But, at the same time. . ." Her voice drifted off.

"At the same time, they're always there," he finished.

"Yeah, they are. And they've always tried their best, and still seem to like each other after thirty-five years."

"OK, that is even crazier than having a wall of Popes."

"Agreed. But it means it's possible, right?"

"To be good parents?"

"Yes. And to fall in love and stay in love."

"That'd be nice."

She fell silent. When he turned to see why, it looked like her facial expression had changed. He wondered if he'd said something wrong — the new melody was demanding more and more of his brainpower. It always made him think of captains on *Star Trek* diverting power to the shields. Had he forgotten to keep life support on? Then she smiled, and he relaxed.

"Have you ever been in love?" she asked.

"Sure," he said, too nervous about this line of questioning to look up from the keyboard.

"When?"

"That first Pretenders record," he said. "Made me want to time travel to 1980 and stalk Chrissie Hynde."

"Someone real."

"Don't tell me she's not real."

"Someone you met. In person."

He shrugged. "I don't know."

"Really?"

"Really."

"You know when you're in love."

"Do you? Because sometimes you think you are but then you realize later you weren't, right? So does that mean you were wrong when you felt it?"

"No." Her answer was quick, her tone decisive. "It means you felt it, but it just didn't last. But you still felt it."

After that conversation, Calvin found himself answering Melli's questions more easily. He shared stories about life in Mayo, even describing those first years he and Grady had tried to find their way musically, complete with playing her their awful version of "Shake It Off." He grew so comfortable during these talks that one night he mentioned his little brother with the mad drawing skills.

"Wait, you have a brother and a sister?"

His fingers stumbled on the keys slightly. He felt as if he'd been caught in a lie, even if he hadn't lied yet. He could make up another sibling, but then Melli might ask why Calvin never mentioned this brother before. Or, he could say he meant to say sister, but that would be unkind to Alex. He wasn't embarrassed by Alex — he could never be embarrassed by the only family member he felt close to — but he worried about betraying a trust. Would Alex be okay with Calvin sharing his story? Calvin thought Alex would like Melli, though, so he decided to just come out and tell her. His explanation started out sounding confusing to even him, and the more words he added the more confusing everything sounded, but Melli just smiled and rested her fingers on top of his fidgeting hands.

"So, the person who had been called Alice — she/her — would rather you call him Alex — he/him?"

He nodded.

"And that's what you're doing, right?"

He nodded again.

"I think it says a lot, that he trusted telling you. That can't have been easy. And," she continued, "it also can't be easy for him to try and figure all this out in the land of Mayo, huh?"

"Nope. It kills me that I had to leave him behind, but when he graduates I'll find a way to get him here."

"Good."

"And he texts, and calls. And I promised I would always find a way to answer quickly."

"That's a good brother." She moved her hands back into her lap. "Give him my number. In case he ever can't reach you."

Once again, Melli made things much easier than he'd imagined they would be. After he cleared it with Alex, he gave them each other's contact information, and they texted occasionally — if some new shoes came in that Melli thought Alex might like, she would send a picture, and once Alex learned Melli had majored in English, he would send questions when he was struggling with an assignment. Calvin has often had an urge to ask each of them what they text about but has so far managed not to. It can only be good for Alex to have someone else to talk to as Alex and not Alice.

Melli and Grady dated for six months before she found out he was also seeing other people. Just like that, their relationship was over. Just like that, she stopped coming to the house. But six months later she sent Calvin a text saying she missed him. His fingers shook, literally shook, as he responded.

me 2

10:30 a.m.

Lunch prep is in full swing when Calvin gets back from his break. The number of employees doubles at 10:30, and a second day manager clocks in. Today it's Andy, who is so young and energetic that he even inspires Big Ron to leave the safety of his office. The two of them wander through the kitchen, Andy taking long strides with his lanky legs and Big Ron moving in small circles. They each pretend to have things to do while uttering banal phrases like, "Who's ready to have a great day?" and "Energy, people, let's see some energy!"

All kinds of people wind up working at Burger Buddies for all kinds of reasons, Calvin has learned, and the only thing they have in common is that none of them ever planned to work at a fast-food restaurant. Random teens, middle-aged men who look confused at where they have landed, the occasional sad-eyed woman of indeterminate age, the younger workers who battle their nerves by being too giddy.

Newbies: when they wake up and find themselves working at a Burger Buddies, the first thing they have to do is survive the 10:30–2:30 shift. It's the most stressful part of the day and quickly weeds out anyone bothered by digging into a grease-clogged sink or mopping up multi-colored vomit in the dining room or hunting down the source of that stomach-churning smell in the men's room. In the kitchen, if you survive those first few broiler shifts, your "reward" is a move to the fry station. Cook too many and they get cold, and management will be angry. Then, if you can't magically make three baskets appear for a sudden rush, management will be angry. Not enough salt? Worthy of a sharply raised voice. Too much salt? Get ready for loud questioning of your worthiness as a human from sweaty, frazzled men in ties.

Calvin has never been stressed out by anything inside the walls of a Burger Buddies. He survived his first week of throwing burgers on the broiler and trying to keep up with fries unscathed. Management quickly realized Calvin would show up when he was supposed to and knew how to count, so he was moved to the drive-thru after Monica was caught skimming off the register. Surviving three months put him in a small minority and sticking around more than two years moved him dangerously close to Little Ron/Annie territory.

Calvin clocks back in after his break, puts his headset back on and heads to the drive-thru window. "My lord hath returned," Kendall says, bowing slightly.

"Bless you, my child," Calvin says. It's their standard patter, a schtick they started the day Kendall caught Calvin staring at the cross hanging around his neck. "Oh, it's real," Kendall had said, hand placed gently on the necklace. "And I promise not to stare at your missing cross if you promise not to stare at my always present cross."

They spend the next half hour taking orders from the lunch early birds, stocking up the drink station and resuming their debates over music. Today, Kendall wants to continue arguing his case that Calvin is underestimating Janet Jackson and overestimating Frank Ocean, while off in the distance Andy goes off on a long tirade about the way a container of mayonnaise had been opened.

Target Dude comes through just before eleven, as usual. Unlike Red Kia, he's not chatty, but Calvin still feels a connection to him. For one thing, he always has loud music going in his car — some days

10:30 AM

Beyoncé, some days old R&B, one day even some Phoenix. Calvin suspects Target Dude has to pretend to be nice to people all day and takes this ride to get lunch as a chance to listen to some music and not say a word. He also suspects he feels a connection to Target Dude because he makes Calvin think of Ken. They lost touch when he went off to college, though Grady said he'd dropped out in his first year. He works at a Target in Nebraska now. Does he talk to the Burger Buddies cashier on his breaks, or just listen to music and wonder what his life could have been, in a fair universe?

Soon the flow of cars is so steady it cuts into Calvin and Kendall's ability to banter, and Joni takes her spot at the register. Some days Joni looks a little younger than Calvin, and some days she looks a little older, but she never says much; he doesn't know what her story is. She maintains an impressive monotone in the headset and punches the keyboard with freaky accuracy. Kendall fills the bags, lining them up on the ledge to Calvin's left; Calvin collects the money and pushes food out. It's been the same weekday drive-thru crew for several months now, and as the lunch rush begins Calvin again thinks of how crucial routine is to getting through the crappier parts of the day. He estimates a maximum of seven percent of his brain will actually be needed for the next two hours.

A Mini Cooper pulls up. Inside, two beefy guys looking embarrassed to be squished so close together, one with a credit card ready and the other fishing around in his enormous overalls for change. The piece of lyric from the morning is still floating around one corner of his brain, fighting for space with the music that he wrote last night. *Crying in my Mini, crying over what I can't see.* He's not sure it's a song meant for "crying" as a verb, though. Maybe if he changes that to—

"We good?" Beefy Guy Two finally hands his money over. It's seventeen cents short, but Calvin just nods, puts the cash in the drawer and prays that Tweedledee and Tweedledum are gone when he looks up.

KING CAL

And they are. Small miracles.

"Heya," Calvin says as the next car pulls up. It's a shiny new Tesla, one of those Too Nice for Burger Buddies rides, driven by one of those Women Who Look Like They Never Eat. "$5.49, please."

Woman Who Looks Like She Never Eats doesn't make eye contact, and the way she barely holds her credit card out the window means Calvin has to stretch to reach it. This kind of passive-aggressive reminder that he is but a servant can sometimes drive him crazy, but one upside to being exhausted is that he does not have the energy to care about these selfish people and their tiny victories. He has to lean out again to return her credit card and to give her a bag with two Double Buddies and a large fry. She drives away without a thanks, of course, immediately replaced by a minivan that seems clown-car crowded with toddlers in various states of dress and cleanliness. A blonde urchin with either chocolate or feces on his face is leaning out the back window chanting "Booger Buddies! Booger Buddies! Gimme da boogers! Gimme da boogers!"

11:24 a.m. Two hours and thirty-six minutes left.

When Calvin first told Grady they needed to make a Plan if they wanted to turn their music into something people other than a few friends could hear, Grady was skeptical. "I mean, I wanna be famous and dance around big stages, sure. But writing a 'plan' doesn't sound very rock and roll. Can't things just, like, happen?"

"Only bad things just happen," Calvin said. They were sitting on the counter in Grady's parents' kitchen, emptying a bag of Lay's. "For anything good to happen, we need to make a plan."

"OK. So what's our plan?"

Calvin had been trying to answer this question since Ken had told him they needed to figure out what they wanted to do. He finished chewing, then held up his right hand. Five steps seemed like a good number for a plan — enough to get them away from Mayo, but not so many Grady would get scared off by how much would be required.

1. Graduate high school.

The first step. Easy for Grady but not a guarantee for Calvin. School had never been an institution that made any sense to him. He managed to go most days, because it was better than being home, but he rarely managed to give a shit. Having The Plan gave him more of a reason to sort of do some of the work some of the time, but there were still days when he just couldn't find the energy to do anything but run chord patterns in his head. His mother and father both said they didn't care what he did next as long as he graduated. They must have been terrified at the idea he would wind up a high school dropout, stuck at home with them, because at the start of senior year they told him there was a new MacBook waiting for him if he actually graduated.

A new MacBook that would be crucial for getting decent home recordings.

Grady would graduate with a 3.6 GPA. It drove Calvin crazy — Grady hated school as much as Calvin, or at least said he did, but he still managed to get everything done in time, with nothing but As and Bs. But once they had The Plan, and could just look at each other in the hallway, or whatever crappy class they were in, and say "Sixteen," and Calvin would try to focus.

Sixteen. P, for Plan, was the sixteenth letter of the alphabet.

Just as it began to look like Calvin would actually manage to graduate, Mrs. Darvish assigned a ten-page paper, instead of a final, analyzing *Mrs. Dalloway*. As soon as Calvin looked it up on Wikipedia and saw that it was a hundred-year-old novel about a rich woman getting ready for a party, he knew he was doomed. He could study enough to guess his way through an exam, but actually create ten double-spaced pages about some ancient novel that managed to please Darvish the Devil? No way.

When Calvin told Grady he thought he'd probably have to go to summer school, because he couldn't even read the book, never mind write about it, Grady said he'd find a solution.

And then he wrote Calvin's final paper.

He made Calvin look it over, in case Darvish got suspicious and started asking questions: the nature of time in *Dalloway*; how the past, present and future all co-exist inside everyone's heads; and how Woolf shows this through one average day in the life of some rich old woman and a crazy war veteran. It almost made Calvin want to read the book.

Darvish loved the essay. Calvin passed the class. The Plan continued.

2. Save money.

Grady thought they should leave Mayo as soon as they graduated. As much as Calvin also wanted to leave, he thought they should stay an extra year and save some money. His fear of having to go back to Mayo because they were too broke to escape was greater than his desperation to leave. Grady's view might have been because his family had money. Calvin never forgot the first time he watched Grady casually ask his mom for ten bucks and she just said, "Sure," and pointed at her wallet.

Calvin's father didn't like the idea of them waiting either and said Calvin would have to pay rent if he didn't move out. That would have defeated the whole point of staying, but his mother, of all people, came to the rescue and said he could stay with her. She made him pay for his own food, cut the grass, clean the bathrooms and help drive Alice around, but all of that was easier than dealing with his father. And since Alice was the only family member Calvin was going to miss, he wanted to spend as much time with her as he could.

Alex was still Alice then. Calvin tries to remember him more as Alex than Alice, but it's hard to go back and change the cast of his past.

3. Get as far away from Florida as possible.

They thought about New Orleans, which seemed like a fun city with lots of music, but Grady had a sister at Tulane who said the summers made her question the worthiness of life, that everything went limp with a damp sweat from April to October. So, they picked

Atlanta: a big city that wasn't in Florida and had a decent music scene. Plus, it would not be as expensive as moving to New York or L.A. or Chicago.

4. Start earning enough money to survive, pay rent and keep upgrading gear.

They'd each find jobs they could quit without any warning when some important musical opportunity suddenly appeared. They didn't think they should work at the same crappy place, because that would make getting time off harder. Calvin had washed dishes, cut grass and bagged groceries during high school. He hated all the jobs, but making money meant buying records and going to concerts. When they got to Atlanta, making money would mean keeping the band alive. He would do anything, for that.

5. Write lots of great songs, record them as well as they could and post them online. Earn universal praise and adoration.

This was the part of The Plan Calvin was least worried about. He and Grady were getting better at shaping their songs. Grady wrote the melodies, sang the vocals and played all the tricky guitar bits; Calvin supplied the music and the words, programmed the drum loops and mixed everything. "Your music needs a voice, and vice-y verse-y," Grady kept telling Calvin. "Can't have one without the other." While Calvin agreed, he knew there was more to it than that. Grady was the voice for the singing, but he would also be the voice for everything else they would need to do as a band, like talk to club owners and carry any interviews they ever gave. Calvin would happily be the quiet one in the background, nodding at all the right times.

Even with The Plan in place, and Darvish appeased by Grady's *Dalloway* essay, Calvin found things to worry about. He worried about whether they'd be able to save enough money to escape Mayo, worried about not finding a job or a place to live once they got to Atlanta. Worried about how people even got stuff like electricity and water turned on. Worried about driving on the highway, and what would happen if some big truck cut them off or threw a tire.

The closer he and Grady got to graduating, the deeper his worries burrowed into his brain, seeping into every aspect of his life. The sound of his own thoughts changed. It was like someone was hitting random piano keys inside his head, with no pattern or melody, no sense of time at all.

Then, one morning, just a few weeks before they were supposed to graduate, he couldn't get out of bed. Literally could not move. His stepmom finally got nervous enough to stop shouting at him to get up already and came in to ask him, quietly, without his father hearing her, if there was something wrong. Dottie sat on the edge of his bed, looking soft and human and full of genuine concern, just like one of those moms he had seen on TV shows. He almost told her the truth, almost tried to explain how he was sure the moment his feet hit the floor, the whole world would just open up and swallow everything he had ever touched, and how even scarier than that was knowing some part of him didn't think that would be so bad actually, some part of him thought maybe having something awful happen was the only way to get rid of the feeling something awful was going to happen.

Instead, he just shrugged and told her he was fine, just tired.

Something in his voice must have revealed that he actually wasn't fine, because instead of warning him of the consequences he'd face from his father if he did not do what he was supposed to do, Dottie continued to sit on the edge of the bed. Calvin waited for her to leave, but she didn't, and the longer she sat there, the weirder it got. Then, somehow, it stopped being weird. It became reassuring. Something about the way she just sat there, softly humming to herself, waiting, allowed his brain to pull out of the dark whirlpool. And then he got up.

For a while he thought of what happened as "The Whirlpool," but then he decided "The Spiral" was a better name. A whirlpool could pull you down and under, but it was an outside force. The dark feeling had come from inside him, and the larger it grew, the tighter it pulled against his chest. Dottie never mentioned it again, but every now and then he'd catch her staring at him, as if looking for some sort of warning sign. It was annoying, but he also remembered the way she just sat there, waiting for him, so he'd try and smile and flash her a thumbs-up.

He worried about The Spiral coming back. He could feel it creeping closer some nights, but he was able to fight it off for the rest of the school year. When he actually graduated, his father kept his promise and handed him a box with a new MacBook inside. Warm relief caused Calvin's cheeks to flush a red so deep his father asked if he was drunk.

The year after high school was the best year he'd ever had in Mayo. He had to suffer through a job at Costco, but it was better than washing dishes, and there was an end date in sight. He and Grady recorded as much as they could and started tracking the Atlanta music scene online. Grady had promised his mother he would stay for one more Christmas, so they escaped Mayo on New Year's Day, a year and a half after graduation. It was the best birthday present he could ever have received: suddenly his dream of being somewhere else, anywhere else, had become reality. Good things really *could* happen, even to him.

Two and a half years later The Plan was working. Not as fast as Calvin had fantasized, but there was no denying the progress: four EPs up on Bandcamp, a dozen gigs and airplay on college and online indie radio stations. Calvin had reached out to a few bloggers who had either mentioned Lords of the Living or seemed like they might dig the music, and some of them had written back. There were even a couple, including some random dude in Australia, who wanted Calvin to send them whatever new music they had as soon as it was ready. Grady got just as excited as Calvin did with each of these small signs of fandom, but he would also wonder how quickly the next sign would come — and when the signs might grow bigger.

Grady was getting impatient. Looking back now, Calvin could

see he should have thought more about what it might mean, that Grady kept pushing crappy drummer and bass player options to fill out the band, like he was willing to settle for anything just to get things moving. But even if Calvin had been more aware of that impatience, he never would have imagined that Grady would go on the road playing guitar for One Four Three. Led by a lecherous egomaniac in a cowboy hat named Roddy, One Four Three was six guys who played their instruments well but never bothered to write what Calvin would consider an actual song; most of their originals involved generic chord patterns and endless guitar leads. Inexplicably, over the past year they had morphed from lower-tier locals who opened for other people on weekdays to weekend headliners.

The band and its followers (Onesies — really?) said it was thanks to their self-released EP, which featured crowd favorite "My Dear Friend, Mr. Heineken." Everyone else credited (blamed) a series of TikToks starring Roddy's Chihuahua, who was posed to make it look as if he was playing miniaturized instruments: behind tiny drum sets, with tiny guitars strung around his neck, paws placed on a toy piano. The music itself went nowhere — a series of basic chords, played over some midtempo groove with lots of guitar solos and the (oh, oh, the pain) occasional squealing harmonica solo. Roddy was also one of the town's most relentless schmoozers, which meant Grady insisted they go to One Four Three's shows and hang out. Grady admitted he was trying to get them to offer Lords of the Living an opening slot, and when Calvin shuddered, Grady waved him off.

"There are worse things than opening for an awful band that has a decent crowd," he said. "Remember, we contain multitudes of multitudes. The same people with bad taste who go to see Roddy could be smart enough to like us."

And now Grady was driving around in a bus with Roddy. Originally, they just wanted to hire him for the first four weeks of the tour, a temporary replacement for their lead guitarist. After less than a week, though, Grady texted that Brian's rehab was not going quite as quickly as everyone had hoped, so he'd be staying with the band "a little longer." Just like that, four weeks turned into four months. Tracking the tour online, Calvin can see there are only a few more weeks left. At least the end is in sight.

As frustrating as it has been to put the band on pause, what really bothered him about Grady taking the gig was the idea that Grady had started to lose faith. It had never occurred to Calvin to lose faith in The Plan. He never expected them to be famous after just a few years in Atlanta and was happy with the progress they'd made. He would never forget the first time he and Grady heard a Lords of the Living song on WRAS, turning the car radio up as loud as it could go and recording the moment on their phones. "Open me up," Grady was singing, and strangers all across the city were listening.

He's remembering that moment as he hands a bag of Double Buddies and fries to an Abercrombie & Fitch ad who does not even look at him. He reminds himself the memory is real, as are other good memories, like the scattered, but positive, reviews of their music, and a dozen shows that went really well. Moments like that are enough to sustain his faith they will keep making progress when Grady finally comes off the road.

"Oh, come on," Abercrombie says, not looking at him as he paws through the bag of food. "You really think that's enough ketchup?"

11:30 a.m.

Eleven-thirty is when Calvin usually starts to believe he can make it through the rest of his shift. Six hours down, two and a half to go, with a constant stream of cars to help the time move quickly. He barely pays attention to the soundtrack made by Joni taking orders, only noticing when something unusual happens — like the thick and slow molasses drawl that asks, "OK, you, you there? Hey, you there, OK?"

"WelcometoBurgerBuddies. Can I take your order?"

"OK, OK, this is gonna be three separate orders, you got me? Three different tickets, OK? Like, there's three of us, and we each just wanna pay for our own?"

Joni looks at Calvin. They're not supposed to take more than two separate orders per car, especially during the lunch rush, but Calvin has learned it takes longer to fight with the assholes who want to do it than it does to just go ahead and let them. He nods at her while he pushes out two bags to the three construction workers squeezed across the bench of a Ford pickup.

"OK, OK, the first one, the first one . . ." The voice starts to go through each order slowly, drifting between too soft and too loud. Molasses Man takes so long to order that only one car is left at the

11:30 AM

window by the time he's done. Gaps between cars in the drive-thru lane during a rush mean the line waiting to order gets that much longer. If a manager notices, he'll panic and start raising his voice to state the obvious. "Hey, we got a backup, y'all! Let's move it!" Half-listening to the tortured release of the third (and please let it really be the final) order as he delivers a Chicken Buddy and two shakes to a skeletal man in an ancient Honda (where do all those calories go, Ichabod?), Calvin works out a Burger Buddies Manager/High School Teacher Venn Diagram. Both have lots of power in a system designed to keep the lower ranks powerless; both involve trying to get those without power to perform and behave in a certain way; both like to remind everyone of their power even when it's not necessary. "Hey, we have a line of cars in the drive-thru" is no more insightful or helpful than "Hey, I think some of you aren't paying attention."

The manager probably makes more money, which is depressing, but the teacher might get more respect. Does either have real power, or do they both just share an illusion of it?

The idea of power floats onto the song he wrote last night, the music still looking for words, as Molasses Man's pickup noisily approaches the window. It could be a song about power, but he should find a word other than power to use, something less obvious. Strength is OK, but it's one of those words that's hard to sing well—maybe "strong" is the answer.

I have just enough power to keep from getting hurt. Or, I hope I'm just strong enough I don't get hurt?

When Molasses & Co. finally leave, Calvin glances up at the camera and sees a line of cars snaking awkwardly into the parking lot. Management's goal is to keep any of those potential orders from getting so tired of waiting they drive away, so it's just a matter of time before someone—

"My drive-thru's backed up, people!" Big Ron says, walking by and clapping his hands. "What's going on?"

Maybe less is more, and he should just leave the problematic word out: *Need to learn to use enough / to keep myself from getting hurt*? Not terrible, but also kind of vague. Squishy. Maybe his brain is too tired today to do any better than vague and squishy. For all the years he's been writing songs, every time he starts a new one he feels like he barely knows what he's doing. Sometimes he thinks that's a good thing, that it can keep him from getting bored with the process. But sometimes it's frustrating, because—

"Calvin! Kendall!" Now Andy has noticed the crisis and wants to offer his brilliant insights. "We have a line! Let's get these cars moving!"

Big Ron grabs a ticket, and Calvin dreads seeing what he comes back with: Big Ron is notorious for being slow, and always leaving out at least one item.

"Calvin, Calvin, I got me an idea," Kendall says, walking over with three bags just as Big Ron walks away, staring at the order ticket as if it were in Russian. "Let's get this food out the window fast as we can, what do you say?"

"See, I knew you were the smart one," Calvin says, matching the first bag Kendall puts down with the large Coke waiting. Standard Angry Woman is glaring at him as she pulls up, but when she sees Calvin holding her drink and wearing his biggest "Just Doin' the Best We Can" smile, she softens and hands him her credit card.

The possible lyrics keep tumbling through his head even as he swipes the Visa and listens to Joni take the next order. Maybe it's a simple fix; maybe "use" is the problem. *I finally learned to lose enough / to keep myself from getting hurt.*

That's almost-maybe good. He'll need to figure out who's singing to get much further. It doesn't feel like him; it feels like a different character's voice. Oh, he's certainly lost lots of things, and lots of people, but for him the losing is always the thing that hurts. This sounds more like someone who deliberately shuts themself off. And, yeah, he's certainly done that a lot—

11:30 AM

Angry Woman drives away just before the thirty-second alarm goes off.

—but he also said yes to the opportunity he knew could have hurt him more than any other if it hadn't worked out.

Six months after she broke up with Grady, and less than twenty-four hours after her text saying she missed him, Melli met Calvin at the Dunkin' Donuts on Memorial Drive. It seemed easier than having her come to the house, where there could be a potentially awkward conversation with Grady.

Driving there, Calvin had worried about whether he should try to hug her hello. Would she think that was weird, or would she think it was weirder if he didn't? And then she walked in, saw him, smiled and greeted him with a big hug. He had a hot chai and a glazed chocolate waiting for her. She hugged him again for remembering her standard Dunkin' order and then they sat down and began talking as if they had just seen each other yesterday.

He'd expected her to want to talk about the break-up with Grady, but she started with everything else. Her parents? Still very much the same: still wishing she would get married, still dragging her to church every Sunday and more during holy seasons — and there are so many holy seasons. They had at least stopped talking about moving to Arizona and expecting her, as their only child, to move with them, but that also meant the pressure to go to grad school had increased. Her job at Abbadabba's? The same, which was fine, but if she did go to grad school she'd have to cut back her hours, or even quit, and then she'd need to count on her parents for all her expenses, even the secret ones. That would not be fine.

When he casually asked if she had a new boyfriend, she took a sip of chai, shook her head, and mentioned Grady for the first time. She had learned a lot from her mistakes there, a whole list of warning signs she should have seen, things she could have done differently. Men lie but don't even know it, because they don't think it's lying if it's just not telling you something they don't want you to know. She was still mad at Grady, but she also felt like she needed to thank him in some weird way because he had taught her to never be so trusting again.

Calvin didn't say much during that part of the conversation; he just nodded. He didn't imagine it would be easy to date Grady but always assumed the best parts of the relationship would offset the more challenging ones. That's what it was like being in a band with him.

Then it was his turn. Melli asked him about Lords of the Living (another EP almost ready to upload, still trying to find a drummer who could keep time and/or was not an alcoholic), Burger Buddies (yes, still there, and yes, it's exactly the same), and Downy (yes, still there, and exactly the same). When she stood up to say she had to go, that it was past ten and her parents still gave her grief if she came home much later than that, he felt that weird stomach churning, that nervous feeling he'd had before most school days. How long was it going to be before he saw her again? He felt better when she leaned in to hug him goodbye.

"I've missed you," she said. "Can we do this again soon?"

"Of course," he said, making himself wait at least twelve hours before he texted her. She wrote back right away (oh, those wonderful little dots), and they met again the next night for two hours, then a few nights later for even longer. It quickly became more awkward to not tell Grady than it was to just tell him. It was so unusual for Calvin to be going anywhere that his best friend knew something was up.

"You're seeing Melli? Like, dating Melli?"

"No, no," Calvin was quick to explain. "Just hanging out, the way we used to when she'd come over here."

"Uh huh," Grady said with a smile. Calvin knew what Grady was thinking, but he thought that his odds of dating Melli were slightly worse than the odds of his joining a band with Thom Yorke. At least Melli could start coming over to the house again now that Grady knew. It was as if she'd never been gone — she would walk in without knocking, ask Downy what he'd cooked her for dinner, make a joke about the ever-revolving cast of characters in the other bedrooms and then talk with Calvin for hours about her parents, or her job, or what would ever change about either. It was a little awkward the first time Grady wandered out to the back deck, which had become their favorite conversation spot, and sat down to join them. But only a little, and that awkwardness soon passed. Watching the two of them together, Calvin was finally convinced that his worst nightmare — Grady and Melli getting back together — was never going to happen.

Calvin learned how to make chai at home, and Melli was so impressed that she insisted he teach her. They started spending the first half-hour of each visit in the kitchen, carefully measuring the powder and milk and sugar, whisking hard enough to generate some froth but not so hard they spilled any of what they called "their precious," each giving their best impersonation of Gollum from *Lord of the Rings* before taking that first sip.

After that, they would move to the porch and talk for an hour or two. Melli always had stories from work or a new podcast to recommend; Calvin talked about music the band was working on, new songs that were especially rewarding or challenging or which of the books she'd talked about he'd finally started reading. It felt odd, at first, to have these long conversations without the safety of his keyboard as a prop, but once he got used to that, he realized they were both saying a lot more. He even learned her full name, which he had always wondered about.

"So, my guess is Melanie."
"Melanie? Who's Melanie?"
"Is that what Melli is short for?"
"No, but nice try." She smiled.
"Melody?"
"Melody? I'm a song, eh?"
"Heh. A catchy tune."

She shook her head. "Nope. Amelia. Named after my mother's mother, as one does."

"Grady never told me."

She smiled again. "Well, Grady never asked."

And then one night when they were on that back deck in the dark, laughing about something for so long he'd forgotten what had been so funny in the first place, she leaned over and kissed him. It wasn't a giddy, caught-up-in-the-moment peck. It was a real kiss, real contact with real lips. The way her lips moved inspired his own to respond in a way they never had before, and it felt so natural that it was clear his lips, his entire mouth, had been waiting for this exact moment.

When she slowly pulled back, he could feel the blush spreading across his face, his cheeks warming from the inside. "Well," he said, "that was unexpected."

"And unwanted?"

"So, so wanted. Just unexpected."

She leaned forward, kissed him again. This one lasted even longer, and he felt even more comfortable responding.

"Good," she said. "Because I have wanted to for a while."

It felt as though his entire head turned crimson. "So have I."

"Why didn't you say something?"

"I was afraid to."

She batted her eyes, as if she were a Southern belle. "Afraid of little ol' me?"

"Yes," he admitted. "Afraid you'd say no."

"Why would I say no?"

He could feel his mind racing through all the things he could say to deflect, to change the topic, to avoid saying anything too close to the real answer. "Because I'm not the kind of guy who gets a girl like you," he said, deciding to see what happened if he just told the truth.

"That's crazy, you know?" She paused, her eyes focused intensely on his face. "You always undersell yourself, Calvin."

He kissed her again, to make sure it wasn't some sort of waking dream. Now that it had actually happened, he could let himself admit, even if only to himself, that he had thought about this moment many, many times, and as amazing as he'd imagined it would be, the reality proved even more amazing. Her lips were even softer than he had imagined they would be. "Why didn't you say something?" he asked.

"I didn't want to risk ruining our friendship. I didn't want to risk losing my best friend."

"So, what changed?"

"I imagined how much fun it would be to have a best friend you could also kiss."

"It is fun, isn't it?"

"It is."

Calvin had already started a list of Firsts with Melli. First time meeting Melli, first time alone with Melli, first time eating with Melli, first time taking a walk with Melli. First time he celebrated his birthday with Melli, who was the first person to make such a big deal of his being born on the first day of the year. After that night, the list evolved in ways he had never imagined possible.

Like kissing. The first time he kissed Melli was the first time he understood what kissing was. He felt like he'd been told he'd been eating ice cream, but he'd really been eating sand — and then had a taste of real ice cream.

Or the first time getting naked with Melli. He'd been terrified to take his clothes off for people before; his body looked especially scrawny and pale when he imagined it through the eyes of others. But it felt as though Melli had seen everything he was, already, that removing the actual clothes was just a formality.

The list grew longer quickly and became his favorite list, ever. He couldn't wait to keep adding to it.

12:00 p.m.

High noon at a busy fast-food restaurant. The line of people inside waiting to order is long enough to make it hard to reach the drink station or tables in the dining room. The angry looks from those having to wait longer than they feel acceptable are growing more intense, and the drive-thru is a solid line of cars from the pick-up window into the parking lot.

The noise volume seems to double, too. Expediters waiting for that Double Buddy with extra cheese shout at the poor souls trying to keep up with an impossible flood of orders, leading to return shouts demanding everyone be patient and stop shouting. Then there's the beeping — the various noises generated in the land of Burger Buddies can be overwhelming. The fryer beeps when it's time to pull the fries out of the oil, but the station gets so backed up that no one ever turns the beeping off; they just take one basket out and put another in. Microwaves at all the sandwich stations beep when they start and when they finish; and, of course, the drive-thru alarm goes off whenever a car is at the window for longer than thirty seconds. There's another alarm at forty-five seconds, then a minute. By the time a car has been there ninety seconds the noise is unbearable — as it was designed to be. "Management by intimidation," Kendall calls it, and that seems right.

12:00 PM

The newbies twitch every time a noise kicks off near them. Calvin feels bad, remembering his own period of adjustment to the sounds (never mind the smells) of life at Burger Buddies. He wonders if they would be reassured or terrified to know that, at some point, if they last long enough at the job, they won't even hear the relentless waves of sound. The only time he notices the noises now is if someone else reacts.

It's just after twelve when the Bigwigs arrive. It had never occurred to Calvin that a fast-food restaurant would have so many layers of bureaucracy. There are shift managers, day managers, divisional managers, regional managers ... all creating some ridiculous feudal hierarchy of food. It still baffles him, the number of men and women in sharp suits who drop in to see how things are going. They like to show up when the restaurant is busiest, too, so of course they walk in right at noon.

Today's group is slightly unusual, because one of the three Bigwigs is a younger woman. Calvin recognizes one of the men, a middle-aged district manager named Tomás, who calls everyone "guy" and always looks bored. Tomás also likes to remind everyone he came from Mexico penniless and unable to speak English, and while Calvin certainly has no problem with the story, it bothers him when Tomás uses it to berate employees he thinks do not work hard enough. Calvin doesn't recognize the older white guy, who's on the phone as they walk in, or the woman. She's dressed in a sharp dark pants suit and looks rail thin, especially compared to the pot-bellied men with her. It makes sense to Calvin that in the corporate world the men can get as heavy as they want, but the women have to stay skinny to keep their power.

"Uh oh," says Calvin to Kendall, who's walking over with the next few orders. "Here come the Bigwigs."

Kendall looks over his shoulder as he starts placing the bag in order on the ledge. "Oohwee," he whistles, in an exaggerated country accent. "Which one of them wigs you figure is the biggest?"

Calvin glances at the first bag to make sure it's the one he needs and passes it out the window with a cursory "Have a good day." When it's this busy, everyone is happiest if he just minimizes the time it takes to get their food and drive away. "Well, the biggest wig is usually awarded to the oldest of the species," he says, as the next car pulls up.

"Yes," Kendall says, assuming a serious tone. "And one can't help but notice the eldest is also the whitest male, which also factors into wig distribution."

"Astute observation," Calvin says, leaning out the window to take the next credit card. "But in this case my guess is that the young female may have that honor. Her strong steps and straight back indicate power. Most telling of all, the males seem to be nervous in her presence."

Joni turns around to study the people from corporate. "What are you guys talking about?" she asks, finger hovering over the talk button on her headset, ready to take the next order. "I don't think any of them are wearing wigs. That's just, like, their hair? Welcome-toBurgerBuddies, may I take your order?"

Calvin returns the credit card after he swipes it and hands another bag of food and a shake out the window. He's checking the next order just as Tomás walks by, headed to the kitchen. He flashes Calvin a big thumbs-up when their eyes meet. Tomás has always liked Calvin and keeps asking him to move into management. The idea of becoming a manager holds no appeal, though. The best part of the job is how unimportant it is, how little of his brain he needs to use to get through the day. Management would mean making a little more money but at the cost of brain space. Walking into Burger Buddies would feel more like walking into an actual job, and just thinking about that makes his palms sweat.

All these words climb in my head / but nothing ever gets said.

Kendall is walking back with two more orders just in time to see the exchange of thumbs between Tomás and Calvin. Kendall has never liked Tomás. "He crushes on you hard, guy," he says, shaking his head.

"I wish maybe he didn't," Calvin says. "He's always pushing me about this management thing." He slides the next bag into position, waiting for the careful white-haired old man driving to reach the window. Slow and steady can lose the race, too, man. "It's online, guy, all the training is online." Calvin tries to make "guy" somehow sound like multiple syllables, the way Tomás does, though only after making sure Tomás is not in earshot. "But what could there possibly be to study before becoming a Burger Buddies manager? And why would I ever want to do it?"

"So, he wants you to have a chance to make more money?" Kendall collects two more tickets from the small printer by the drink station. "Get some health benefits? How is that so awful?"

He walks away before Calvin can answer. Calvin had just assumed Kendall would be as appalled by the idea of moving into management as he is. One of the reasons they got along so well, he thought, was because they both understood this was not any sort of "real" job — not if a job needed to have genuine stakes to be "real." More money would be good, and having his own health insurance would keep him from worrying that his mother would eventually make good on her threat to take him off her policy. But what he wants most of all is to be in this building as little as possible and to never have to think about it when he walks out.

After passing a large bag of food to a sharp-dressed man in a tiny BMW, seated next to a woman in a low-cut tank top who is either his daughter or girlfriend — the body language is confusing — Calvin turns around to wait for Kendall to return. Thinking about how to make his next point, he is interrupted by a short stab of a horn and then a louder, more sustained honk. He's surprised to see Mr. Beemer still at the window though not at the look on his face. That air of condescension from customer to employee is built right into the fast-food career.

"There's no chicken sandwich."

Calvin speaks calmly, in his best Aim to Please voice. "It's in there, sir. Check the bottom of the—"

"If I said it's not in here, it means I have checked, and it is not in here." Mr. Beemer holds the bag up in the air, as if that somehow proves his case.

The first drive-thru alarm has already gone off and more will follow if Calvin can't get Unhappy Chicken Man to leave. Bigwig Woman is by the fry station, and Calvin knows she will be looking over after hearing the alarm. He can also see the driver of the next car in line, a red-faced man in a cargo van, clutching the steering wheel tightly and mouthing something that doesn't look like praise for Burger Buddies. The easiest solution would be to grab another chicken sandwich, allowing Beemer to have his victory and getting the drive-thru moving again. Today, though, Calvin does not want to let this three-piece suit, or his child bride, drive away talking about the dumb Burger Buddies employee who couldn't even check an order. After however many hundreds of lunch rushes he has now completed, Calvin can confirm the contents of a bag by its weight and shape, the same way a doctor is able to know immediately what that lump on your neck means. "Can you check one more time, sir?" he asks, taking on that extra-polite tone he needs to pull out when he feels himself desperate to start screaming at someone. Kendall has noticed what's happening and is hanging nearby in case he needs to get another sandwich to shut this guy up. Today, though, Calvin wants a victory — or at least not have a loss. "On the bottom of the bag, you'll find—"

"I told you I checked. Perhaps it is your ears that need to be checked?"

"I was just—"

"You think I cannot count?"

"Sir, I never—"

Beemer cuts him off so he can start riffing about all the things he

12:00 PM

can do that clearly Calvin can't. All Calvin can do is smile and nod, even as he senses Bigwig Woman approaching from behind. "What's the goddamn holdup," she whispers in Calvin's ear, her voice sharp and cutting. Then she steps forward to wave out the window and smile. "What can I do to help, sir?" Her voice is glazed in honey. "Remember," she adds, "at Burger Buddies we make good food and we make good friends!" The emphasis on the "and" is perfect, sounding just the way it does in the commercials.

Just as the Bigwig is speaking to him, though, Beemer finally reaches in to check the bottom of the bag. Calvin is focused on his face, waiting for the change when — ah, there it is. "Humph. I don't know why you put the rectangular box on the bottom." Beemer hands the bag to his girlfriend/daughter. "That makes no logistical sense."

"None," the woman says.

"You're right, sir, of course." Bigwig places her hand on Calvin's shoulder in an undeniably condescending manner. "I'm sure our associate—" She pauses just long enough to glance at Calvin's name tag. "Alvin understands and would like to apologize."

These are the moments that almost break him. The idea of saying he is sorry to this entitled asshole, while his smug superior looks on, generates an immediate island of nausea in his stomach. What he wants to say is, "Alvin would very much like to tell this asshole to suck on his chicken sandwich," but he knows that would get him fired, and finding another crappy job that gives him nights and weekends off will be impossible. These calculations must be worked out in a matter of seconds, while Bigwig's nails poke into his uniform, as she taps heels that probably cost more than he makes in a month.

Telling her to stop fucking touching him is something else he suspects he should not say out loud. There's really only one thing he can say.

He looks at Beemer Man with the most sincere look he can summon. "So sorry, sir. Have a great day."

Beemer and his young companion both shoot a final, aggrieved stare at Calvin. As they pull away, Bigwig turns to Calvin, drops her Customer Smile and whispers, "Stop wasting my fucking time and get this line moving." Her lips don't even seem to move, allowing her face to be frozen in her faux smile. "Can you do that, Marvin? Or do I need to find someone who can?"

Calvin nods without a word, the behavior expected from all employees, and gets back to work.

Number 9 on that list of Things He Never Imagined Learning How to Do: apologize for shit that wasn't his fault. It used to be hard enough to say he was sorry even when he'd done something wrong.

When Kendall comes back, dropping off two more orders, Calvin returns to the conversation they were having before the Beemer Battle. The time and energy wasted searching for a chicken sandwich that was there all along has only reinforced his belief: this job is worth having only if it minimizes the amount of time and brain power wasted. "Manager? Working nights, called in for weekend emergencies, dealing with all the worst customers? Really? Who would want that?"

"Uh, me. I need the money, man." He matches the drinks Calvin has staged with the next two orders. "I would love to make enough here to stop Ubering at night. No more driving drunk yuppies from one bar to another, through Buckhead and the Highlands? Give me the dumb online course and a tie for that, never mind some fucking health care."

Kendall grabs some tickets and walks away. For the next ten minutes or so, Calvin focuses on pushing out orders so Bigwig can go bother some other underpaid employee. He's in one of those angry-at-everything moods, and that makes him angry at himself, since he'd vowed he would never let this crappy job get to him. He's ashamed to realize he's angry because he's embarrassed, since Kendall watched Calvin grovel before Bigwig Woman and Beemer Man. And sure, Kendall has to perform the same act, everyone who works

12:00 PM

there does, but something about having a friend watch you dance on command makes it even harder to bear. There's a big difference in motivation, though. All Calvin had to worry about was scraping together enough money for rent, gear, pot and food (in that order) while Kendall's salary was crucial for his family.

No wonder Kendall reacted the way he did when the management offer went to the white guy who didn't need or want it. The white guy who could afford to say no.

He makes eye contact with Kendall when he turns around to check the next bag, relieved that he doesn't seem angry. Before he started working here, Calvin knew the amount of power someone had was connected to the amount of money they had, but here he is reminded daily. Since most people pay by credit card it also feels unreal, like play-acting kids selling pretend goods for invisible money. Some of these people come through every day, which means their twelve-dollar lunch is sixty bucks for the week. The list of better things people can do with sixty dollars is endless, he thinks. Cables for the keyboard and the mics. Enough pasta for weeks. New bundle of digital recording effects.

All of those are things he currently needs, which makes him wonder how he's ever going to earn enough money to pay for it. And that makes him wonder how much longer he can survive in this drive-thru window — how much longer before he really does snap and says something that allows someone like Bigwig Woman to fire him? And if no one fires him, how much longer before he has to quit for his own sanity? How much longer—

"*Hey!*"

Calvin turns to look at the source of the angry voice behind him, a blonde teen in a Mercedes playing Coldplay much too loudly (though, Coldplay at any volume is too loud). "Yes?"

"I need some ketchup, chief. Ketch. Up. I mean, three? You gave me three? What the actual fuck?"

"So sorry," he says. When he turns to reach into the container of ketchup packets next to the window he sees Bigwig Woman staring at him. He nods at her, working hard to control the part of his brain that wants to command his arm to hurl all the ketchup he can hold at Coldplay Mercedes. "My mistake. How many would you like?"

1:05 p.m.

During the peak of the lunch rush it's hard to imagine the cars ever stopping, but all of a sudden they do. That's when Calvin allows himself to look at the time. If it's after one p.m. the end of the day is clearly in sight.

Today it's 1:05. Less than an hour left. That's a win.

While they work on restocking and cleaning, Calvin and Kendall banter about music. Any earlier tension is gone, thanks to another unspoken rule of Burger Buddies survival they both follow: never let anything related to the job ruin anything more important.

And everything is more important than Burger Buddies.

Today Calvin returns to the topic of Prince, whose records he has been studying obsessively. What he's been trying to figure out, as he listens, is how Prince managed to make the tracks where he played all the instruments sound like a full band. Since Lords of the Living might keep making all their records with him and Grady doing everything, Calvin would love to learn how to make some of the songs sound more like a "real" band.

When Calvin mentions listening to *Parade* last night, Kendall pretends to be annoyed. "What is it with you and always asking me about Prince? Ask the Black guy about the Black guy, is that it?"

KING CAL

"Of course," Calvin says. "If you were Mexican, we'd have to talk about Santana records."

"You're welcome for dodging that one, amigo."

"Yeah, exactly, thank you."

"And if I suddenly get into, like, old Bing Crosby shit, you're my go-to guy?"

"Got you covered," Calvin says, before starting a discussion about "Kiss" between the stray post-lunch orders they get. They move from the choice to have no bass in "Kiss" to how much Prince stole from Michael Jackson and vice versa, which leads to a discussion about whether Michael's legacy is forever tarnished by the accusations against him. Kendall is a firm "yes," but Calvin is surprised to find himself defending the music — not Michael himself, but the music he made. "When we're gone, we're gone. But the stuff we made, that still exists, right? So, what's most important, our lives or our art?"

"You creative types," Kendall says on his way to get more cups and lids. "Always sticking together."

Calvin wonders if that's it. Maybe he's worried someday he'll make some terrible mistake as a human and not want all of the music he leaves behind to be tarnished. Which makes him wonder just how much music he is going to leave behind, and whether it'll be any good. These are not questions to ask yourself toward the end of a long day of working at a Burger Buddies.

Too many words inside my head / hiding from me, playing dead.

Kendall returns with the cups and lids, drops them next to the drink station and takes off his headset. "Congratulations on another day of serving fine food to fine Americans," he says. "I'm gonna get some lunch before you disappear."

If Kendall's headed for break it's 1:30, so there's only half an hour left. Kendall's making his drink when Calvin decides he should say something. The last thing he wants is any lingering weirdness between him and the only person in the restaurant he actually likes. "You should ask Tomás about it. The job. They're definitely looking for someone."

Kendall raises his eyebrows. "Just walk up to Tomás and announce I want to be a manager?"

"Yeah."

"Not how it works, Calvin."

"Why not?"

"Come on, man. If he wanted me to do it, he'd've asked me."

"He just asked me first."

Kendall points to A.J. on the sandwich station, the sign that he's ready for his custom cheeseburger. "We know why he asked you first."

"I've been here longer?"

"There's more to it than that."

"What?"

"Come on. You must have noticed, right?"

"Noticed what?"

"That most of the managers and assholes in suits are white, right? And by most, I mean all."

Calvin scans the restaurant as Kendall talks. "OK, you're right about that. But me and Little Ron are the only white people who aren't managers."

"Exactly. And everyone but Little Ron knows Little Ron is never gonna be a manager, like, never ever. That means you're a real live unicorn — a chance to get some more white power in the place."

"White power?"

"I'm not blaming you, man," Kendall says. "Like, I don't think you're part of the problem or whatever."

"But I am white."

"So fucking white, believe me." He starts to walk over to grab his sandwich. "You play it low-key and everything, but it sure serves you well."

"You think so?"

"Oh, of course. Your man Tomás thinks the place does better when there are white people in ties walking around telling everyone what to do."

"But he's from Mexico! How many times have we heard that story?"

"Too many times. But even though he's brown he thinks he's white." A.J. offers Kendall a fist bump and then hands him his cheeseburger. "Need proof?" Kendall asks, turning back to look at Calvin. "How about the way he's always talking about how hard he worked right after he bitches out some Black employee. We're lazy, he's not. There it is."

Calvin *had* noticed, but what he realizes now, talking to Kendall, is that he just assumed the bias of someone like Tomás wouldn't extend to someone like Kendall, that even people with entrenched prejudices would be able to see Kendall as, well, as Kendall. Which means he's stopped seeing Kendall as Black, which means he's guilty of soaking in his own white privilege. Because, of course, most of the world, especially people like Tomás, will always see Kendall as Black.

"Don't beat yourself up," Kendall says with a shrug. "I don't expect you white boys to understand everything, even the smart ones. Because even here, man, when you're in the minority? You are still part of the majority power."

Calvin does beat himself up, though, as he handles the drive-thru by himself his last half-hour. Just a few minutes ago he was sticking up for the role of the artist in society, imagining himself very much a part of that group. Aren't artists supposed to notice stuff other people don't?

He tries to think of other meaningful insights he's missed while working. *Just because I never said it doesn't mean that it's not there.* Too on the nose for use in a song? *What do we miss if we pretend to see it all.* He's got plenty of time to run over everything in his head, because it's one of those slow stretches, when the last thirty minutes can feel like three hours.

Tomás wanders over before Kendall gets back. As soon as he's in sight, Calvin pours a large coffee from the pot he just made — he makes a pot around this time every day that Tomás is on site. Is it slightly degrading, to be making coffee for his superiors? Sure, but Calvin never has trouble getting days off when he needs them, either.

"Guy. You're killing me. We need a new day manager here, and soon. Like, yesterday soon. This place is losing money every lunch rush. When you gonna do that training?"

"Ah, I told you, I can't do it." Calvin lines up three sugar packets and rips them open.

"Of course you can, guy. You could run this place."

"It's the time." He dumps the sugar in, starts opening and pouring three creamers. "Like, I need my nights."

"I need my nights, too, guy. You think I don't have nights?"

"But I'm in a band."

Tomás looks confused. "Band?"

"Yeah," Calvin says. He hands Tomás his coffee. He knows he's explained this before, but Tomás never seems to remember. "I'm in a band, and—"

"OK, guy, OK." Tomás takes a sip of coffee. "I get it. I'm in a bowling league."

"Bowling?"

Tomás nods, puts his cup down on the counter. "Bowling. I have the second highest average for the Dunwoody Dynamos." He walks a few steps away, then turns and starts walking toward Calvin as if bowling, back hunched, right arm swinging. He mimes releasing the ball, then triumphantly throws his arms in the air as he stands back up. "Those pins don't stand a chance."

"I believe it," Calvin says, wishing a customer would come along to save him.

"So, I get you, guy. We have our passions, we are passionate creatures. But you won't have to work every night."

"I know," Calvin says, trying to think of how to make it clear, without being offensive, that Lords of the Living is more important than a bowling league. "But if I get a chance to play a gig, anywhere, anytime, I have to take it, you know that. I can't afford to turn it down because I'm working."

"It just seems crazy to me, guy. You need the money, and I need someone who can do the job to take the job."

"What about Kendall?"

Tomás takes a sip of coffee, then shrugs. He looks confused. "Who the hell is Kendall?"

"My runner for lunch."

"The girl taking orders is Kendall?"

"No, no. The runner. He's great."

"The Black guy? Where is he now?" Tomás asks, looking around.

"Break. After I leave, he'll run things over here."

"Huh." Another sip of coffee. "And you can vouch for him?"

The question feels wrong — like, why should he have to vouch for Kendall? And why should it even matter if he does? He wants to say the question is ridiculous, Kendall is smarter and more capable than anyone else in the whole building, but instead he just nods. "Of course. Totally. 110 percent." The bottom line is Kendall wants the gig, and he would never have to know Calvin had to "vouch" for him.

Tomás nods and says, "OK, guy," before he walks away. Calvin can't tell whether that was, "OK, I'll take your suggestion," or, "OK, you turned me down again so you're dead to me." For Kendall's sake, and his own, he hopes it's the former. It would be great if Tomás would stop bugging him, and it would also be great for Kendall to not have to Uber every night.

When Kendall walks back right at two o'clock, rubbing his belly as if he just finished a gourmet meal, Calvin wonders if he should warn him Tomás might talk to him about management. He can't think of any way to say it that doesn't sound awkward, though, like

1:05 PM

he's looking for some kind of praise or something. "Welcome back. Your fans are ready for you."

Kendall picks his headset back up, burps. "You outta here, Batman?"

"Outta sight and outta mind," Calvin says, using the drive-thru register to clock out.

"Tonight's your boy's show, right?"

Calvin turns around, nods. "Yup."

"It's at the Variety?"

"Yeah. Why, you gonna go?"

"Please. Lame white-boy jam band is not my scene."

"Is there any other kind of white-boy jam band?" Calvin never fails to be happy when Kendall mocks One Four Three. He said he'd made it through thirty seconds before he had it all figured out, and knew he never needed to hear it again. They didn't talk about Lords of the Living too much, but Kendall had listened enough to point to some favorite moments, like the opening of "Digital Meltdown."

"Fair point. 'Lame' is redundant. But their drunk fans who need some Uber love? That's fish I can catch real easy." Kendall holds up a peace sign. "Welcome to Burger Buddies," he says into his headset. "What can I get ya?"

Calvin pushes open the front door and steps outside. The heat coming off the parking lot never stops feeling insane, even after almost three years in Atlanta. The smell of warm tar rises up to blend with the smell of grease baked into his uniform, and the combination never fails to make him wince. At the same time, the moment he steps outside, done for the day, he feels himself floating, a trapped bird discovering that the window he has been slamming against for hours is suddenly open.

Being in management would make it that much harder to feel that sudden freedom. The extra money wouldn't be worth the pain of being forced to stay late if there was some sort of problem, or coming in on a day off because the store was short-handed. Being on call to this place would be like agreeing to go to Hell whenever the Devil felt like torturing you. Once again, he thinks of Grady's brother. The last time Calvin saw Ken, he was moving up the Target ranks and making more money, but didn't seem exactly thrilled with how his life was working out.

The text from Ken, about a year ago, had caught Calvin by surprise. He and Grady hadn't heard anything directly from Ken since they left Florida.

> *Hey how u doing*
> *Livin large in Stn Mtn wyd*
> *Here for a conference need to escape. Up 4 dinner? Expense acct!*

Ken had tried Grady first, but he wasn't answering. This was during Grady's Tessa Phase, Tessa being a bartender at the Yacht Club who he started seeing not long after Melli broke up with him — so quickly, in fact, that Calvin suspected the Tessa Phase started before the Melli Phase ended. Tessa shared a small apartment in East Lake, and Grady could be gone for a day or two at a time when he went over. Ken had shown up during that six-month period when Melli had disappeared from Calvin's life, too, so he'd had no plans at all. And a free dinner sounded amazing.

They went to a Jamaican place Ken had read about on Memorial Drive. It was tiny, hidden in some run-down strip mall, but Calvin tried to keep himself from looking as unsure as he felt. Ken proved as good at picking restaurants as he'd been in suggesting albums Calvin would like. The Formica table filled up with plantains, jerk chicken, rice and peas, even something called oxtail. The name filled Calvin with dread, but it turned out to be delicious.

"So, you're like a Jamaican food expert?"

"Nah. Dabbled here and there."

"How did you know what to order?"

"Searched around, saw what other people ordered and raved

about. I'm starting to travel for this job, and sometimes a good meal out is the thing that saves the day." He stabbed a plantain with his fork. "All part of adulting. Don't waste time and money and calories on crappy food."

"Seems I have much to learn."

"Indeed, grasshopper. Did you know I'm buying a house?"

"Buying a house?" Neither of Calvin's parents had pulled off that feat, renting every place they lived in. "How'd you pull that off?"

"Omaha's not as expensive as, say, Atlanta. And I make a real salary, and everything."

"You gonna hire a butler?"

Ken shook his head and said, "No. Two butlers," before taking another swig of his ginger beer.

Calvin raised his bottle as a salute, and the rest of the meal passed comfortably. He'd been just as nervous about the two of them having stuff to talk about as he had been about walking into Sunshine Jamaican, but Ken kept the conversation moving, from recapping where the other members of Ken's high school band, Gunsmoke, wound up (the only one still playing was Jumbo, the drummer, who Calvin remembered as being awful), to winters in Omaha ("I'd like to say you get used to it, but you don't, you just lie and say you do"), and the worst part of working at a Target ("People who clearly have too much money arguing over fifty cents they feel they were overcharged"). When dinner was done, Ken reminded Calvin it was on the Target expense account.

"Expense account, buying a house. What the hell do you do?" Calvin asked. "Do you own your Target, or what?"

Ken laughed and explained that his Target had lots of "assistant managers," the title just being a way to try and make people feel important. He casually asked if Calvin had ever smoked Nebraskan weed.

"Wait — you can keep smoking pot even after you buy a house?"

"Given the stress level involved, I think it's actually mandatory."

When they got back to the house, Downy was watching one of those real-estate shows he loved, and everyone else was out. Calvin grabbed a lighter from the bowl on the kitchen table and then led the way out to the back deck. They sat on the wooden bench built into the railing. Ken pulled a joint out of his back pocket, carefully lit it, took a long hit, then passed it to Calvin.

Just as Calvin inhaled, Ken asked, "You really still working at Burger Buddies?"

The question caused Calvin to cough as the smoke hit his lungs. "Jesus, man. Never ask about someone's dead-end job when they're getting stoned."

Ken started laughing. "My bad, my bad," he said, holding up his hands as if in surrender. "Not trying to be a bummer."

Was Ken about to lecture him about getting a "real job"? He'd never imagined Ken saying something like that, but this was a Ken who was planning to buy a house. "Well," Calvin said, exhaling slowly and anxious to keep the mood light, "I will be clocking in at that fine establishment at five-thirty a.m., thank you very much."

"Oowee, 5:30." Ken took the joint back. "Though, for the record? I think it's a smart play."

"A smart play? Five-thirty is a smart play?"

"Well, not the 5:30 part, maybe. But that crappy, disposable job part."

"Oh, so it's a smart play to put on that clown outfit and push toxic food to annoying Americans?"

Ken paused to take a hit. "It's meaningless, man. Which means for you, now, it's good. Taking a more serious job, like, so quickly, just for the money? Probably was the final bullet in my fucking guitar."

"You think so?" Calvin was relieved enough to be honest. "Because most days I wonder what the hell I'm doing there."

"You're making enough money to live, without giving anyone too much of your actual, like, self. Right now, right now you just need to be writing songs." Ken pointed at Calvin dramatically. "I've been keeping up with Lords of the Living on Bandcamp, you know."

"You have?"

"Of course. Jesus, I'm the one who told you to go for it, remember?"

Calvin did. "I do," he said. "I never forgot it," he added, the weed loosening his tongue.

"Really?"

"Yeah, man." He took a hit. He'd never expected to have a chance to thank Ken, and he didn't want to be too timid to say everything he wanted to. "You were the first one, besides Grady, to tell me the songs were good, you know? The first."

"Only because you were afraid to let anyone else listen." Ken held the last of the joint between his fingers carefully. "And the songs are really good. I gotta admit, when Grady said you had a song about 'Drowning in Mayo,' I was afraid you'd jumped the Weird Al shark. But it works."

"Thanks," Calvin said. "It started off as kind of a joke, I think, but then it's like the song got more serious without even trying."

"When I talk to my friends who write songs, or books, or anything, that seems to be how it goes. Like, the writing sort of takes over the brain, like they can't control it." Ken inhaled deeply, trying to get the last bit of life out of the joint. "And your stuff is already, like, top ten percent. And that's why I want to push you again now. Both of you — but mainly you."

Calvin wondered if Grady had complained about how long it was taking to find a drummer and bass player. "I know, we're supposed to be filling out the band, but I just—"

Ken waved his hand like a movie director stopping a bad take. "Fuck that. What you guys are doing now, when you play, works just fine. You've worked up some cool loops, and you can handle some bass lines and keyboard stuff at the same time. Grady looks great up there singing and has become decent at guitar. So don't worry about dealing with drummers until you have to, trust me."

"So what—"

"It's the songs, man. That's what you guys need to be all about right now. It's what you can do that I never could, and why you're still making music, and I'm not."

"But, shit," Calvin said, staring at Ken, whose fingers could move at a speed Calvin's brain could barely process, who held a guitar as naturally as if it were an extra limb attached to his body, some bonus part that instantly did whatever his brain told it to — and was in town for a Target conference. "You're amazing. Like, the way you play? I really thought you would be famous. For real."

"That's one of us, then."

"You never thought it? Like, you never just wanted to go for it?" As soon as he asked the question, Calvin was afraid he'd maybe gone too far. But Ken just smiled and shook his head.

"When I was fourteen, fifteen? Sure. I thought about it all the time."

"So what happened?"

"I learned the truth."

"What truth?"

"That there are a lot of amazing guitarists. A lot of people with fast hands. Too many, really. But if I didn't find a good band, or write some good songs, there was nothing for my hands to do. We can't all be Elliot Easton."

"Elliot Easton?"

Ken groaned. "You kids! Did I teach you nothing? Lead guitarist of the Cars."

"Oh." Calvin nodded. "'Best Friend's Girl'?"

"Yep. Thing is, Easton was just lead guitar. Didn't have to write much because the band had a lead singer and songwriter. Still crucial to the band, because almost every song had a lead break that wound up being important. And that, that's what I never found — some band with good songs that just needed someone to play leads."

The pot made Calvin's two contradictory reactions even more

intense. He was happy to hear Ken talk about his songs the way he was, but he was also sad to hear Ken talk about the loss of music in his life. "So, what should we be doing next?"

Ken studied the dwindling joint, holding as little of the end as he could, to steal one last hit. "I never wrote songs myself, but I've been lucky enough to meet some great writers. My favorite writers talk about not thinking while they're writing. They also seem to think about what kind of writer they want to be. So, Calvin — what kind of writer do you want to be?"

"Oh, man." Calvin shook his head. "That's a big question for this particular moment in the universe."

Ken stood up, stretched. "Good as the songs are, I feel like you're sort of holding back." He looked at Calvin. "You should be focused on songs that only you can write. That no one else could write."

Calvin closed his eyes, scanning the songs he had written, wondering which ones fit that description. Ken's voice continued out of the darkness.

"I'm not saying you even have an idea of what that means, yet. But you should think about it. Push yourself to go even deeper."

When Calvin opened his eyes, he saw Ken staring off the back deck. There were enough trees in the backyard that it was almost possible — at night, during spring and summer, when the trees were thick with leaves, if the houses behind 4630 weren't burning too many lights, and if you looked at just the right angle — to imagine you were at the edge of some woods. Calvin stared in the same direction, wondering how to find a way to the songs only he could write, the way a Stevie Wonder song or Elliott Smith song could only have been written by them.

"But what if there is no special Calvin Only song?"

Ken looked back at Calvin and shook his head. "Then I'd call bullshit. I already know that's not true."

Calvin wanted to have as much faith in himself as Ken seemed to have. "So how do I find it?"

"You're the songwriter. Might as well ask me how to paint a bowl of fruit." Ken shrugged. "Maybe spend a little more time on each one, see what else can be done. Try different things — like, do you always write the same way?"

"Yeah. I start with a loop, then work a keyboard part on top of that."

"Cool. But you should try some other method, too," Ken said. "Pick up a guitar, or skip the starter loop."

"I can't play guitar like you," Calvin said. "Starting on guitar—"

"See, that makes it even better," Ken said, turning to look at him again. "Limits can be great. And it'll let you focus more on the writing, less on the playing. I think that was my problem — I always had so much fun playing, I never wanted to take a break and try writing, which I was not good at."

"Did you try? Writing songs?"

"Once or twice," Ken said. "But it was hard, and I have never liked hard. Guitar was easy."

"Heh. Opposite for me, man. Guitar has never been easy."

"Trust me, of the two, the songwriting is more valuable." Ken looked at his watch. "I gotta jet, but keep looking around the curve. Keep seeing where else you can go."

"For sure. And thanks again for taking our music seriously."

"I do," Ken said. He started to walk to the back door, then paused. "But promise me you'll keep going, even if you have to slide into that curve alone."

"Alone?" The image of a cartoon version of himself, wiping out as his bobsled hit an icy curve, flashed into his head. "I'm not planning on doing this myself. Did Grady say he—"

Ken held up his hands, smiled. "No, no, Grady didn't say anything. But I know my brother, man, and he's like me in a lot of ways. He's never liked hard stuff either, and what you guys are trying to do, to get recognized for making cool music in a world where people think, like, songs should be free when you hit a button on your phone? That's gonna be hard."

1:05 PM

Calvin knew it was gonna be hard, and knew Grady would get frustrated sometimes, but Calvin got frustrated sometimes, too. One of the many great things about having a music partner was knowing that the two of you would be able to share everything, the good and the bad. He had no doubt that Grady would stick it out as long as Calvin did. And Calvin had no doubt that he would stick it out as long as it took.

2:10 p.m.

Many things about working at Burger Buddies are crappy, but the commute is not one of them. It's only a mile from the front door of the restaurant to 4630 Central Drive, where he and Grady have been living for two and a half years. If he catches the light for the only left turn, Calvin can be home before he's even finished listening to a single mix.

4630 looks decidedly average from the street: a two-story suburban home with a short driveway on the right leading to a two-car garage. Dark green, with black shutters and tired-looking bushes along the walkway to the front door, the house offers no hint that anything other than a very average family lives inside.

It was not the kind of place Grady and Calvin had imagined when they plotted their escape from Mayo, but the first serious test of The Plan was finding someone in Atlanta willing to rent to two unemployed twenty-year-olds. They didn't want to take jobs too far from where they wound up living, since they would be sharing one car. So, they downshifted from finding their own apartment in some hip part of the city to moving in anywhere that would have them. That turned out to be a shared bedroom in a house in Stone Mountain, a city Calvin had never heard of. Grady had, though: "Yeah,

2:10 PM

Stone Mountain — where the Klan was reborn, about a little over a hundred years ago."

At least sharing a house meant spending less money on rent than they had expected. They quickly saved enough to buy two cheap mattresses to replace their sleeping bags and then started upgrading their home recording gear. A new vocal mic revealed hidden layers in Grady's voice, and buying a secondhand bass meant they didn't have to use a keyboard for those parts.

The better the recordings sounded, the more music Calvin started to write. Within a year after they'd moved to Atlanta, they had written and recorded a dozen new songs, put up a Bandcamp page and even gotten played a few times on WRAS, the Georgia State radio station. Things went so well, Calvin admitted to Alex, a few months after he moved out, that 4630 felt more like home than either their mother's or father's places. "Is that weird?" he'd asked.

"I mean, not so much weird as offensive to those of us left behind."

"I didn't mean that—"

"I know, I know," Alex said quickly. "I'm kidding, doofus. It's actually good news, to think there could be a place for me, somewhere."

He's remembering that conversation as he opens the door, ten minutes after he clocked out. One thing that makes it possible for him to survive a long day of dealing with fried food and the American public is walking into a place that feels like a home.

The kitchen is visible at the end of the front hallway; when Calvin steps inside, he sees Downy sitting there with a bowl of cereal. He's not surprised that Downy's home — Downy so rarely leaves the house that Calvin has stopped trying to figure out what he does for money. What's surprising is finding him awake, since he usually sleeps until three or four.

"My man." Downy offers a salute and returns to his Cheerios.

"And good morning to you." Calvin walks into the kitchen, tosses his Burger Buddies cap on the counter, yawns. Does he want to sleep, or eat, or both? "What has you awake so early in the day?"

"Had a most unsettling dream, involving giant mice. I rolled a joint to put me back to sleep, but then I was hungry." Downy pauses, then lifts the bowl to his mouth to drain the milk. "So here we is."

"Here we is," Calvin repeats, opening the pantry door and studying the contents, as if the answer to what he should do next could be found inside. Each bedroom was assigned its own shelf to eliminate fights about who had purchased what food. Downy called this the "Treaty of Tordesillas" approach, and even though Grady had laughed like he knew what that meant, he later admitted to Calvin he had no idea. The shelf the two of them shared was sparser these days, but he could not deny it was nice to have Pop-Tarts and cereal that didn't disappear at Grady speed.

Calvin shuts the pantry door, deciding to leave the last packet of Pop-Tarts for breakfast tomorrow. He steps over the sticky spot in the floor, where the linoleum has completely peeled away, and heads to the sink. If he drinks some water, he might be fooled into thinking he's not hungry and be able to sleep.

Like everything else in the kitchen, the paneling on the cupboards needs work, the faux wood covering peeling away in several spots. Downy has an unspoken arrangement with the landlords, though; he makes sure the rent is paid on time, and in exchange the property owners only come by once a year, to drop off a new lease. They never even come inside. They don't have to do any repairs on the house, and the renters don't have to worry about things not looking exactly like a normal home.

Calvin takes one of the last clean mugs — NO. 1 OM, thanks to a missing M — and fills it with water. He turns his head when Downy dramatically clears his throat.

"But how rude of me," Downy says, putting his spoon down on the edge of his bowl. "How was work, dear?"

Calvin shrugs. "How was work? 'Welcome to Burger Buddies, where we pretend to be your friend so you'll give us money. Want any fries with that?'"

2:10 PM

"Capitalism, my friend. Remember that you have signed up to play the game of Capitalism."

Calvin makes an exaggerated sad face. "But what if I don't want to play that stupid game?"

"Too late. You were born in the U.S.A., you play Capitalism. Until something else takes its place, that is."

"But what -ism can take its place?" He drinks the water quickly. He hadn't realized how thirsty he was until he started drinking.

"For now, it is the only -ism we have. Which does remind me, good sir — today is that special day of the month."

The fifteenth is tomorrow: he needs to have the rent in Downy's Venmo by midnight tonight. "Ah, it is, it is," he says, pulling out his phone, and praying he has enough to cover it. Thank God Grady remembered to send his share. "Sending now," Calvin says, relieved he actually can. The amount left won't even cover a cheeseburger meal at Burger Buddies, but he gets paid Friday. Being broke has become his superpower, so forty-eight hours shouldn't present too much of a challenge. Maybe he can snack on some of One Four Three's catering at the show.

Downy checks his phone, nods. "And once again technology successfully moves data around, and keeps our economy moving," he says.

Calvin has to give Downy credit: no one sharing the house seems to make much money, but the bills always get paid on time, and none of the utilities has ever been turned off, which means he's already better at running a household on a tight budget than either of Calvin's parents were. He's also done more to teach Calvin how to do it himself than his parents ever had, explaining everything from which utilities are strictest with their deadlines ("Don't test the water company") to how to get that last bit of toothpaste out ("Straight edge of a comb, my friend, and some elbow grease").

Calvin puts his phone away and runs his hand through his hair to see just how greasy it is. Answer: very. "So, after your breakfast, back to sleep?"

"Believe it or not, my good fellow, I have a few phone calls to make." Downy burps, shrugs. "I wage my own battle with capitalism from time to time, and today I must armor up again, and ready myself for the inevitable slings and arrows."

Calvin raises his eyebrows, pauses. It's not the word choice that catches him by surprise — Downy lapses into a faux Victorian dialect at times, and Calvin has learned to just roll with it. As with most things Downy it is harmless, and even a little amusing. The first few weeks they had lived here, he and Grady kept wondering if Downy was for real, or if his whole life was some sort of performance art. Eventually Calvin had decided it didn't really matter, because there were certainly worse roommates they could have been stuck with. What's surprising is that it sounds like Downy is pursuing a real job. "What arrows will you have to fight off today?"

"I have a phone interview. Terrible concept, really — so much of all that I am benefits from being experienced in person, wouldn't you agree?"

Calvin pauses, then shrugs. "OK, I was gonna make a joke, because there must be a million possible jokes here, but I got nothing. Good luck, brave warrior." He puts the empty mug in the dishwasher — another house rule — picks up his cap and heads for the stairs. It's time for a long shower and a desperately needed nap. Seeing Grady and Melli will be easy, but watching Roddy bask in the glow of a sold-out show's crowd, and then telling Roddy after the show how great he was, will require more energy than he has at the moment.

They'd been in Atlanta for a little over a year when they got their first really good gig, opening for an indie band from New York at one of their favorite dives, 529. Sunflower Bean was putting together the kind of career Calvin believed was in reach for Lords of the Living: they put out records every couple of years on a small but cool label and toured the country, playing small but cool clubs.

He couldn't deny the show was the result of Grady's determination to be friendly with everyone in every club in town. He had become tight with the soundman at 529, bonding over *Lost* and early Pink Floyd records, and that had led to a few Tuesday-night gigs there. Lords of the Living had never played to more than a dozen people, but the soundman was still impressed enough to suggest them for the Sunflower Bean opening slot.

The night the gig was confirmed, Calvin and Grady sat on the back porch with Downy, sharing a celebratory joint. Downy offered to make a poster, and Calvin wondered how many songs they could squeeze into a forty-minute set.

"It's gonna be great, no doubt," Grady said, passing Downy the shrinking joint. "But we need a new closer."

"What's wrong with 'Mayo'?" Calvin asked. "Drowning in Mayo" was the song they ended all their sets with, and they played it so much that there was no doubt they'd play it well again, even with the nerves and adrenaline that could come with a larger crowd than they were used to.

"Everyone's tired of 'Mayo.'"

"But this should be a lot of people who have never seen us before. They've never heard 'Mayo.' It's a great closer."

"Agreed. It's still time for something new."

"Like I can just write a new closing song on demand?"

"Sure you can. Just make sure it's exciting. And catchy as fuck."

"That's all. Just a new exciting song that is catchy as fuck, finished in time for us to learn it before the show in two months." Calvin shook his head, once again impressed at how Grady could make the complicated things sound simple.

"The crowd's gonna be biggest for the last couple of songs of our set. So, after 'Mayo' we kill the room with this new one."

"This new one I haven't even started yet."

"Exactly!"

Downy started laughing as he exhaled. "Your boy has faith in you, young Calvin."

"Full of fucking faith," Grady said.

"That's one of us."

"Come on, Calvin with the secret superpowers." Grady waved in the air, as if brushing away a gnat. "You can do it."

Grady could be stubborn when he had an idea he was convinced was good, and Calvin knew that he wasn't going to let this drop. He also knew that Grady's instincts about live shows were almost always correct. So even though he wasn't sure he had enough time to pull it off, Calvin promised to try. If he could come up with a song that worked, they would be especially excited to show it off, happy kids playing with a new toy.

By the next night he had become pretty obsessed with the idea of writing a new closer. Calvin had a hard time resisting a challenge like this. Even though he knew that Grady knew he'd get obsessed, he didn't mind being played, not when he was being played for a good cause.

Calvin wasn't sure there was enough time to pull something new out of thin air, so he started looking for an existing piece of music to inspire him. Sifting through the most recent dozen or so led nowhere. "Fleetwood Mac Mistake," "Lost Ramones," "Waltzing Horses." They all had interesting moments, which is why he'd saved them in the first place, but the best one — the one that sounded like a missing chorus from *Rumours* — would not work as an exciting closer. So, he decided to go back in time a little and see if any of the older pieces would work. He didn't remember writing "Scary Chorus," but as soon as he hit play it sounded like he might have found his starting point.

Calvin usually put the music together in isolation, hesitant to let even Grady hear anything until he had a complete draft, but after he worked on "Scary Chorus" for a while, making the drums a little bassier and adding another layer of keyboards, he wasn't certain he was heading in the right direction. He played it for Grady, who suggested speeding up the tempo. That proved to be the answer — still big and a little ominous, but also a little more manic and exciting.

"Where the hell did that come from, anyway?" Grady asked, after they had listened again to the faster version.

"Some old file called 'Scary Chorus.'"

"No, I mean, like, when you first wrote it? Where does that even come from?"

"Oh." Calvin had been writing songs long enough he'd stopped thinking about the mechanics of the process. How often do you think about what your feet do when you walk? The first answer that came to his mind was, well, it wasn't like writing, at first; he told Grady it was more like looking for a secret wall.

"A secret wall?"

"Like there's this wall, and I just sort of put my hands out, hoping to find it. When I find it, I run my hands along it, tapping. If I find the right spot the wall opens up, and the music comes out."

"Comes out? Like you hear it in your head?"

Calvin had nodded. "Yeah, it's in my head but my fingers are playing it on the keyboard, as I listen? It's more like I'm just playing a song I've already heard."

"Uh, that's a bit woo-woo."

"Hey, you asked."

"But it sounds so easy. Why can't I find the secret fucking wall?"

"That's just the first step, man." Calvin had moved to the keyboard and slid headphones on. He quietly ran through the chorus, so he could work his way backwards to find the verse. Or would it be better to figure out what came after the chorus — maybe a bridge? Or a solo? As he played, he tried to explain to Grady how hard he had to work to turn the bits that had tumbled out from behind the wall into an actual song. Finding the sound was the first step, but then he had to shape that sound into something satisfying and complete. That could take days, or weeks. "Or, like, with this chorus, even longer. It's something I wrote a couple of months ago."

As he finished, Calvin realized he had been talking more to himself than Grady. When he looked up, he saw Grady surfing his phone. "All I can say, man," Grady had said, grinning and shaking his head, "is that I'm glad I met you and your fantastic brain. Because I could never work my way through those particular weeds."

Two days later, the music was done. Grady had checked in as Calvin laid out the pieces, so he had melody ideas ready to go. All that was left was the lyrics. The two of them had been in sync on every decision to that point, from how long the intro should be to whether to go back to a chorus after the lead or straight to another verse. Grady never wrote any of the music, but he had a great instinct for fine-tuning arrangements, and helped Calvin know when a song was finished.

When it came time for the words, though, they had different ideas. While singing random syllables for the melody, Grady had ended the chorus with "It's party time" and then sung "Party / in A-town" during the dramatic break before the lead. Calvin had smiled, it sounded so ridiculous, but Grady thought he'd stumbled onto something they could actually use.

"There's your hook," Grady insisted. "'It's Party Time.'"

"We can't have a song called 'Party Time.'"

"Sure we can."

"Uh, maybe you can. I can't."

Grady shrugged. "It's a fucking winner, in my book. But if you can come up with something better — and nothing that's some end-of-the-night bummer — then maybe I can be talked out of it."

It took a few days, but eventually Calvin worked up a chorus around the idea of "Digital Meltdown," and it worked so well that Grady eventually, if a bit reluctantly, gave up on his "Party Time" vision. The track was completed four weeks before the Sunflower Bean show. They decided to upload it to Bandcamp the night of the gig, announcing the new release just before they launched into the song.

When they started "Meltdown" there were about a hundred people in the crowd, which is all it took to make 529 feel packed. Calvin

2:10 PM

vamped on the opening chords, while Grady said their name and website address one more time. When the first chorus hit, it really did seem like everyone Calvin dared to make eye contact with was locked onto Grady, heads bobbing in time. Driving home with an especially jazzed Grady, a dozen hot Krispy Kremes and the final mix of "Digital Meltdown" blasting, Calvin had to admit that the whole thing had gone off even better than expected. Who was to know that the next time he'd see Grady play it would be in front of a much bigger crowd and with another band?

2:30 p.m.

The bedroom Calvin and Grady share is at the end of the upstairs hall. Whenever someone comes to visit their "studio" for the first time they like to dramatically throw open the door and say, "Welcome to the TARDIS." The room should feel cramped with the two of them and all of their gear, but it never has.

One reason is their beds — or, more accurately, their lack of beds. Sleeping on mattresses, without a frame or even a box spring, stuck in opposite corners created an open area in the middle of the room. It's here that they've set up the nerve center of their home studio: a Nord keyboard; a guitar stand with two electrics, one acoustic and a bass; the MacBook Calvin received for graduating; and the recording interface he and Grady had saved up to buy before they left Mayo.

They'd sacrificed other things a normal bedroom might have. They share a single dresser left behind by whoever had the room before them; only two of the drawers actually open and close, so they each use one and have a small spot in the closet/vocal booth designated for the few "nice shirts" they hang up. No night table, no art on the walls, no bookcases, no chairs. Calvin doesn't miss any of it. He finally gets to stay in one place, and it feels like he has more space in this tiny room with his best friend and all this recording stuff than he'd had in any of his childhood homes. There was probably a lesson in there somewhere if he was ever in a mood to look for life lessons — something about how the stuff you need takes up less space than the stuff you just have because you think you're supposed to.

The first thing Calvin does when he walks in the room is take his uniform off and toss it into the big Amazon box that serves as his hamper. He has two uniforms now, a reward for working at Burger Buddies for so long. It feels more like a punishment, though, a threat that if he stays long enough he'll have a shelf full of the damn things. It's supposed to allow him to wash the one he's not wearing, but really it just allows Calvin to go twice as long without washing either. Maybe four times as long — wasn't that how exponents worked?

He calls out to the Alexa that sits on the ground next to his bed. "Alexa, what time is it?"

"It is 2:30."

Dottie had given him the Alexa as a going-away present. She handed the box to him out of sight of his father, probably because she didn't think he would approve of spending the money; even getting him to pitch in for his share of the MacBook, something he had agreed to do, had been a pain in the ass. Calvin thought it was silly for her to risk his father's anger for something he didn't need, but he now has to admit he's grown dependent on it, especially for waking up in the morning.

He stretches, holding his arms up above his head while he counts down from ten slowly. It's something he's started doing a few times a day since Grady left with One Four Three. The change in the room, and in his life, has hit him harder than he expected, and his mind has been working overtime.

He worries about, well, everything: whether the songs he is writing are any good, whether Grady is having so much fun touring he won't want to stop, whether Atlanta is the right city for them, whether Alex will be OK without him. The more he worries, the less he sleeps. The less he sleeps, the more he worries. Exactly the conditions The Spiral needs to return, and he is desperate to keep that from happening.

It has only found him once since they escaped from Mayo. It happened on a night Grady took Melli to see *2001* at the Plaza. After two hours of trying to work on a new song, Calvin had decided it was all shit. None of the loops he'd made sounded any good, no new chord patterns came to him as he ran his fingers over the keyboard. Nothing he tried sounded like it would ever be worth anyone's time. The headphones began to feel like a vise, squeezing so hard they would eventually flatten his head, as if he was nothing, a mosquito who wasn't fast enough to avoid being smacked between two hands.

He took the headphones off, but instead of breathing becoming easier, it only became harder. Going to bed seemed like a good idea; he liked his bed, he never wanted to leave it in the morning, so going there would calm him down, would let him breathe. That didn't happen. The blanket felt like a dead weight on top of his chest, too heavy to slide off.

Calvin didn't know what time it was when Grady came home. Lying as still as he could manage, hoping Grady would think he was asleep, Calvin created a silence so loud in his head he thought his brain would explode. He could feel himself twitching, aware of how hard it was getting for him to keep from moving. He was desperate for Grady to think he was asleep; if he knew Calvin was awake, Grady would start talking — probably about Melli, who was harder and harder for Calvin to talk to him about. And whatever they talked about, the weather or new guitar strings or whose turn it was to clean the shower, Calvin worried that as soon as they started talking he would not be able to hide how dangerous his own mind was being at that moment. But maybe that's what he needed to do? Maybe the only way to escape The Spiral was to—

"Hey." He hadn't planned on saying anything; the word just came out. His voice must have sounded as strange as it felt inside his head, because Grady turned on the bathroom light and looked in Calvin's direction.

"Dude. You OK?"

"Yeah, yeah."

"Really?"

He paused, debating whether to keep the lie going, say everything was fine or he just had a headache, but decided to say the truth. "I mean, no. Not really."

Grady pushed some cables out of the way and knelt down on the ground next to Calvin's mattress. "What's up?"

Calvin began to describe The Spiral. He didn't look at Grady at first, because he was too worried he might see confusion or pity, or, even worse, a look that made it clear Grady was thinking he'd made some terrible mistake moving to Atlanta with this basket case. When he finally made eye contact, though, Grady just nodded.

"Man. That must suck. You told Dottie about it, right?"

"Yeah."

"And what did she do?"

"She just kind of, like, sat there."

"And that worked?"

Calvin nodded. "I guess it just, like, helped pull me out of my own head. Or something."

"OK," Grady said. "Then that's what I'll do." And he did.

Buzz.

The vibration of his phone pulls him back into the bedroom. 2:34. *Home yet working man?*

He can't wait to hear Melli's voice, but he needs to shower first. Something about talking to her while smelling like french fries feels wrong. He settles for texting her (*working class hero is home but smells like a fryer*) before heading to the shower.

The water needs to be as hot as possible; he doesn't step in until steam is visible. The initial sensation burns, but that's the only way to defeat the grease. *The heat does the trick, the heat does the trick.* Or, what if it's too hot? *The heat can do the trick, or it can make you sick.* Or, *if it don't make you sick?* He stands under the water and runs variations of the line through his head. It's so hard to know at first if he's had some cool new insight that he can work into a song, or stumbled onto a cliché a million people have already bled dry. A whole list of things that could possibly "do the trick"? *Love could do the trick, if it doesn't make you sick.* Need a new rhyme, already. *If it doesn't fade too quick?* Sometimes he doesn't know for sure until he's tried placing the words on top of some melody he's working on, and sometimes he knows right away he's headed down a dead end. *The heat does the trick* sounds like a ticket to Bon Jovi land, so he abandons it.

What were the lines from this morning? *All alone in my Volvo, where did all my words go?* He speeds the words up and slows them down in his head, trying to match the tempo of the music he wrote last night. Maybe the word "Volvo" should go. Combine those lines with the ones he thought of on his break — *There's too much in my head today, too much for my words to say / There's too much that I don't know / Where did all my words go?*

Not awful, but a bit whiny, and that last line still isn't close. Grady and Melli both ask him why he doesn't write anything down, but he believes if the lines are worth using, they'll stay in his head. The bit about words was better, wasn't it? *Words climb into my head / But then they hide and just play dead / My head's too full of words today / My head's so full it has nothing to say.*

His arms and chest are turning red from the heat, which is a good sign. The showers get longer and longer, especially when he's tired, but he needs to make sure the water and soap have enough time to work their magic. Melli will be waiting for him to call, but she could be in the shower with him, right now, if she lived here.

Melli doesn't want to move into a house with other roommates, though. "My parents—" is usually how she starts. Calvin understands that he is not the engineer or doctor her parents expect her to marry, but it worries him to be some secret she has yet to share. She keeps assuring him she will tell them about him, but she hesitates whenever he brings it up.

"Your parents will have to deal with it someday, you said so yourself. Why not sooner rather than later?"

"Because I won't be able to stay there once I tell them. So, I need to have a new home lined up and ready to go."

"You can stay here."

"What about Grady? All three of us in that room? That's some fucked-up French-movie shit."

"Nah. Another room will open up, they always do. Then he can have his own space."

"But if I'm gonna lose my parents by moving in with my boyfriend, I don't want to have three or four strangers hanging around. I'll risk being disowned when we can afford our own place."

Back when they'd had that conversation, the logistics of finding an apartment they could afford seemed impossible. Imagining it felt like he was back on the playground talking about forming a band, everyone planning to play instruments that they didn't own.

Then he remembered what he and Grady did to escape Mayo.

"Maybe we need a Plan." They were on the back deck, having chai. He wanted rituals like this to happen every night.

"A plan? Like a war plan?"

"Yes," he said. "I haven't thought of it like that before, but that's it. A war plan. Exactly."

"That sounds so official."

"It is. It's what helped me and Grady escape Mayo."

"You needed a secret plan to escape? Was this some sort of military-industrial complex city?"

"If only. Just a crappy city in Florida. Having a plan just, like, made it feel less overwhelming."

"Heh. Well, if it helped you escape Mayo, it must be strong stuff.

What did you do?"

Calvin quickly summarized The Plan he and Grady had developed. "I mean, none of it's Einstein or anything," he added, "but it helped me stay focused. And not panic."

"Panic?"

He had never told Melli about the way his mind could get stuck in loops of worry, and was hoping he would never have to tell her about The Spiral. "I was in high school, and thinking I'd never graduate, never mind figure out what to do next. I panicked sometimes."

"Who wouldn't?" She paused, then asked, "But the plan helped?"

"It did." He was relieved that she hadn't asked if he had ever panicked thinking about what the two of them would do next. Because of course he had.

"So, we need a plan of our own."

"Exactly."

She leaned forward to kiss him, then clapped her hands together. "OK. Let's plan. What's the first step?"

He tapped his chin with his finger, as if deep in thought. "Well, it's simple, really. Money."

"Money," she repeated. "Of course."

"Any place we rent will need first and last month's rent, right? Security deposit?"

"Yep. Money to turn the utilities on. And furniture?"

"Furniture?" He grinned. "I mean, all we need is a bed, right?"

"Well, that's first. But we'll need to sit sometimes, too."

"Yeah, I guess so. And all this needs money."

"Money."

"Fucking capitalism."

"Hey," she said quickly. "My father loves capitalism, so that might not be the best line to take around him."

Calvin nodded. "Capitalism doesn't suck, OK, got it."

"My parents' parents had to flee Castro's Cuba, remember. Capitalism doesn't just not suck — capitalism good. Capitalism holy."

"More holy than Jesus?"

"Just about."

He mimicked writing something on the palm of his hand. "Noted."

"But that does remind me."

"Yes?"

"Another step of the Plan."

"Oh." He knew where she was headed and made a nervous face. "The parents. We have to meet them, huh?"

"You know the deal. You show me yours, I show you mine. It's gonna be hard for me to tell them, and I just — I don't think I'll be up for going through more drama with parents after it's over, you know?"

She had mentioned this before, that she wanted to meet his parents before he met hers. He'd always resisted, but not because he was worried about their disapproval. They would probably be relieved he brought anyone home and would love Melli — if they didn't, he wouldn't care. What he didn't want to do was ever go to Mayo again in his life. It was a steel trap he'd escaped once, and he didn't want to push his luck. "Would a Zoom introduction count?"

She thought for a moment, then said, "Sure. Easier than going to Florida."

That could work. As soon as it began to get uncomfortable, he would just pretend the connection had frozen and log out. "OK, mine first. But is that before or after we find a place?"

"I think after," she said. "Maybe this is The Plan: 1. Save money. 2. Begin to look for a place. 3. Tell your parents. 4. Put money down on a place. 5. Tell my parents. 6. Move in. Etcetera."

He raised his eyebrows. "I like the sound of etcetera."

"I thought you would."

"How much money do we need, anyway?" He watched Melli think, and he knew that unlike his pretend thinking earlier, she was really running numbers in her head, trying to find an answer.

"Five thousand dollars?"

"Whoa."

"Rent, security deposit, cushion? It's more than we have now, sure, but totally doable, right?"

"Yes," he said. If he was honest with himself, it didn't feel doable at all — none of it felt doable. Dating Melli seemed impossible, and even more impossible seemed the idea of not making some horrific mistake that would cost him the relationship he never thought he'd have. Saving thousands of dollars, when he usually had trouble surviving from one paycheck to the next, seemed as likely as completing his training for a mission to Mars. Still, here she was sitting next to him. If that was possible, maybe everything else was? "Totally doable."

"I agree." She paused, then held up her hand. "We also need a step seven."

"Seven?" He narrowed his eyes. "Grady and I only had five. Seven, is like, two more."

"But the last step is important: not lose track of our own shit. You should have your own goals, and I should have mine."

"Fair enough." He paused. "Does that mean I need to think of goals, like, right now?"

"I figured you were easy."

"Oh, I'm easy like Sunday morning for you."

"I mean," she said, intercepting his hand as it moved for her shoulder, "it's music. It's keep working on the band and writing songs. Keep working, keep getting better."

"Yeah." He nodded. "I never realized that was my plan."

"Because it's like breathing for you. I need to respect that and help you."

"Thank you," he said. As Alex had reminded him more than once, not every girlfriend would be as supportive of a starving artist. "And I'll support you."

"Good," she said. "I've decided I want to go to grad school."

"Cool. English?"

Melli nodded. "English. Maybe I wanna teach?"

"Teach?" Calvin was surprised — not because it didn't make

sense, because it actually made perfect sense. He had just never heard Melli say it before.

"I think I resisted the idea because all my friends assumed I would be a teacher someday. But Diane's little brother comes by after school, and I've started to look forward to working with him. I've also enjoyed helping Alex with his papers, so, yeah. I think I wanna teach."

"OK, then," he said. "Then we'll make sure you get to grad school."

"It means we'll be broke, so the apartment will have to be small. Like, we'll-be-on-top-of-each-other small."

"I was hoping that would be the case," he said.

"And if we're unhappy, or pissed off, we have to just say it. Talk about stuff. No going to bed angry, or anything ridiculous like that."

"Oh, if I'm going to bed with you every night, how could I ever be angry?"

"It's hard to imagine, I know. But think about it — even your parents didn't think they'd ever stop being in love with each other, never mind being able to talk to each other."

"Huh." He was reminded that when he was with Melli, he should not think of himself as the smartest person in the room. "I admit I'd never thought of that."

"And it didn't just happen. The level of bitterness you describe takes years of practice."

"Maybe," he said, "we shouldn't be talking about my parents while we work on our Plan."

"But maybe we should. Because it's not going to be easy all the time." Her voice grew softer. When he remembers this conversation, which is one of the many Melli conversations he replays in his head often, he can feel the way her hand grazed his cheek, before gently landing on his chest. "I just want to know it's something we can do."

This time when he reached for her shoulder her hand dropped down, so he could gently pull her close enough to kiss. "This is oh so doable, with you."

3:00 p.m.

The phone is ringing when he steps out of the bathroom. "I should warn you, I'm just wearing a towel," he says.

"Well, my day just got a lot better," Melli says. "I love the sound of your naked voice."

"Good to hear you, too," he says, and it's the most honest thing he's said all day. "How's work going?"

"Same as it ever was," she says. "Would you like a new belt to go with that, ma'am?"

It's one of their many gags: he's always pushing the fries, she's always pushing the belts. She had to fight her parents to be able to take a job at all, but the fact that Abbadabba's closed at 7:30, and she wouldn't be in a restaurant or bar serving people alcohol, had convinced them.

"Do you do personalized fittings?"

"Only for very, very big tips."

He laughs. "You know what my next line has to be, right?"

"Yes, something like, 'Oh, I got a big tip for you right here.'"

"Well, then, I don't need to say it. Just think it."

"So," she says, "tonight. Let's plan before some random rush of customers."

3:00 PM

"Yeah," he says, exhaling. "Tonight." As fun as hanging out with her will be, watching Roddy bask in applause will be exhausting. "Tonight."

"I'm working until 7:30. Want me to pick you up?"

Driving to the Variety with Melli would be fantastic; being with her makes him feel like he's wearing a bulletproof vest. But it would be silly for her to drive all the way from Little Five to get him and then drive back, when she can walk from work to the show. "No, I should meet Grady at soundcheck, like he asked."

"Doesn't Daniel have the car?"

"Yep." Daniel is the newest member of the house, a quiet kid from the Dominican Republic who has found a job at Chili's. When he has late shifts he uses the car Grady and Calvin drove up from Florida, which can be a drag, but Calvin needs the money Daniel pitches in for the insurance. "I still have something left on that Uber gift card, though. I have enough to get there, but maybe you can drive me home?"

"Oh, I'd love to."

"Thanks." She always says she doesn't mind, and he believes her, but it's still embarrassing to not even have the money for a ride home. It's one of those months with the worst timing, though. Paying Downy for the rent broke him, and his one credit card is maxed out from the new guitar amp they splurged on, just before Grady took off. "You could even linger, when you drop off?"

"I do like to linger."

"I mean, you could even spend the night," he says quietly.

"You know I want to. And you know I can't."

"I know. But a man can dream."

"So can a woman. Trust me. But now, I need to get back to work. And you should nap. And dream."

"I love it when you order me around."

"There's more where that came from. We can talk about dreams and commands tonight."

KING CAL

"OK."

"I love you."

"I love you, too," he says. He's stopped being surprised at how easy it is to say it to her. Now he just wonders why it was so hard for so long.

Calvin tells Alexa to set the alarm to go off in thirty minutes and closes his eyes. He imagines — and not for the first time — how great it would be to have an on/off switch for all of his thoughts. He tries to distract himself with the music he wrote last night, trying to match it with combinations of the lines he was thinking about at work. *There's so much that I don't know, there's so much I can't say.* Maybe by the time he wakes up his brain will have figured something out.

3:45 p.m.

Calvin wakes up to subhuman whistling, the terrifying intro to "Moves Like Jagger." He has finally found a song so horrific it always wakes him, a sonic slap in the face.

"Alexa, off."

Yawns, stretches. A little more sleep would have been nice, since he will be out so late, but considering how many questions were looping through his brain — does the melody for that new song work, is there enough on his Uber gift card to get to the Variety, what will Melli be wearing today, how many more weeks until One Four Three's tour ends, anyway? — he's lucky he managed to sleep at all.

As he's sitting up in bed he gets a call from Alex. If it were anyone else, he wouldn't answer. Before he moved out, though, he'd promised Alex he would always answer his calls. "Alex."

"Calvin."

"How was school?"

"Interesting opening question. So insightful. I mean, do you write these down ahead of time? You should put them all into a book, so you can sell them."

"Ouch. Thing is, as much as my question may have sucked, you didn't really answer it."

"I didn't? Perhaps I'm going Socrates on you and waiting for you to realize you know the answer already."

Alex is smarter than Calvin, just one of the many reasons talking with him is so rewarding. "Maybe I need to rephrase the question. Did you further your education by attending class today?"

"Well. No. There were too many parts of the day I found objectionable. We're reading *Lord of the Flies*, for one, and I fail to see how a novel about spoiled English prep school boys written more than seventy years ago, mind you, is worth my time. 'Ooh, little boys are really little savages!' How insightful."

"Ah, another skip day." Alex is supposed to be going to summer school for the lit class he somehow failed. "You must be at Mom's."

"Are you implying our mother is less-than-attentive as a parent?"

"I think we are both aware of her skills in that department."

"Hmmm. Let's just say as long as our mother doesn't ask too many questions when she gets home, no one will notice my day of relaxation. I have mastered the art of the low profile to the point that I don't think the teachers even notice when I'm not there."

School had been impossible for Calvin to sit through, but he wishes Alex liked going more. There was an Advanced Drawing option in middle school, and Alex was so excited when he found out there might be a class he actually liked going to. There was only one section, so you had to enter a lottery to take it. The idiocy made Calvin's head hurt. If a class was popular, wasn't the solution to make it easier to get into, not harder?

If school couldn't be set up in a way that worked for the kind of smart and wonderfully weird people who were often ignored or undervalued by everyone else — the Alexes of the world — then what was the point of it? If Alex, who loves to draw, can't take an art class, and loves to read but fails his lit class, there's no hope for anyone else.

"And you, brother of mine?" Alex asks. "Did you once again serve the hungry of the world?"

"I successfully pushed bags of food through a small window in exchange for swiping plastic cards."

"And to think Mom and Dad thought you'd never amount to anything."

"I mean, if they could only see me standing in that drive-thru window in my smelly uniform, right?"

"Oh, I bet they imagined you in just such a uniform many times."

That line is good enough to make Calvin laugh out loud. "This is when I start to hope you called to work on your new stand-up routine about some fictional loser brother."

"Well, to be honest. . . "

"Yes?"

"I really called so you could help me settle one of those questions for the ages."

"Isn't that what happens every time we talk?"

"Fair point. But today's question, your honor, is important. So, let's stay on track shall we?"

"We shall," he says, holding his phone out for a second so he can see the time. 3:58. He should be in an Uber in half an hour. "What is this question?"

"SoundCloud, YouTube, TikTok: where do the coolest underground music types post their shit?"

"You should know better than me. Isn't each generation supposed to be hipper than the one before it?"

"Well, I used to spend most of my time chasing leads on YouTube or TikTok, but I just found some really cool shit on SoundCloud. Sometimes the algorithm actually sends me something I like."

The reference to the algorithm makes a stone skip across Calvin's chest. It no longer sounds like Alex is sharing a random new music tip, which the two of them do a lot. "If the computers get smart enough to pick good music," he says, hoping banter can save him again, "we're all doomed."

"I'm waiting for you to tell me, but I guess you don't want to, right?" As Alex talks his voice rises slightly in pitch, the way it does when he's upset. "Like, there's this whole new thing in your life, but you didn't want me to know?"

Calvin rubs his head. He has to think about getting dressed, to start moving and plan his Uber trip. But that will have to wait. It sounds like Alex has discovered King Cal, the SoundCloud account where Calvin has secretly been posting new music. Music he sings.

"It's not like I tell you everything, right? I mean, not like I've been telling you every important thing for years. Oh, wait, that is what it's like — I mean, you're only the first one I asked to call me Alex. That's all. Nothing important, or anything."

A day he will never forget: his little sister, the only one in the family he liked, never mind felt any sort of familial connection with, calling him in tears. It was so early in the morning Calvin assumed someone had died, but instead, after she stopped crying, Alice told him she wanted to be called Alex. "He/his" would be his pronouns, but he didn't know how to let the rest of the world know. Not yet. Because yes, Alex could be a girl's name, but it could also be a boy's name, and Alex wasn't sure yet what felt right. He needed to tell someone, though, and the only person he could tell was Calvin. Calvin was relieved to feel like he may not have totally fucked up his response, which mainly involved telling her — him — that nothing had changed. Alex or Alice or Apricot, he or she or they was still one of Calvin's favorite humans. ("OK," Alex had said, "but if I ever change my name to Apricot, please put me out of my misery.")

It kills him that Alex sounds so hurt. "It's not that I didn't want to tell you," Calvin says.

"But—?"

"But I haven't talked about it with anyone."

"Really?" Alex pauses, and his tone softens. "You haven't told anyone?"

"No. Just posted something I'd just finished recording. And then did it again. Like, it sort of became a thing before I really knew what

I was doing." It feels silly, now, talking about the way he kept it secret. He must have wanted people to hear, since he uploaded the songs on SoundCloud. So why not tell Melli, or Alex, or Grady? Oh, that's right: in case it sucked. "I haven't even said the name out loud."

"So, say it now."

"What?"

"The name."

"Out loud?"

"Yes. I wanna hear you say it."

He's trying to think of another way to stall, to redirect the conversation, but he stops himself. Saying the name will make it more real, which must be why he's nervous — but which is also a good reason to just say it.

"King Cal."

Alex exhales melodramatically. "Now that wasn't so hard, was it?"

"No. But now that I've heard what it sounds like, I'm worried about that k-k sound. Cheesy? Or cool?"

"It's neither, but that's perfect. The music will decide it, right? Like, if the music keeps being good, the name will be good."

Ken had said that about the name Lords of the Living, Calvin remembers. More alliteration — he must have some secret alliteration fetish. He stands up, looking for a clean and sufficiently cool shirt to wear. "So, the music is good?"

"Of course, asshole. That's not the question. The question is, when did you start this secret life?" Alex asks. "Like, the first one I found was posted three months ago."

"Three months?"

The number surprises him. "I guess so. There was no plan, or anything. I just." He pauses, spotting his black GENERATIONALS T-shirt. He holds it up, sniffs and decides it's suitably clean. "I just finished a song and thought I should do something with it."

"OK, that's the posting to SoundCloud story. But what happened before that?"

Calvin puts the shirt on. "What happened?"

"Yeah. Come on, Calvin. I have never heard you sing before. Ever."

"I'm sure I sang you happy birthday."

"Doubtful."

"I must have." He's relieved to find a pair of jeans in the closet/vocal booth. He sniffs, shakes them out and starts to sing to Alex. "Happy birthday to youuuuu…"

Alex laughs. "Nope, doesn't ring a bell."

"I owe you fifteen renditions, then. You want them now or later?"

"Uh, later. Maybe even never. But thanks."

"Happy birthday, dear Alexxxxxx…"

"So, what does Melli think? I mean, you changed the name from 'Melli' to 'Mary,' but that one about watching her sleep is gorgeous. If a little stalker-y."

"I haven't told anyone, remember?"

"Well, yeah, but I didn't think you meant Melli."

"Why not?"

"I thought couples told each other everything."

"At the risk of making you more disillusioned than you should be at such a young age… Couples do not necessarily always tell each other everything."

"Fifteen is not young."

"Fifteen is so young."

"We're the TikTok generation."

"What does that have to do with anything?"

"You multiply our age by 1.4."

"Because?"

"Because of the shit we've seen. And will see." Alex changes tone. "But stop deflecting, bro. You need to tell Melli."

"Why?"

"You're a couple. And this is important to you. And it's really, really good."

The phrase "really, really good" bounces around inside his chest,

3:45 PM

popping little balloons of tension he hadn't even noticed filling up. "The songs are good? Or the singing? Because I'm worried that—"

"The singing is good. The songs are good. Not good — great, actually. I wouldn't have said anything if it had sucked."

He smiles. Yes, if Alex had stumbled on King Cal and been disappointed, he would have kept it to himself. "I wasn't sure it was ready to share yet."

"But you didn't make the tracks private, either. The algorithm found me."

"I didn't think anyone I knew would hear them. Maybe some randos in New Zealand or something?"

"And the small number of freaks who follow Lords of the Living, Vijay Iyer, and the Generationals on SoundCloud? Something triggered the machine to send it my way."

"Stupid machine."

"You need to tell Melli, Calvin. If you don't, then I—"

"You can't tell her either, OK?"

"I won't tell her."

"Thank you."

"As long as you do."

Calvin sighs. The only opinions that matter as much as Alex's are Grady's and Melli's, which means he can't wait for them to hear songs that he is also afraid to play them. "I will."

"And hurry up. Because my promise has a pop-up timer."

"How do you know what a pop-up timer is?"

"I've seen old TV shows. I know shit."

"When does it go off?"

"No one ever knows — that's the whole point. It just pops."

"OK. Just don't pop this second." Pants on, Calvin checks the time. "Hold on, I have to order an Uber."

"An Uber! Mr. McMoneyPants, huh?"

"As if. We played a party before Grady left and got paid in Uber cards."

KING CAL

"That's right. The Grady gig is tonight."

He puts the phone down next to him on his bed, alternating between answering prompts and putting on the least smelly socks he could find. "Yes, tonight."

"Grady on the big stage. Melli going, too?"

His Uber confirmed, Calvin slides on his always-tied Keds, grabs his wallet and heads for the front door. "Yeah, she's gonna meet me there."

"Grady's the best. Say hi for me, and like, really say it. I've spent my whole life wishing I could have a best friend."

What Alex says, and the way he says it — so open, and warm-sounding — turns a movie on in Calvin's head. He can suddenly see, very clearly, all those years he spent hanging out with Grady, the two of them in his room listening to music or getting stoned and playing checkers. "Checkers with a buzz is harder than chess could ever be," Grady used to say, staring at the board with fingers pressed into either side of his forehead. Alex, then Alice, is in those memories, usually at the edge of the frame, hair still longer but already insisting on pants and the baggiest T-shirts she could find. She must have been watching the whole time. "He is the best," he says, feeling less tired than he had before the phone call began. Once again Alex has reminded him how lucky he is to have a best friend and a girlfriend and to be on his way to see them.

"And Calvin?"

"Yes, Alex?"

"That King Cal shit is really, really good. I'd like it even if you weren't my only brother."

As often happens, Calvin has no idea how to respond to praise. "Thanks."

"Now go. And text me after the show."

"It'll be late. You'll be asleep."

"Asleep? Have you met me?"

"Fair point." He opens the door and steps outside, looking for the black Nissan that will bring him to Little Five Points. "You'll probably sleep now, so you can miss dinner."

"You have met me."

"Once or twice."

"Well, have a blessed day," Alex says. It's what Dottie used to say to them when they left for school from their father's place, and ever since then they've used it as their goodbye.

"Have a blessed day."

4:35 p.m.

Every time he hangs up with Alex, Calvin feels guilty about not being there. His parents always had something to complain about when he was around. He hopes they're not making life too hard for Alex and hopes Alex's ability to make himself invisible can help.

He wonders, as his Uber driver pulls up, when Alex will listen to King Cal again. Sheila, a middle-aged white woman, has the classic rock radio station cranked and what appears to be an entire pack of gum in her mouth. Years of serving the public have made him aggressively pleasant in dealing with anyone else in that position, though, so he pockets his judgments and offers a big smile and hello. Sheila waves, pops a bubble and gets back to mouthing along with the "na na na"s at the end of "Centerfold." Calvin looks out the window, trying to pay as little attention as possible to whichever Bon Jovi travesty is lumbering onto the airwaves.

Which King Cal song was Alex's favorite? He wants to text and ask but doesn't want to come across as needy. Even though he does want to know. Very much. Now.

Sheila drives slower than she chews gum, but Calvin's not in any particular rush. Grady said five, but no soundcheck ever starts on time. The last thing he wants is to be there early; he wants to minimize awkward small talk with everyone who isn't Grady. They'll all have road stories to share, and then someone will turn to Calvin and ask, "So, what have you been up to?"

WelcometoBurgerBuddiesmayItakeyourorder.

That's not all, of course: there's also King Cal, who had not been planned or expected. Alex knows now, but Calvin still isn't sure when or how he will tell Grady, even though King Cal might never have been born if Grady had never left for tour.

That first week Grady was gone it felt like time had broken. The hours at Burger Buddies stretched out further than he ever imagined possible, cruel taffy that never broke. Melli was suffering through one of those stretches where her mother insisted she come right home to help with dinner; she'd decided that poorly developed cooking skills were the main reason she was not married yet. Even Downy had his first steady boyfriend since Calvin and Grady had moved in, an older guy who drove a Tesla and usually appeared at the front door in a suit and tie, carrying takeout. The other two roommates were both new arrivals who worked nights, so the house felt emptier than usual.

After two weeks away, Grady sent word that things were going so well One Four Three wanted to hire him for all four months of the tour. He had to keep doing it, he said — the money was too good, and it was easy work after he'd spent all that time learning the songs. He was picking up road tips from the other guys in the band and meeting lots of people who asked who else he played for, so he had plenty of chances to spread the word about Lords of the Living.

All Calvin heard was "four months." Four months where nothing would get done for the band, just when it seemed like maybe they could start getting a little traction. He read the text twice, then went to lie face-down on his mattress in the corner. Which is where he was when Melli woke him up with a slap on the back.

"Get up," she said.

He rolled over. "Excuse me, did you know that actually hurt?"

"I hope so. That was the point. You're supposed to shower me with affection when I show up."

"Well, you're supposed to be going home to practice arroz con pollo."

"I got out early, so I wanted to spend my bonus hours with my boyfriend, but he's still in his smelly work outfit."

He told her about Grady's new plan, and how it bummed him out so much he couldn't even shower. Instead of covering him in sympathy and kisses, as he expected her to, Melli just shrugged.

"Grady's gonna do what Grady's gonna do. I think we both should know that by now. That doesn't give you an excuse to sit around and mope."

"Four months, Melli. Four. Months."

"Which is really not that long."

"It sure feels like it."

"The more stuff you do, the faster it will go by."

"What else am I supposed to do?"

"What else? I mean, there's lots of stuff you can keep doing for Lords of the Living, right? Don't you have all those spreadsheets, with stuff to work on?"

She was right. After she went home to perfect her latest cooking assignment, he took a shower, then sat on his bed and opened his Lords of the Living files. He had spreadsheets for places he had sent music to, clubs he needed to follow up with, and, most importantly, songs in progress.

He had discovered the joy of spreadsheets during their senior year in high school, when he was stressed about The Plan and whether or not it could work. Writing what they needed to do, with due dates and color coding, became a great source of comfort. Laying steps out in little text boxes calmed his brain, kept the thoughts from running wildly through his head. Striking through each completed item was a tiny bit of reassurance that someday, if he just kept working, all goals could be met.

He continued using spreadsheets when they moved to Atlanta, tracking new stuff that came up, like set lists they had used. And while Grady joked about Calvin's "spreadsheet addiction," he kept texting stuff to add to "one of his crazy lists" from the road: websites and bloggers to send music to, online radio stations worth checking out, new tools for mixing someone mentioned that might be worth exploring. At first Calvin had been annoyed at all the suggestions, feeling like some sort of housewife given a to-do list by her absent spouse, but then he realized it was a good sign, a way of Grady trying to pitch in for Lords of the Living even from the road. He decided to finally go through all of those texts and put the best suggestions into their proper spreadsheets.

And then he felt better.

But what he really needed to do, he knew, was keep putting together more music for Grady to sing to when he got home. When he opened the files from his last recording session and saw it had been two weeks since he had done anything, Calvin decided he couldn't go to sleep until he'd drafted something new.

For the first hour nothing had sounded worth pursuing — it all sounded tired, ideas he had tried before. It reminded him how much he missed Grady, and not just because the room felt too big and empty without him, his clumps of dirty clothes and his stack of dirty dishes. Grady was the one who pushed Calvin, got him to think about what he was doing and why. Grady was also his first audience, his guaranteed beta-tester, the one who would instantly pass judgment, be it harsh ("Haven't we done this kind of thing before?") or complimentary ("I can't wait to sing this thing"). Knowing Grady would not be there to listen right away made it harder.

He almost gave up, but when he asked himself what he'd be doing instead, he didn't have an answer — so his fingers kept forming chords, shifting a finger or two at a time to see what change he could create, reminding himself that it was impossible to know when the music would suddenly open up. This time it came when he slowed down, when he held a couple of chords he'd been circling around for longer than he'd planned. Something about the sustained notes allowed the door to swing open, and out stumbled something that sounded like it could be alive.

The sensation reminded him of a safe-cracking scene in some French movie he'd watched with Melli one night. The first few moments of a potential new song that fit sounded like a tumbler falling into place, letting you know you are officially on your way to cracking the code. It can take a long time to get that first number, and sometimes it can take even longer to find the second number, the second piece of the sequence, but sometimes the pieces fall in line very quickly. He got lucky this time, and less than an hour later he had a musical skeleton laid out. It turned out poppier than he'd planned, but he'd learned that the tone of music was hard for him to steer. It was better to let the music do whatever it wanted instead of trying to make it do what you imagined.

This is when he would usually force himself to take a break. Once a song was sketched out, it was best to step away, to go do something else and then come back later to listen; that was the only way to hear what he had actually written as opposed to what he *thought* he had written. He did not want to stop, though. Since he knew where the lead break would go, he decided he would run down a few passes with a keyboard solo, then dared himself to try it with an electric guitar. Grady was a much better guitar player, but once Calvin relaxed and let himself think as little as he would think when playing a piano, he found a riff that sort of echoed the keyboard. After comparing the two, he combined them. That worked well, and their melodies gave him ideas for verse and chorus vocal lines .

He knew he needed to stop if he wanted to have any time to sleep before work, but he was spinning a ball on his finger and stopping would risk letting everything fall. There was only one verse, so if he could just write a chorus, the whole song would be almost done. He closed his eyes, the way he did when he was searching for the music, and this time, he waited not for a sound but an image, something he could describe.

It was Melli, of course. He remembered their long embrace before she went home, the way she'd felt in his arms and the sound of her breathing and how amazing it was to be allowed to hear it.

I close my eyes
To hear Melli breathe
I hide behind
The shadows she sees
Well, I'm so grateful
Yeah, I'm so grateful
That I get to hear Melli breathe again

The words themselves came pretty quickly, and after a few minor tweaks, lined up neatly with the melody line in his head. The biggest challenge would be singing. It seemed an impossible job for him, but it was either that or wait for Grady to come back, and he was afraid the longer he waited, the harder time he would have making it sound the way he wanted it to.

Could he sing it himself, at least well enough to have a full demo for Grady? Just thinking of trying made his head hurt, so he decided to treat singing the way he treated playing a guitar lead and think as little as possible. He took care of the logistics first, moving the laptop into the closet so he could sing and engineer. He then forced himself to record a mic test, singing the chorus to "Old Man," because surely his voice would sound passable if he compared it to Neil Young's.

When he listened back to check the recording levels, he worked hard to switch from singer to recording engineer, forcing himself to coldly evaluate his success in capturing the sound while forbidding himself from passing judgment on the quality of his voice. Maybe one key to being able to sing well was simple: just assume you can. Sure, everyone screws up a line every now and then, but that doesn't mean you can't sing. So, engineer Calvin just checked the levels on the guy croaking "Old Man," pretending it was someone else, and focused on making the raw track as good as the limits of his equipment, and the singer's natural tone, made possible.

When it came time to switch his brain again, from engineer Calvin to singer Calvin, he had to resist the urge to climb into his bed, to remind himself it was late, that he needed to get up for work very soon. Surrendering to the feeling he was in way over his head would confirm he did in fact need Grady to finish anything. He refused to accept that.

So, he put his headphones on and took a deep breath. It was the worst time to think about Mrs. Morris, but there she was, frowning inside his head. Sixth-grade chorus, a class he signed up for thanks to Cindy Overstreet, who'd moved into the house next door over the summer. He'd ridden bikes with her, shown her the shortcut to the library and the Dairy Queen. She'd said he should sign up for chorus so they'd have at least one class together. He had no idea the first day involved singing for Mrs. Morris, in front of everyone. Owl glasses around her neck on a chain, face in a permanent state of annoyance, seated at the piano, hitting notes he was supposed to echo with his voice. He froze, then finally sang in a broken whisper.

Cindy was placed in the Advanced Chorus. Calvin was sent off to regular Chorus, which everyone called "Bore-us," because the primary activity was surfing your phone while the student teacher tried to get everyone — anyone — to pay attention. And now Mrs. Morris was in the closet with him, glaring at him as she ran through a sequence of impossible notes.

He shook his head like it was an Etch A Sketch. Clear the frame. He did not need Grady to finish songs. He was not Middle School Calvin anymore. Maybe he needed to pretend he was no longer Calvin, at least long enough to track the vocal. He couldn't pretend to be Grady, though, because that would represent some sort of fucked-up identity crisis — and also, he knew who Grady was, and knew he could never be Grady. He would be someone else. Someone new. After all, if Alice could become Alex, then Calvin could simplify and call himself Cal.

Cal is more direct. More confident. Cal thinks a lot less than Calvin. He put the headphones on and hit record in Reaper. Cal takes a big swing; if he misses, Cal swings again.

The first attempt at singing the chorus was weak, his timing OK but his voice too hesitant. He made himself record the second chorus also, and then he went back and did two more passes of each without stopping to listen. By the third time through, Cal had completely taken over Calvin, and he no longer worried about each syllable being perfect, no longer visualized some pretend audience making faces of horror. He listened to the last take first, and when he managed to hear with the ears of the engineer and the songwriter, and not the mind of the nervous singer, he had to admit that it sounded almost good.

By four a.m. he had edited a few moments from the second take in to replace the weak spots of the third and made himself try to get an hour of sleep before he had to go to work. As tired as he should have been, it was the most painless day of Burger Buddies life he'd had in months. He'd forgotten to make an MP3 to listen to on his break, but that just made him even more excited to get home.

That afternoon, he hit play on "Hearing Melli Breathe" before he even took off his uniform. He was relieved at how much he liked it. It still sounded incomplete, though, and not just because it was under two minutes. The song needed more than one verse, and as happy as he was with the chorus, even his vocals, he decided he needed to change the name. It could be bold and cool to leave the name as Melli, to lay it all out there as openly as Lennon did on "Oh, Yoko," but it could also make her uncomfortable — maybe it crossed the line from love song to stalker song? And never mind what would happen if her parents somehow heard it. "Oh, you're that boy who wrote that creepy song about listening to our baby girl breathe?"

Over the next few days, he started working on revisions as soon as he got home, only stopping to talk with Melli or Alex. He tried it faster, then slower, sometimes with more guitars, sometimes with more keyboard sounds. He wanted to finish it before he met Melli for dinner on Friday, and once again a deadline was key. "Melli" became "Mary," and the song became more about the way just knowing she existed, just being able to dream about her, even when they were apart, could make him feel safe.

It began to seem like it could be finished late Thursday night. There were things he might change, but there always were. It would have been a good time to have Grady walk in so Calvin could play it for him; Grady had a gift for knowing when things were complete and when a little more could be done. Calvin listened one more time and decided he was more likely to make it worse than better if he kept tinkering with it. He had always felt a song wasn't officially complete until he released it, though, and he didn't want to put it on the Lords of the Living Bandcamp page; without Grady, it was not a Lords of the Living song. Instead, he created a SoundCloud account for "King Cal" and posted "Watching Mary Sleep." No graphics, no other info. Terrible marketing, but he didn't think there would ever be another King Cal song, so there wasn't much reason to push it.

For the first time, he was posting a song just to post a song — no expectations about what it might do for the band's career, no worries about how much anyone liked it. He hit play, and as he listened back, he suddenly remembered that conversation with Ken on the back deck. For the first time, he felt sure he had finished a song only he could have written.

He and Melli went to La Fonda Friday night, but every time he got a chance to mention the birth of King Cal, he stopped himself. Telling Melli would make it real, would mean he was ready for people he knew and cared about to hear his singing — and he wasn't ready for that. Writing had put him in a better mood, though, something Melli commented on more than once at dinner. That put her in a better mood, too. They strolled through Candler Park after dinner, holding hands and trying to guess what was happening in the houses they passed, debating which homes had happy vibes and which looked more melancholic. Even if he was the only one who ever heard "Mary," feeling so much better meant the whole process had been worth it.

He refused to let himself check the listening stats for a week. There were many moments when he imagined himself as an alcoholic, tempted by that bottle hidden in the toilet tank, but he managed to make it six days before he looked. Twelve listens. His ego took an initial hit, but he reminded himself he had not told anyone about the song. There was no bio or art on the page. For an unknown random musician, King Cal had done OK for himself.

After he posted that first King Cal song, he didn't imagine he would ever record another; doing it once and not hating the final product had been enough of a win. He would keep writing songs for Lords of the Living, and King Cal would be a one-hit wonder — well, a one non-hit wonder, an answer to a trivia question no one would ever ask. It was fun to watch the listens slowly increase, but he didn't worry about the number stalling at some point.

But then, not even a week later, things changed. It started when he laid down for his usual post-work nap. Too restless to sleep, too tired to sift through the bits and pieces of songs he had waiting to work on, he sat on his bed with his acoustic guitar. Normally it was one of the last instruments he recorded, an extra layer added when the rest of the song was done. This time, after running through the standard things he played when he held an acoustic — highlighted, of course, by a decent impersonation of Neil Young, butchering "Heart of Gold" — he found himself working through a few new chord patterns. He was tempted to switch to keyboard to follow this new idea but remembered Ken's suggestion that he try new ways of writing. So, he kept working his fingers on the fretboard of the acoustic, stumbling his way slowly through.

Before he finally went to sleep he had the sketch of a new song. It had a lot of open spaces and no vocal melody, but there was enough to call it a song. As soon as he got home from work the next day, he ran through it a few times, remembering the parts and trying to settle on the right tempo, then started trying to hear where the vocals could go. As with "Mary," it was easier to find the melody for the chorus first. He'd had an idea of a keyboard part that could slide under the guitar, and the vocal line could follow that.

It wasn't until he looked up that he saw it was after one a.m., or about four hours before he had to be up for work. He wanted to record a voice memo of what he had so far, and when he reached the chorus, he sang the first lines that came to mind so he could have an idea of what the melody might sound like with actual words. *Inside my head, the world makes sense, it makes sense to me.* He played that section a few times, and it felt like the last five syllables were wasted, just repeating the same idea. It would be better to reveal something more about the singer — *what* is making sense? Eventually, the first number in the combination for the safe appeared: *Inside my head, the world makes sense, I know who I am.*

Maybe it was because he'd written the song on guitar, or because he'd already had to sing it a few times, or maybe it was just because Grady was still gone and he was still alone, it felt like it might be another King Cal song, not a Lords of the Living song. A few days later, after he finished the lyrics, he was thinking he had written a song about Alex. That meant he would have to be the one to sing it. Something about having a second song under that name made it feel more permanent, more like a new band. But could it be a band, if it's just one person? Whatever it was, that it was all him made it scarier and more exciting, all at once.

He looks up to see the marquee of the Variety Playhouse looming on his left: ONE FOUR THREE, and just below that, SOLD OUT. He thanks Sheila, who pauses bobbing her head to some awful Aerosmith ballad long enough to shoot him a thumbs-up. Already a few diehard Onesies are loitering around the front door, even though no one will be allowed in until seven. Straight ahead is the parking lot, and off in the distance he can see the classic black tour bus. King

4:35 PM

Cal gets a random listen or two a day on SoundCloud, while Grady plays in a band that tours in a bus, just as the two of them had always dreamt of doing.

5:15 p.m.

Calvin is standing at the edge of the parking lot, trying to decide what to do. He texted Grady from the Uber, but Grady hasn't even read the message yet, probably because he's in the middle of soundcheck. The band will already have loaded in, so the back doors are probably locked. If he starts hanging around behind the club, looking for a way in, he might be mistaken for a fanatical Onesie hoping to get an autograph.

He looks to his left, in the direction of Abbadabba's. Nothing would make him happier than to drop in on Melli at work. Get a hug, banter, have dinner, then go in to the show together. Diane will be there, too, though, and he's pretty sure Diane views him as unworthy of Melli. Whenever he hangs around the store waiting, she makes lots of comments about how much work they still have to do. Plus, Grady asked him several times to make it down for soundcheck and would probably be annoyed to find out Calvin went to hang with Melli instead. Calvin also needs to make sure he made it onto the guest list, plus one, or he risks not even getting in. Even if he had thirty dollars to buy his own ticket and could allow himself to spend that much money on One Four Three, it's sold out.

The math is obvious. He starts walking toward the tour bus, hoping he can find a way into the venue.

5:15 PM

He catches a break when he finds Little Dee in the parking lot. If he could choose anyone associated with One Four Three besides Grady to see it would be Little Dee, one of the first Atlanta music scene regulars he and Grady met. He had stopped them one night as they wandered from the 529 to the Earl. Didn't even say hello, just asked what the name of their band was. When they asked how he knew they were in a band, he laughed and said he could smell it on them from across the street.

The aging roadie is rummaging through the trailer, cigarette dangling from his mouth, cellphone pinned between chin and shoulder. "I don't care if it's the Queen of fucking Sheba, or England, or even Queen Freddie fucking Mercury back from the dead. No mas ticketos." Little Dee looks up, grins when he spots Calvin. He hits a button, slides the phone into his fanny pack, motions Calvin in for a hug. "Come here, asshole."

Calvin leans in and accepts a sweaty embrace. "How you been?" he says when Dee lets him end the hug. "How's life on the road treating you?"

"Oh, every day is different in the same old way, you know what I mean?"

"Not yet," Calvin says. "But I sure hope to, someday."

Little Dee laughs, slaps Calvin's shoulder. "Oh, you will, my man. Just promise me you'll remember Little Dee, OK? When I come looking for a job."

It's always hard for Calvin to know if Dee is joking or serious. He's told Calvin several times he thinks Calvin is going to be more famous than all of them someday, and he was even sober for some of those conversations. At the same time, Dee has one of those voices that kind of always sounds like it's laughing, so it comes off like he's never serious about anything. It's nice to think he means it, though. "No one could forget you, Little Dee."

"Ha! And we both know that could be for reasons negatory as well as pository."

KING CAL

Calvin stands next to the trailer, watching Dee moving bags and grunting. "So, how's my man Grady fitting in?"

Dee nods. "Fine, fine. Grady's smart and eager. He's figuring it out." He hands Calvin a duffel bag full of cables. "And the ladies love seeing him up there, I can tell you that." Little Dee takes one last look in the trailer, shrugs, then shuts the door and loops the Master Lock through the latch. "Come on," he says. "Let's get you in for the big reunion."

Calvin follows Dee over to the Variety Playhouse, listening to complaints about the weather and how traffic screwed up their timing for soundcheck. When they reach the side door, Little Dee pauses. "One thing, though. I gotta say, I didn't know your boy liked the weed so much."

Calvin shrugs. "I mean, we both partake, sure. But we never have enough money for it to be, like, a problem."

Hands held up defensively, Little Dee quickly says, "I mean, it's not a problem, or anything. Yet. But it is being noticed. So if there's some way for you to mention it? Without, like, letting him know I said anything, because that would be no bueno."

Calvin shifts the bag of cables from one hand to the other, trying to think through all the dominoes this information knocked over. First, that Grady is a big pot smoker, which was never an issue before. Second, that others are noticing. And, finally, it sounds like something that needs to be fixed for Grady to keep playing with them — when Calvin was thinking the time with One Four Three was almost over. He wants to ask Dee a series of follow-up questions but doesn't. "Sure."

"That's my man," Little Dee says.

When Dee pulls open the door a wave of noise hits them; Calvin can hear the band running through a song. They step inside and Dee takes the bag, leaving him free to roam. He hasn't been to the Variety in a few months, not since seeing Sharon Van Etten with Melli. He's disappointed, as he walks toward a row of seats in

5:15 PM

the middle of the floor, at the impressive wall of sound One Four Three is generating. Grady is set up stage right, and Calvin is surprised at how different he looks. He couldn't have actually grown taller, but he looks taller, standing so confidently on that large stage, playing a riff on a gold Les Paul. His hair has grown down to his shoulders, so it flops nicely in time as he bobs his head. Calvin feels a burst of pride watching him — that's my bandmate, looking so cool up there. All the years they have been friends, Calvin has listened to people comment on Grady's good looks, but this is the first time he has seen the power those looks can have on stage. The combination of his easy grin and chiseled jaw makes him look like one of those people you've known your whole life, and his light brown hair seems to glow under the stage lights. Watching him move so naturally, Calvin can immediately see how much he's benefited from his time on the road, which will only help Lords of the Living next time they're on stage.

Right behind Grady, on a low riser, shades on even for an indoor soundcheck, is Greg, who switches between keyboards and guitar. Calvin can remember his name because he always looks like he's auditioning to play Gregg Allman in some dreadful bio-pic, his ponytail falling halfway down his back, leather jacket and cowboy hat carefully arranged to look casual. The other side of the stage is manned by Eddy Harsch, a serious-looking older guy with a ZZ Top beard and fisherman's cap, playing a Hammond B-3. The drummer, on a riser in the middle of the stage, looks like a graduate from the Bland & Bearded School of Workmanlike Rock; it could be the same drummer they had last time Calvin saw them, but they go through drummers like free samples at Trader Joe's, and none has been particularly memorable. The bass player is Roddy's younger brother. He writes and arranges all the music, but Calvin can't remember his name. He couldn't look more different than Roddy, with his short, skinny, accountant kind of vibe, but he has some sort of similar-sounding name — Randy? Robby?

KING CAL

Roddy himself? Not on stage yet. A true diva only appears when all the musicians have their sounds worked out.

When the song ends, the bassist nods, mumbles in Eddy's ear, then looks at the drummer and tells him something. Grady, switching to a Strat for the next song, catches Calvin's eye and grins. Calvin shoots him a peace sign. It's hard to deny that his friend looks happy to be on a big stage, several roadies floating around to tend to everyone's needs.

After a short break, Roddy's brother — and Calvin really hopes he hears someone say the guy's name before they talk, because he's definitely been introduced a few times already — nods at the drummer and gives a four count. As the band begins, Roddy appears from backstage, dressed in the same basic outfit he's worn every time Calvin has seen him, on stage or off: black suit jacket and vest, white button-down shirt, black jeans, black boots. With his cowboy hat, neatly trimmed beard and thick confidence, he could just as easily be strolling onto the stage of the Grand Ole Opry. He's handed an acoustic guitar by one of the roadies, and confidently moves to his mic in the center of the stage.

Once Roddy starts singing, Calvin recognizes the song. It's one he's heard them do live a few times, and he has to admit the chord pattern isn't bad. For the first verse and chorus, Roddy's voice is relatively restrained. He's not going for drama, or doing that goofy, almost-scatting thing he does when he's trying to sound more "exciting." He indulges in a little bit of that over the next verse and chorus, but it's still reasonable. Grady sings along in the second chorus, and hearing his friend's voice through a good PA reminds Calvin how clear and strong that voice is. He has to admit, it blends nicely with Roddy's.

The song seems to go on forever, though. Calvin wanders to the back, hoping it looks as though he wants to hear how the music sounds in different places and not as though he's bored. There's no bridge, just a long guitar solo that morphs into an extended outro.

5:15 PM

Roddy strums his acoustic aggressively, Grady plays a busy guitar riff, the rhythm section tries to cram in as many notes per second as humanly possible and Eddy delivers a dramatic organ solo. Everyone's technically playing well, creating a big wall of sound, but there's nothing for Calvin's ears to actually listen to. Those decent opening verses and chorus feel like they ended a half-hour ago.

When the song finally ends, the bass player again issues notes to everyone, except Roddy. None of the band members gives much response beyond a nod, though after Grady gets his comments, he picks up a small notebook from the top of his amp. Before he starts writing he scans the theater, and when he finds Calvin he grins and waves him up.

Every time Calvin has seen a show at Variety he's dreamed of being on that stage someday. This isn't the way he imagined it happening, but he has to admit it's satisfying to be up here for whatever reason. The stage is deeper than he expected, but also somehow smaller. Or maybe it just feels smaller because so many people are moving around. He counts four roadies, each wearing baggy black sweatpants and a black T-shirt with either a band name or a musical instrument logo. One is marking spots on the floor with gaffer's tape; one is looking over the half-dozen guitars lined up off stage right; one is talking to the drummer about what seems to be some sort of monitor issue; and Little Dee is on the phone again as he coils up guitar cables. There's a fifth member of the crew, too, and it's clear he has a more important job because he's wearing slacks and a black polo shirt and carrying a briefcase.

"That's Tommy," Grady says.

Calvin turns around.

"Caught me staring at the guy with the nuclear codes."

"Tommy the Mommy," says the roadie next to Grady. He takes the Strat from Grady and heads to the side of the stage.

"He runs the show." Grady hugs Calvin. "Man, it's good to see you."

"You, too," Calvin says.

Grady pulls back, waves his arm around the stage. "Welcome to the One Four Three Revue."

"It's a big old machine." Calvin pulls back and pokes his friend's belly with his pointer finger. It's hard to imagine Grady ever looking fat, but he's definitely more solid. "Um, they feed you on this tour, huh?"

"Damn straight," Grady says, squeezing his belly. "Like, there's always a magical deli platter in the dressing room, and this thing called a 'per diem.'"

"Hold on, hold on, that's that Latin talk."

"I know! They give us Latin money every day. To buy food and shit."

"You get paid in pesos?"

The roadie walking by laughs at that, and Grady grins. "I told you guys he was funnier than he looked."

"And not just funny-looking," Calvin says, enjoying the rush of banter. Is that what a best friend is, someone you have fun saying dumb things with?

"Well, we can't all be as good-looking as Groovy Grady."

Calvin feels a hand on his shoulder and turns to smile at Roddy, who has a good six inches on him. "Roddy," he says. "Welcome back to the ATL."

"No place like home, my man." He squeezes Calvin's shoulder, then points at Grady. "Thanks for lending us this pretty face."

"I'm all about sharing the love." Calvin works hard to sound casual, like he doesn't hate Roddy, like it's no big deal Grady's already been gone for so long. He's also trying too hard not to think about what kind of universe bestowed success upon someone like Roddy. The first time he and Grady saw One Four Three, opening on a Wednesday at the Star Bar, they figured the band would last six more months, tops. "Just stop feeding him so many doughnuts, OK?"

Roddy laughs, shakes his head. "Gotta keep my band fat and happy, you know? The gaunt emo thing scares the children."

5:15 PM

"I need all the doughnuts," Grady says. "All. The. Doughnuts."

As Grady is talking, the roadie who took his guitar calls him over, leaving Calvin alone with Roddy at the front of the stage, the exact worst-case scenario he had feared. He turns his head to look out into the room and decides to keep it simple — like being stuck with a relative you hate and talking about the weather. "Nice view from up here, huh?"

"Man, it sure is. I love venues this size. There's talk of moving to some bigger places down the road, and that'll be great — but I'll miss these smaller rooms."

Calvin figures he's been alone with Roddy for seven seconds. A mere seven seconds, and the man is already showing off his insufferable ego. Ah, yes, these "smaller rooms," that only hold twelve-hundred people. He imagines some British narrator telling viewers this could be a good chance for Calvin to examine his own feelings. Why is he so bothered by someone else's success? So, what, Calvin is right about Roddy, and the fans who sold out this place are all wrong? Yes: Calvin knows he's right. He also knows he needs to be polite, because kissing Roddy's jam-band butt could pay off with an opening slot somewhere down the line. "You guys are killing it," he says, choosing a verb he can tell himself has a second meaning Roddy won't guess. (Killing melody, killing music, killing the souls of all who hear you.) He turns back to Roddy. "That's a huge sound you make."

"Thanks, brother," Roddy says, placing his left hand over his heart, as if he's been blessed. "We all know it's just a matter of time before you guys make it happen, too."

"Thanks." Calvin looks behind Roddy, hoping to see Grady riding to his rescue, but he and the roadie are standing in front of a guitar amp, twirling knobs. "How's my boy holding up?"

"He's aces, man. A road warrior in training."

"Good to know," Calvin says.

"He is a young man of voracious appetites, and not just for doughnuts. But these things usually balance themselves out, as one adjusts to the rigors of being a professional musician."

Calvin nods, even as his brain fills up with reasons to be annoyed about everything Roddy said. Faux erudite language? Check. Subtle dig at those who are not "professional" musicians? Check. While also implying Calvin's best friend is not yet fully trained? Check.

"Though, I gotta say, sometimes I wonder if we hired the wrong Lord of the Living."

Roddy's comment breaks the loop of thoughts inside Calvin's head. "What do you mean?" he asks, trying to maintain his chill fellow-musician look and not reveal how confusing the sentence is.

"I mean, until Ronny told me," Roddy says, speaking a little more quietly, "I didn't know you, and not your friend with the golden pipes, were the wiz who wrote those songs. And you guys have some great fucking songs."

Ronny, Calvin thinks to himself: that's the brother's name. What kind of parent names their kids Ronny and Roddy? He wishes it didn't feel so rewarding to have Roddy call their songs great, but it does. He's trying to think of how to answer when he feels Grady playfully slapping his shoulder.

"Ready to go eat, amigo?"

"You know it," Calvin says. He nods goodbye to Roddy. "Let's amscray."

6:45 p.m.

"Why are we going out to eat, anyway? Don't you get, like, some sort of magical platter of food in the dressing room?"

"Yeah, usually," Grady says, "but not tonight. Everyone has so many people to see in Atlanta, Roddy just got a buyout from the club." He holds up a fifty-dollar bill. "Dinner's on me."

"You get fifty dollars for dinner?"

"Oh, not usually," Grady says. "Sometimes it's a hundred."

"Sure it is," Calvin says. "And that's what I make an hour at Burger Buddies."

Grady laughs. "If only, right? But, nah, Roddy slipped me fifty tonight instead of twenty — said I should make sure 'my boy' is taken care of. He must like you, you sly dog."

Between the money for dinner and that talk after soundcheck, Calvin supposes Roddy does like him. That's not necessarily good news; Roddy only likes people he wants something from. What does he want from Calvin? Songwriting help or Grady, or both? "Not as much as he likes you," Calvin says. "He was raving at soundcheck."

"He's really not so bad, man," Grady says. "And not just because he likes me."

"Uh huh."

"No, really. He's really harmless and not even around a whole lot. Ronny is the one who runs soundcheck and debriefs after the shows."

"'Debriefs'? Sounds like you have some fucking office job."

"I can use big words, too," Grady says. "It's just what Ronny calls it when we go through the set on the bus ride."

They finish walking through the back parking lot and reach Euclid Avenue. Calvin looks to his left and nods in the direction of a restaurant Melli likes. "Elmyr?"

"I just can't do Mexican, man. My stomach will be making noise the whole set."

"Happens when you get older?"

"For sure. I'm only three months ahead of you, remember, so I am your future." He motions to their right. "Thai?"

"Sí."

Calvin texts Melli with their plan so she can meet them after work, and they start heading toward Thai 5. Grady downloads months of road stories on the way: some celebrity sightings (a confusing conversation with someone who may or may not have been Sheryl Crow); an aftershow party with a very chatty Billy Corgan; a dressing room drop-in from that guy who had the big hit about ice-cream dreams; some good meals (pays to hire roadies who know where all the secret places are, like this ribs place in Memphis that didn't even have a sign out); some lessons learned about touring on a bus (walking around on long rides is amazing, the wi-fi is great, but the smell from twelve guys on a bus is as bad as you'd imagine, if not worse); and even a summary of how Ken is doing (came to see them in Omaha, engaged!).

He's finishing up a story about winning *Simpsons* trivia on the drive up from Florida when they reach Thai 5. After they sit down and order lots of dumplings and a basil chicken to split, Grady holds up his palms as if caught red-handed. "Man, I'm sorry, I've been rambling on and on."

"Nah, it's all good," Calvin says. "You're the one out there having adventures."

"It's your turn now," Grady says with a smile. "How's Melli?"

Calvin shrugs. "You know. Fine."

"Fine?" Grady raises his eyebrows. "Fine, like OK, or fine like, good?"

The waitress drops off their IPAs, and Calvin starts to summarize the last few months. As well as things are going, he still hasn't met her parents, and he worries about that.

"It's not like she's met yours, right?"

"That's what she keeps telling me," Calvin says. "And, sure, fair point. I told her I'd set up a Zoom."

"A Zoom? Like a crappy job interview?"

"No, but who wants to go to Mayo?"

"Not I, said the fly."

"Exactly." Calvin raises his bottle so he and Grady can toast to that. "But setting up the Zoom involves talking to them again, so I'm stalling."

"You are fond of stalling awkward conversations, my friend."

"Heh. Maybe you do know me."

"Oh, I do."

"But it's also not like I'd give a shit what they thought, or stop seeing her if they didn't approve, or whatever. But Melli does care what her parents think, and if they freak it might be too hard for her to keep going."

"Yeah, I can see that. I worried about that, too, you know. Only child, super-religious family, deadbeat musician boyfriend."

"You left out atheist."

"Oh yeah, atheist. Manage to tick all the negative boxes." Grady laughs. "I mean, I'm sure it'll be fine when it happens."

"If it happens."

"Oh, it'll happen someday. It'll be hard for her, though."

Calvin nods. "Yeah, I think it will be. It took me a while to realize that as much as she complains about her parents, she actually loves them."

"Yeah, she does," Grady says. "It sure sounds funny the way you say it, though."

"Funny how?"

"Like, it's unusual or something. But don't most people actually love their parents? Melli's mom and dad sound, you know, normal, if super-intense with the expectations thing. It will be hard for her to go against them. I'm not saying, like, it will never happen or anything. But sometimes I think you forget it can be trickier for some of us, to go against our parents. Even when we know we're right."

Calvin nods. He forgets that some people had parents they worried about disappointing. It was harder for Grady to tell his parents about The Plan, hard enough that he was afraid Grady might find it too hard to go against his parents and would just go to college. Calvin hadn't thought he would be able to go ahead with The Plan on his own, which meant that for the first time he was really relying on someone else. That was terrifying. Then he'd gotten a text from Grady, saying *dun n dun*, and being part of a team was exciting. Ken helped them out again; after pushing Grady's older brother into college and watching him drop out, Grady's parents were more inclined to let Grady try something different.

And now he knows how much he is counting on being part of a team with Melli, but she could love her mother and father enough that she finds it impossible to break free. This is not something he wants to think about, so he changes the topic. "What about life on the road?" he says. "A woman in every town?"

"Oh, there are lots of beautiful women in the world, my friend."

"You may have mentioned this before, too."

"But truth is, I'm usually too tired. There's maybe one day off a week, and that's usually some long-ass drive to the next city. These guys run a tight ship, and I still feel like I'm struggling on a few songs."

"Same setlist every night?"

6:45 PM

"Maybe a different encore sometimes, or a new cover to shake things up, but same main set."

"Radiohead changes the set every night. Wilco, too."

"Heh. Well, this ain't Wilco or Radiohead. But I can see why you'd want to — like, to keep everyone sharper?"

Their food arrives, so Grady pauses. They each nod yes when the waitress points to their empty beer bottles. "Four more weeks with the cowboy hats?" Calvin asks. "That's what I see online."

"That's what I hear," Grady says.

He knows Grady's voice well, and he's surprised to hear something else behind the words, some other sound buried in the mix. "You don't sound certain about that."

"I have learned," Grady says, picking up his chopsticks and eyeing the plates of food, "that the substitute guitar player does not get band updates right away. I roll with it."

"Huh." Calvin uses his chopsticks to slide some basil chicken on to his plate. He had not prepared himself for anything more than another month of downtime for the band.

"It's nothing to worry about, right? I'm making money, getting good life-on-the-road intel. Learning a shitload about playing live."

"It's just been a long time, man," Calvin says. "Longer than I ever expected."

"I know, I know?" Grady pops a dumpling into his mouth. "But I want you to trust that I have a plan. We've been good with plans — so can you trust me, when I say I have a plan?"

Calvin wants to trust Grady. Needs to trust Grady. Without Grady, he might never have had the confidence to write songs, never mind record them and put them out for the world to hear. He probably wouldn't have even had the confidence to leave Mayo, Florida, for that matter.

Actually, he would have failed that *Mrs. Dalloway* essay and then gone to summer school, and who knows how that would have gone. So, of course he should trust Grady.

KING CAL

"OK," Calvin says. "I trust you have a plan. What is it?"

"Now that is a fair question, amigo," Grady says. "How about we save it for after the show? We have lots of other things to talk about first. I've got more stuff for your spreadsheets, like names of smaller places to play that looked cool. Gear tips from Donkey and Mikey, who have been roadies for longer than your father's been a dick. Drummers and bass players to check out from Ronny, who knows, like, every musician in Atlanta. Even restaurants to hit, those places no one knows about except road warriors." Grady tosses one of the last two dumplings onto Calvin's plate and stabs the other with a chopstick. "But your turn. What have you been up to? How many new songs you have cooking for when I do get back?"

He should have been ready for the question. All the music he's finished during Grady's absence has been used for King Cal, and he hasn't decided what he'll do with those songs when Grady comes back. He could turn them into Lords of the Living songs, but he doesn't know how Grady will feel about singing Calvin's melodies, since melodies were the one part of their songs Grady has always written. More than that, Calvin worries about the lyrics. King Cal lyrics feel different than the lyrics he'd written for Lords. Knowing he is going to sing them means Calvin hasn't worried about writing words that could feel weird for Grady to sing, or weird for Calvin to hear Grady sing.

Calvin does not want to hear Grady sing "Watching Mary Sleep." It's King Cal's song.

He dodges the topic by quickly saying, "Oh, I'm working on lots of new stuff, don't you worry." And it's not a lie — lots of pieces of music are always being recorded and stored, waiting to be assembled. "You'll have plenty to do when you get back." And then he pivots, asking if Grady has heard anything new he's interested in, what they listen to on the bus, have there been any great openers? He senses that Grady suspects he's dodging the question, the same way

Calvin suspected Grady did not want to talk about how much more time he'd be spending with One Four Three. After being friends for so long, they each know when the other does not want to talk about something, but they also let the other get away with it, trusting that eventually everything will be said.

They've just about polished off the chicken when Melli walks through the door. Calvin is always happy to see her, always amazed when she looks his way and smiles. Now, after an especially long day, and a day with more tension than he is used to feeling, her presence feels even more miraculous than usual. He stands up to hug her hello and kiss her, in spite of his continued unease at public displays of affection. As he sits back down, he points to the almost empty plate of chicken. "There might be some crumbs left there," he says, "but we're carnivores. We could order something else?"

"No, thanks," she says, sitting down. "Amy brought in this, like, huge salad thing — something left over from her baby shower. We just nibbled and noshed on that all day."

"Wait, you 'nibbled and noshed'?" Calvin asks with a smile. "Who are you?"

"I," Melli says, reaching over to take a pepper from his plate, "contain multitudes."

For a moment Calvin worries that Grady will need to show off in front of Melli and start telling stories of road success and excess. He's long since stopped worrying about Melli going back to Grady, but sometimes Grady's competitiveness causes him to puff up his chest. Tonight, though, Grady just banters, asking for updates on Downy ("A job interview? Wait, is this the same Downy?") and offering random insights from the road ("The best thing about having a road manager is I don't have to think about anything. Someone just tells me what to do next week."). The next half-hour or so passes easily, and when the check arrives Grady takes care of it, as promised. Then he leaves to get ready, with an exaggerated wave and bow.

Melli turns to him as soon as Grady is gone. "Now," she says, giving him a kiss on the cheek, "let's go for a walk."

"That," Calvin says, standing up, "is the best plan I've heard all day."

7:45 p.m.

Melli wraps her arm through his as soon as they step outside. For the first time today he is alone with her, and it feels like a piece of iron is finally removed from his ribs, allowing him to breathe more easily. "Well, hello," he says.

Melli smiles, gently touches his right ear with her hand. "Well, hello," she says.

He leans down to kiss her. Kissing in public: something else the Calvin of Mayo, Florida, never imagined doing. Ever.

"So," she says. "How was dinner with your boy?"

He pauses, takes her hand. They begin walking, that sloweddown, relaxed pace they naturally fall into when they don't need to rush anywhere. He should try to tap out the bpm sometime — Eighty? Seventy? Maybe even as slow as sixty? Part of his brain tries to work out their tempo while the rest thinks about her question. He has spent most of his life saying "fine" to anyone who asked him any question that required evaluating his mood, because it was the quickest way to end the conversation. The conversation with Melli never ends, though, just has pauses when they are not with each other, so he takes his time and gives honest answers. "He talked a lot. Seems to be having a good time. And at soundcheck, he seemed, like, even more confident up there on stage."

"A more confident Grady? Is it possible?"

"I didn't think so, but yeah."

"But is it a good thing? Is the world still safe?"

Calvin shrugs, grins. "As long as he uses his evil powers in the service of the Lords of the Living, I am OK with it."

"'In the Service of the Lords.' Good name for an album."

"Only if we're willing to resort to controversy to sell records. Which we are."

"Thank God." She squeezes his arm, the gentle press she uses when excited. "Oh! And I got a nice message from Alex earlier."

"Oh? How is he?" He knows Alex wouldn't be messaging about King Cal, not when he promised Calvin he wouldn't yet, but it is a reminder the clock is running. He should just tell Melli. He knows she would say she liked the songs, no matter what, but he also knows her so well he knows he could tell if she didn't mean it. So, he talks himself out of telling her, but that just makes him worry about her finding out some other way and getting upset. The whole thing has become a perfect circle of worry.

"He's hating summer school, but no one should be surprised about that. And while he's complaining about *Lord of the Flies*, complaints that are perfectly valid, of course, my mom is sending me a half-dozen websites for golf-course communities in Phoenix."

"Phoenix! I thought they'd given up on this Arizona craziness."

"So did I. But whenever she has time on her hands, it seems to come back up again."

He tries not to panic. Phoenix might as well be fucking Mars. "Would they really expect you to go with them?"

"They might expect it, but it's never gonna happen."

He believes she believes what she's saying, but he also knows that Grady is right: she loves her parents. Which means there could very well be a chance she won't say no to them about moving, or about

7:45 PM

not dating some Burger Buddies atheist — never mind living with him. Is that one of those things you can never know about someone else until the moment comes, the people the other person would never be able to say no to? Maybe it's something we don't even know about ourselves.

Listening to the sound of her voice as they wander down Euclid, riffing on everything from the permanent scent that lingers in the air in Little Five Points ("It's body odor for sure, but there's a touch of, like, french fries mixed in?") to the current state of Taylor Swift (Melli remains fonder of the folkier stuff than Calvin), it seems silly to remember how worried he was that the talking might suffer after their relationship became physical. He reminds himself that he'd never really had a model to follow. His parents had never talked, and he'd never had a serious girlfriend in high school to practice with. He would have graduated a virgin if not for some random New Year's Eve party his senior year, when Donna DiGirolamo made a drunken move on him, saying they should celebrate his turning eighteen by putting on their "birthday suits." He'd been too desperate and drunk to say no, and he and Donna never said another word to each other.

But now he and Melli talk more than ever. He even lets himself imagine, sometimes, what they will still be talking about in twenty years. Thirty years. On one hand, it would be all new stuff, it would have to be; on the other hand, he would also be happy still talking about the same stuff they are talking about now. Why not? Once you write a good song, why not keep playing it over and over?

During the next shift in topics Calvin asks if it would bother her to have to sing her hit song forever.

"If I had a hit, and I liked it, no," she says. "But if it was something like that Heineken song?" She shudders.

He shudders, too. One Four Three ends every set with "My Dear Friend, Mr. Heineken," a singalong nightmare that seems to last for hours. "You, you would never commit such a crime," he says. Soon they're talking about what exactly makes a song good, or not good,

KING CAL

once again debating the various stages of Taylor Swift's career. Melli approaches these discussions like the English major she was, and he loves to hear her break down what lines she thinks work especially well. The way her brain works always impresses him, but it also makes him nervous when he thinks of her listening to King Cal songs.

For a moment he convinces himself to bring it up, to just tell her, but she'd want to hear the songs right away, too, which would mean listening on a phone, and that would suck. The whole King Cal story has gotten more complicated than he ever imagined; it's becoming harder for him to control.

8:35 p.m.

The passes Grady gave Calvin work like golden Wonka tickets. A doorman spots them in Calvin's hand and motions to the exit doors, away from the long line of people waiting to get in. As they are ushered in, Melli whispers, "We walked in through the out door, out door," and Calvin adds "Ability to Reference Prince Lyrics" to the long list of Things He Loves About His Girlfriend.

 He leads Melli up to the balcony. The second floor of the Variety is small, a few cramped rows of narrow seats, but they get lucky and arrive as an already wobbly drunk couple abandons two seats at the end of the front row. When Melli sits down next to him and leans her body against his, Calvin feels simultaneously refreshed and exhausted. Some days feel like multiple days, one of those double-albums that would have been better as a single. Or a horror movie, maybe, where you think you've buried the last body, but as you turn to walk away a zombie hand bursts out of the dirt to grab your ankle.

 The opening band, with two energetic women playing bass and guitar, has started. They have strong, pleasant voices and big smiles, but their enthusiasm is offset by the drummer, one of those dudes who always looks tired, with a blank face and slumped shoulders.

 Halfway through the second song, Melli nudges him. "So? What do you think?"

"Hmm," Calvin says, rubbing his chin as if thinking carefully, his standard move when assuming his Thoughtful Critic persona. "I mean, they're inoffensive, but I've already forgotten everything we've heard."

The next song starts, and Calvin remembers conversations he and Grady have had watching bands. As soon as they moved to Atlanta, they started trying to see as many people play as they could. Thanks to Grady's force-of-nature personality, he made fast friends of the doormen at the Earl and 529, two small clubs in East Atlanta that a lot of indie bands hit on tour. Two or three nights a week Calvin and Grady would be ushered in with no more payment than a fist bump.

Going out so often was a little overwhelming for Calvin, who was not used to so much activity and small talk, especially once he started clocking in at 5:30 every morning. If he ever tried to take off too many nights in a row, though, Grady would remind him that they had moved to Atlanta to become a better band, and that studying other bands was the way to do it. "It's like going to school, if school taught shit that really mattered," he said one night en route to 529. "This time we're learning what we want to learn."

"But most of them suck, you have to admit."

"Sure, yeah. But I'm telling you, we can learn something from each of them, even the crappy ones. Learning what not to do is important too, right?"

And he was right. Watching so many bands was the quickest way to appreciate the little things that could make a performance seem much better. They developed lists of don'ts (waste too much time between songs, tell self-deprecating jokes) and do's (make lots of eye contact with each other and with the audience, keep the adrenaline in check so your tempos don't get all fucked up). Tonight's openers introduce themselves before starting their next song, but they say it too quickly, like they're embarrassed to be so pushy. That broke one of Grady's key commandments: Thou shalt make thy name known to all, several times over.

The word "fine" runs on a loop in his head as he watches the band. Would it be better to be bad than to be fine? At least bad might be more memorable than whatever's happening onstage. His mind is running laps around the Variety, and Melli looks like she's getting ready to nap, curling her back slightly and leaning her head against his shoulder — not that he's complaining. So, is One Four Three bad? Or just fine? And what does it mean, then, that One Four Three is so popular?

One Four Three's version of its success — told by Roddy repeatedly, loudly — is a tale of a hardworking group that played whenever and wherever they could, getting better and better live, making more people want to come see them. If it was that simple, though, if that was really all it took, wouldn't more bands just follow the same formula? That formula simplifies things too much, while also implying that everyone who doesn't make it just doesn't work hard enough. He knows it isn't like that. Lots of musicians practice all the time, write great songs, say yes to every opportunity and still play to small crowds on Tuesday nights. If they get any gigs at all.

After the opening band finishes, Melli shifts in her seat. The switch to Beyoncé through the PA must have woken her up. "So, is it really just luck?" he asks, when her eyes open.

"Good morning." She stretches. "Is what just luck?"

He points down to the crowded floor below them. People are beginning to move closer to the stage in anticipation of the headliner coming on soon. "That."

"I mean, as much as I want to be petty about everything Roddy is a part of," she says, leaning forward slightly for a better view, "this can't all be the result of luck, can it?"

"Maybe not. Maybe you need luck and a song about beer. And videos with tiny dogs."

"The dog is more the symptom than the disease, isn't it? An example of a gimmick?" She yawns. "Americans like their gimmicks."

"I guess. But you'd still need that chunk of luck." Watching the roadies preparing the stage for One Four Three — imagine that, having other people set up your gear — Calvin remembers the debates he and Grady used to have about the most important ingredients for a band. Musical talent or vibe? Good songs or good chemistry? "But I don't think of it so much as a formula as a recipe."

"Oh, I like that," she says, wrapping her arm through his. "Calvin's Recipes for Success. I'd watch that show."

"It's all about proportions, right? You need more of some ingredients than others. Like, some perfect blend of talent, determination and songwriting."

"So, the talent is the flour? Biggest ingredient in most cakes."

"Could be." He pauses, trying to visualize an actual recipe for Musical Success. "Though I think the flour might be the songwriting. Talent is important, but practice and determination can compensate for some lack of natural talent?"

She nods. "But without songs, you got nothing."

"Exactly."

"So maybe the songs are the flour, and the talent is sugar. And you need a little more if there's not as much natural talent/sweetness." She leans back in her chair. "But you're right, luck must be a part of it. Some small, but also crucial ingredient."

"Small but crucial. Exactly."

She snaps, smiles. "It's got to be salt, right?"

"Salt. Of course."

"Makes all those other flavors more intense, right? And without it, everything just tastes a little more — flat."

"No salt, no flavor."

"No luck, then, well, no luck."

"That's depressing," he says.

"My Aunt Vicky used to say, 'Better have fun making the cake in case it burns.'"

He gives her a skeptical look. "Your Aunt Vicky? I've never heard of this aunt with funny sayings."

8:35 PM

"Still in Miami, with most of my other cousins," she says. "Of course, I may have heard it on a TV show. But I heard it."

"But what does it—"

"If you had fun making it, it doesn't matter as much if the cake burns and doesn't taste good."

Calvin tries to imagine if he'll be happy if the Lords of the Living cake burns. What would that mean — never become any more successful than they are now? Maybe their career peaks with opening slots at clubs no more than an hour from their house. If that's the future, but they have fun recording and make stuff they like to listen to but everyone else ignores, aside from a few oddballs scattered across the globe, would it still be worth it? He wants cake, and he likes making it — but he also wants it to taste great. He wants someone to listen to a Lords of the Living record twenty, thirty years from now and be as impressed as he was listening to Elliott Smith. But now he also wants that for King Cal, which means he's getting greedy. As much as he wants Grady to come off the road and devote himself to Lords of the Living, Calvin now wants two kinds of cake.

The lights go down. Calvin's best friend is about to take the stage in front of twelve-hundred people. Hard to go back to burnt cake after that.

9:45 p.m.

The lights dim, the crowd cheers wildly and the "Looney Tunes Theme" starts to play. It plays three times, actually — the first time slower than normal, then standard speed, then faster. When the last note hits, the lights come up, and One Four Three is onstage. Roddy counts off loudly and the band kicks into its first song, a generic bit of midtempo Americana that somehow makes the whole place explode in delight.

The end times, Calvin thinks. We are living in the end fucking times.

And there's Grady, stage right, Les Paul in hand, bobbing his head in time. As the band rolls through its first three songs seamlessly — OK, Calvin concedes to himself, they are tight as a snare drum — he watches his friend closely. When he plays, his body moves in a steady rhythm, shoulders fluid and hands moving so comfortably they seem to float above the guitar strings. He grins when he makes eye contact with the other band members, closes his eyes during dramatic moments, as if lost inside the music, and steps forward to sing background vocals for most choruses, all the while never breaking a sweat. Even the cowboy hat, which appears to be required of everyone onstage, looks OK on him, though Calvin will be sure to give him shit about it after the show.

9:45 PM

They launch into the standard One Four Three closer. Roddy stands in front of the mic without an instrument, while Grady—*Grady*—strums the opening chords on an acoustic. His best friend is grinning in what sure looks like delight as the crowd joins in the opening lines:

The end of a long night, the end of a long day, the end of a long week
I got nothing to say but that's OK because we don't need to speak
You and me still as close as can be, bittersweet until the bitter end
Now I raise my glass to you my dear friend, Mr. Heineken

Calvin has seen the band half a dozen times, and every set has ended with this song. But this is the first time he has watched Grady sing along like he means it, instead of in the mocking tone he and Calvin usually take. It's also the first time the lyrics in the bridge are clearly audible, since the Variety has a much better sound system than the smaller places One Four Three usually plays. He hadn't noticed the melancholic edge before; if he winds up finding something positive about the Heineken song, his whole universe will need to be re-ordered:

My father knew you well, the stories he could tell but now he's gone
But I'm not all alone, as long as you're in the house, it feels like home

As the band runs through the outro, Roddy strolls the length of the stage, pointing at different sections of the crowd and bowing, hand held over his heart in melodramatic gratitude. "Heineken time?" Melli asks, stirring awake.

"Heineken time is almost over, thank God."

She sits up, still holding his arm. "Did they play for three hours?"

"It feels like it." The band is finally leaving the stage. "We'll have to sit through an encore, still." He turns to her; she looks as tired as he feels. "Sorry, I need to stay and talk to him."

She sits up a little straighter to kiss him on the cheek. He focuses on the feel of her body leaning against his, to distract himself from the hundreds of people urging this terrible band to play one more.

"He looks happy," Melli says.

"He does," Calvin agrees. "Maybe this is what he should be doing."

"It is. We all know Grady belongs onstage."

"I mean," Calvin continues, "onstage like this. In front of lots of people."

"Yes. But with you. With Lords of the Living."

Calvin tries to think of the way to explain the thought that has come to his head. It's not a good thought, but it is clear, and at the moment he can't imagine it not being true. "Grady belongs on a big stage, but I don't think we're ever gonna sell out a place like this. Maybe he should just give up on me and find some band like this. Or stay in this band, awful as they are."

"You can't say for sure you will or won't sell out a place like this. There's so much left to do, and plenty of time to do it."

Calvin is not sure Grady thinks they have plenty of time, but he doesn't want to talk about this anymore. Below them, the band is back, and the crowd is dancing awkwardly to a jam-band take on "Party in the U.S.A." that seems alarmingly serious. As they mercifully reach the end, musicians begin to leave one by one, until it's just Roddy, singing the final few lines a cappella. The crowd loves this guy, and the inexplicable love of a mob has made even lesser talents famous.

The balcony starts to empty out, revealing a sea of crushed plastic cups and empty beer bottles — lots of them Heineken, of course. Melli yawns, stands up and holds her hand out for Calvin. "Come on, my love. Let's go see your friend in the cowboy hat."

11:10 p.m.

The dressing room is packed with well-wishers: women in tight and tiny outfits, accepting free drinks with a laugh and a smile, and a fair number of local musicians, dudes who spent years making fun of One Four Three but are now desperate to catch the eyes of anyone associated with the band. A few older men in suit jackets and T-shirts, an outfit that screams Trying Too Hard to Be Young and Hip, give off the scent of would-be managers. (Roddy and Ronny have been doing most of the business stuff, but Grady said they were looking for some outside help.)

Calvin takes hold of Melli's hand, as if to make sure she does not get pulled out to sea. "It's hard to breathe," she says. "How long do you think we need to stay?"

"Let's just see him and then disappear," he says. When he turns around to look for Grady, though, he bumps into Roddy, grinning from ear to ear and holding an almost-empty bottle of wine.

"Calvin, the Lord of the Living himself," he says, wrapping his wide arms around Calvin long enough to pass some damp sweat from his shirt to Calvin's neck. "And the beautiful young woman with the most beautiful name I have ever heard," he continues, bowing in Melli's direction, "Melli, Melli. Melli the Magnificent. Melli the Marvelous."

Melli smiles and nods but remains slightly behind Calvin. He knows she does not want to get any closer to Roddy, who has a reputation as being handsy with women. She says nothing has ever happened to her, but the stories are plentiful and believable.

Roddy turns back in his direction, and Calvin digs into his bag of standard post-show phrases. "You guys were amazing, Roddy. I mean, that was just a massive sound up there." The second sentence isn't even a lie — the sound may not have been something Calvin enjoyed all that much, but it *was* massive. He's hoping he said enough, but the look on Roddy's face makes it clear the man's ego is expecting more. "And, I gotta say," he continues, remembering something else positive he can say that isn't a lie, "'Almost Time to Fall In Love.' Is that new? Man, it's just great."

Roddy's face brightens. "Ah, thank you, brother. That's one me and Ronny have been working on a long time. It's making me very happy to play it."

"Well, you gotta record it soon," Calvin says.

"Plans are afoot, plans are afoot."

"That's good to hear," Calvin says, another true statement: if One Four Three is planning to record, they'll get off the road, and Grady can come home.

Roddy takes a drink and exhales slowly, as if the action has exhausted him. "Who'd've thought, right? All those crappy club gigs, and here we are, man, backstage at the Variety."

Watching Roddy's face, Calvin knows he imagined this very night many times, despite the "What a surprise!" act. "Oh, I bet you thought about it, man. I bet you thought about it a lot."

"Ha! Caught me. Of course I did. A lot." Another swig from the wine bottle, followed by a fairly hard tap on Calvin's shoulder with his free hand. "But I bet you have, too."

Calvin nods. "Yep. Of course I have."

"We're more alike than it might seem. Thing is," Roddy says, leaning down as if to share a secret, "you could be closer to making that happen than you think. Had a chance to talk to your boy yet?"

"Not yet." Calvin looks around a little more energetically now, hoping Grady will appear soon and provide him with an escape hatch. What does he mean, "closer to making that happen"? In a flash he remembers Melli asking, when Grady first took the gig, what Calvin would say if One Four Three offered Lords of the Living some opening slots. At the time he had dismissed the idea out of hand, because he could not imagine a worse audience than frat bros. Now that he's seen how many frat bros there are — and how much merch they buy after a show — he thinks it may not be the worst idea in the world.

He feels Melli tugging his arm. "I need to get out of here," she whispers. "Text me when you're on your way. My car is in the back lot."

"OK," he says, kissing her before she turns around to leave. Something about the way she pushes through the crowd, politely but deliberately, reminds Calvin of the first time he'd watched her walk away, at that party he and Grady played for Downy's friends. After coming to talk to them on their break, she'd parted a sea of drunken men with a flick of her wrists, a woman confidently forging her own path.

Calvin is relieved to see that Roddy has wandered off, in search of more wine, or more women, or both. The dressing room is getting more crowded, the air growing thick with the smell of beer, pot and desperation. As much as he wants to follow Melli out and go home, he can't leave before he finds Grady. He can at least get out of the Frat Bro storm, though, and the back corner of the room seems to have the lowest population density. It's also in the opposite direction from where Roddy had headed.

Over the course of his short walk, Calvin turns down two Heinekens and a joint; the last thing he needs, in a room full of people who should never hear his unfiltered thoughts, is to be drunk or stoned. He finds an empty stretch of wall and leans back. It's like he's been awake for a week, so his entire body feels a wave of relief when he can take some of the pressure off his legs. He also has a clear view of the crowd from here, so he should be able to spot Grady as soon as he appears from wherever he is hiding; in some private room with a pretty girl and/or some pretty good weed, is Calvin's bet.

A guy to his left is in the middle of a heated debate with someone on his phone ("I did not say that, and you just saying that I said it doesn't make it so. You have to say things to actually say them"), but the guy to his right is alone and without a drink in hand, like Calvin. He turns and nods; the guy nods back, and the vibe is instantly more relaxed than anywhere else in the room. Calvin wonders if it's safe to make a crack about hell being stuck in a crowded room with frat dudes and sorority girls. As soon as the man starts speaking, though, Calvin is glad his brain was slow to work up the joke. He's standing next to Ronny, who has ditched his cowboy hat and changed into an Atlanta United T-shirt.

"Thanks for loaning us Grady," Ronny says.

Calvin nods, trying to remember if they've ever had a private conversation. He's taller than Calvin remembered; Roddy seems to tower over him on stage, but now Calvin thinks the brothers might be closer in height. Maybe it's the cowboy hat that makes Roddy look so much taller? The extra-large ego? "Thanks for showing him how the other half lives," he says, gesturing to the noisy crowd. "This is not a usual Lords of the Living dressing room scene."

"Not our usual dressing room scene, either," says Ronny. "Normally just a bunch of smelly guys fighting over a box of Ritz and the last Bud."

"That's a vivid image."

"Well, we are supposed to be the writers."

"Oh, you're the writer," Calvin says, trying to sound deferential. And it wasn't hard to do: as much as he may believe his songs are better than One Four Three's, there's no denying Ronny has been writing longer and with more tangible success. "You're the guy whose songs sold out the Variety."

Ronny shrugs. "That was the band. And Roddy. And the Chihuahua."

He's surprised to hear Ronny bring up the role the dog videos played. "You write the scripts for the videos, too?"

"I stay away from that dog, man. If he's not trying to bite you, then he's pissing on your shoes."

"Size-wise, more cat than dog, really?"

"Or rat?"

As much fun as it is to joke about the Chihuahua videos, and although Ronny is being even harsher than he is, Calvin decides to change the subject. If anyone overhears him, he could get Grady in trouble. "I told Roddy, that new song? 'Almost Time'? It's great. So fucking great."

Ronny's face, which has been decidedly neutral even when he was calling their mascot a rat, softens. "Really? Thank you. And thanks for telling Roddy — I had to talk him into that one."

Calvin remembers Roddy saying he and Ronny had written it together, and how happy he was to play it. Does the man ever tell the truth about anything? "Why didn't he like it?"

"He hated my demo." Ronny laughs, shaking his head. "He said it sounded like a song a chick would sing."

"Really?"

"Yeah. I mean, I almost saw what he was trying to say. The vibe is more . . . I think it's more of, like, an emotional song than we normally go for."

"Which is one reason it works so well."

"Thanks," Ronny says. "It's nice to know the fight was worth it."

"I also wanna say," Calvin continues, still thinking about the song, "that it sounds, like, more mature, if that doesn't, like, piss you off?"

"Doesn't piss me off at all, and thanks. That was satisfying to write, for sure." He holds up his right hand and points at Calvin. "Reminds me of what I felt the first time I heard one of your songs. 'Digital Meltdown'? Is that's what it's called?"

KING CAL

Calvin nods, trying to look casual. "Thanks."

"I'd seen you a bunch of times already, and that one just sounded like a step forward for you guys. That chorus just explodes. And I love when a song has music that gets people dancing even when the words are kind of dark."

He's flattered Ronny remembers that one and even paid attention to the words. "Thanks. I actually had to talk Grady into those words."

"Really?"

"He wanted to call it 'Party in A-town.'"

"Frontmen, right? Can't live with them, etcetera." Ronny shakes his head. "But we both have good ones, even if they can be pains in the ass. That helps get the songs out there, and we both know it's all about the songs."

"Always," Calvin says. He's still finding it hard to believe Roddy's brother can be this open with him.

"'Heineken,' same problem. Roddy didn't like the words."

"What? But that's like, your closer, every night."

"I know. Even Roddy could tell that chorus was gold. It's the bridge — he thought it was depressing."

"'My father knew you well,'" Calvin quotes. "'Now he's gone but I'm not alone.' Yeah, beer as solace of the next generation? Pretty dark."

"I mean, it's not really about our father." Ronny shrugs. "But our mother sure had some problems with her wine. And, for me, the bridge was the whole reason to have the fucking song at all."

"I gotta say," Calvin starts, suddenly more impressed with the song than he ever expected to be. "It's pretty impressive, turning a song about alcoholism into a drunken singalong."

"Like having a dance song about technology leading to the end of the world." Ronny smiles. "But that's what we do, right? Take our shit and try and turn it into something people want to hear. I have also learned," he continues, "that it works best if I forget Roddy is gonna sing what I come up with. Just write the song I need to write, and then let Roddy and the band have it."

Calvin wonders if he has been overly conscious of the fact Grady was going to be singing their songs and if that has been shaping his lyrics. Maybe the King Cal songs feel different because he's not thinking about who will be singing. He's going to have to add "Have a deep conversation with Ronny about songwriting" to his List of Things He Never Expected to Do.

"And I gotta say I'm impressed with how you can get the songs to sound so full, you know? With just the two of you."

"Thanks," Calvin says. "The beauty of technology."

"That is one thing to keep in mind, though. Like, OK, maybe this band you saw tonight isn't exactly your number-one jam—" Ronny pauses, holds up his hand when Calvin starts to protest. "It's a safe space here, Calvin. I've heard your music, I know your songs, and I don't think our stuff is, for you, destined to be mentioned in the same breath as 'Fake Plastic Trees.'"

Calvin nods. "No. But few things are, right?"

"Fair." Ronny shrugs. "I'm just saying these players give me a lot of toys to play with. A lot of sounds that can be made. Which can be pretty great for a songwriter. And maybe someday you might want to see what it's like, to have toys like that to play with."

The conversation has officially gone from surprising to confusing. Is Ronny asking Calvin to write songs with him? Why would he ever do that? It also sounds like Ronny is saying he does all the writing, even though Roddy has always hinted he played a large part.

Calvin is trying to figure out what to say next when he feels a friendly slap on his back. When he turns, Grady is standing close, grinning with what Calvin knows is his Very Stoned face.

"I am shocked, stunned I tell you," Grady says, wrapping his arm around Calvin's shoulder, "to find my bandmate hiding in the corner."

"Caught me. I was just chatting with Ronny." When he turns back to say goodbye, though, Ronny is gone.

KING CAL

"Nerding about transition chords and best ways to write a bridge, no doubt."

"No doubt."

"And I know what you're thinking," Grady says, waving his arm around the drunken scene in front of them. "It's not like this every night."

"It'd better not be," he says. "This is nuts."

"Home field advantage, trust me." He looks over Calvin's shoulder. "No Melli?"

"Oh, she saw the show. Even came up here with me, hoping to see you," Calvin says. "But Roddy made her a little nervous."

Grady looks around, probably to make sure Roddy isn't nearby, then makes a pinching motion with his hands. "He didn't get too close, did he?"

"I was her human shield," Calvin says, puffing up his chest.

"Calvin the Enforcer, for the win." As Grady talks, he's bumped from behind by a woman in a pink dress. "Let's go somewhere we can actually hear each other," he says, motioning to the door.

They push their way to the dressing room door, then down the narrow staircase back to the main floor. Even the stairs are crowded with various friends of the band — and after a sold-out show, everyone is a friend of the band. Harder than pushing past all the people is stopping to listen to all the compliments Grady gets. Calvin doesn't want to deny Grady the chance to hear he did a good job because Calvin knows, objectively, that Grady did play well, but it's still a drag to keep hearing "You guys sounded great," because that means Grady is part of the "guys." It's hard not to feel like they're back on the playground, where Grady can easily slide into the group of popular kids, while Calvin hangs out at the edge, alone.

11:50 p.m.

It's amazing how much quieter the world is outside the theater. As Calvin's eyes glance around the parking lot behind the Variety, something about the way the lights hit the uneven pavement, reflecting off broken bits of glass, reminds him of the parking lot in the Waffle House near his mother's. He and Grady would walk there in the middle of the night when Grady slept over. They'd each get coffee and, if they had enough cash, a waffle. They'd stay for an hour or two, talking about songs they were working on, music they were listening to, the pointlessness of school and, more and more as they reached the end of their high school years, The Plan, and their approaching freedom.

Calvin and Grady walk toward the bus. An impressive amount of gear is lined up in the parking lot. Roadies are packing the trailer, speaking loudly in shorthand. "Alpha? I got the Alpha, but who's got the Beta? And I need that fucking Boogie now." Meanwhile, Grady is grilling Calvin for reactions to the show. Could everything be heard clearly or was it a muddy wall of sound? What about that slide solo — was it OK? It's hard to answer, because Grady keeps talking faster and faster, something he does when he's A-level stoned.

Once they pass the bus and reach a quieter section of the lot, Grady stops and stares at him. "I feel like you're dodging. How did it sound, really?"

"It was good, I told you. You guys were really tight — like, that was a machine up there."

Grady waves the words away. "I don't want the bullshit lines you'd say to anyone. Tell me the stuff you'd only say to me."

Grady's face has the look he uses when it's just the two of them. It's the look that says he thinks Calvin is holding back, but there's no need for either of them to not just say what they really want to say. It's annoying that Grady knows him so well, even if it's also nice that someone has gotten to know him so well.

"I was really impressed with the way it sounded like a real band," he starts, looking for something more specific that won't sound like a lie. "Like, you're new, and that's a different drummer than I remember seeing them with last time, but it still sounded like a band that's been playing together for a long time."

Grady smiles. "Yeah, thanks. I was worried about that. What else?"

"Middle of the set," Calvin continues, trying to think of something less positive to convince Grady he's being honest, "it did seem like some of the tempos lagged. Even Roddy lost a step or two, for a few songs."

"Fair, fair. Sometimes we get so amped at the start of the set we wind up underwater in the middle. Need to work on that." He claps his hands together. "This is great. I knew you'd have good stuff to say. What else?"

"It was really satisfying to see you in front of so many people. That's how I always imagined you, you know? In front of a big crowd. And you owned it."

"It's a rush, for sure. But this was a hometown show, right? There are plenty of nights where we have much smaller crowds."

Calvin winces to hear Grady say "we" so much. The tumbler clicks. "But then you keep saying 'we,' and I wonder if I'm not just watching you sit in with other people. I'm watching you in your new band."

"What? No, that's not it." Grady looks genuinely surprised. "These guys will never be my band. It can't be my band if you're not in it." His face softens. "You know that, right?"

Until he said it out loud, Calvin hadn't realized how worried he was. "After tonight, I'm not so sure."

"What, you think I'd give up on our band?"

"Not give up, as much as, like. I don't know — be tempted by something else? Isn't it gonna be hard to open on a Tuesday at 529 after a show like this?"

"First of all," Grady says, holding up a finger, "not all the shows are like this. Like, we've played to fifty people in clubs that hold a couple of hundred."

Fifty is not such a bad night, but Calvin nods.

"And second," he continues, adding a second finger, "all this shit is experience for me, right? And could be helpful experience for both of us." Grady smiles. "I have a way for us to both be on this next leg of the tour."

"Both of us?" Calvin remembers Roddy hinting at something earlier. Is he going to be asked if Lords want to open some dates? His mind tries to calculate the math of that offer, adding up the column of positives and subtracting the column of negatives. "What do you mean? Roddy mentioned something—"

"Ah, man. I told him to let me ask you." Grady holds his arms out to his sides, like he's about to announce Calvin won a new car or something. "I suggested you for the open spot."

"Open spot? What open spot?" It's not what he expected, and he's not sure what Grady means, so it's impossible to hide his surprised look.

"Yeah. Greg wants to come off the road, so they need someone to handle the utility spot. We have a few days off in about a week. Gonna head to Nashville to break in a new drummer. You'd meet us there, learn the set, then come out to California."

Calvin is confused. "Greg plays guitar and keyboards."

"Yeah."

"Have you met me? I'm not any kind of good guitarist."

"You're better than Greg, trust me."

"But—"

"You sell yourself short, man. You always have. You just watched the set — you'd be perfect."

Calvin leans against an old Ford that looks like it hasn't been moved since the '90s. "I gotta say, this is something I never imagined needing to think about. I need a second."

"But you said Roddy mentioned something?"

"I mean, all wink-wink, nudge-nudge and vague. To be honest, I thought he meant having us open a few shows."

"Ah, yeah. Well, I did ask Roddy about that, but those sisters are, like, cousins of his or something, so we're gonna bring them to California."

Again with the "we."

The adult thing would be to not say no right away, to not just run through the parking lot looking for Melli so they can flee in horror. The adult thing would be to run the numbers.

1. Riding across the country in a tour bus with Grady is a life goal, so getting a chance to do it much sooner than he expected is tempting.

2. He would start to get more experience playing live, which he knows he needs.

3. He might make more money than he does at Burger Buddies.

"How much?"

"Same as me: four hundred bucks a week, with twenty bucks a day per diem. Sleep on the bus most nights, but if I can get used to that you can."

He makes nine dollars an hour, which is three-sixty a week. One Four Three could be four-fifty, even five hundred dollars a week if he is careful with the per diems.

"How many days would I get to practice with the full band to make sure I don't suck?"

"Three. But you can get this shit, you know you can. You'd listen and practice on your own and be good to go."

He tries not to think about the injustice of the universe, that a band as awful as One Four Three can make enough to pay its members that much money. Instead, he focuses on the hard truth: it's decent money, and he could save a lot.

4. He has always wanted to see California.

"There's nothing about shows out west on the website," Calvin says.

"It all just got confirmed."

"You're just telling me now?"

"Like I said," Grady says, his tone defensive, "it all just got confirmed."

"How long we talking?"

"Hard to say. Through the Midwest, up the West Coast, then into Canada. There's a week in England now, but maybe some more stuff in Europe? A few days off here and there, to work on stuff for the next record."

"But — like, how long is all that gonna take?"

"Six-month commitment. That's it."

"Six more months?" The searching for positives ends in an instant. Six months of not seeing Melli? Six months of seeing Roddy many, many hours of the day? Six months of not working on Lords of the Living or King Cal? "What the fuck?"

"Roddy is lining things up to start recording in February, so for sure no longer than that. Maybe some small shows in January, to play some of the new stuff live."

"So. through January? That's seven months. That's almost like having a baby."

"It's really not that long, man. Say it is seven months — that's seven months of good pay and saving most of your per diem, too. Money for playing music, not flipping burgers."

Calvin stops staring at the smashed ketchup packet at his feet and turns to Grady. "You're gone until February. And what if they ask you to play on the record?"

"I don't think they will. Ronny actually plays a lot of the guitar in the studio."

Calvin studies Grady's face. "That doesn't mean they won't. Need you, I mean."

"Don't know."

He can tell Grady is just pretending to be casual. "But that's what you want. To go record with them."

"It could be cool," Grady says. "They're looking at a couple of kick-ass studios. It's all hush-hush for now, but Sub Pop's talking about a two-record deal, man. They'd pick up this one to distribute it better, and then pay for the next."

Calvin makes a note to never buy another album put out by Sub Pop, an independent label he had respected until this moment. "That's nuts."

"You were there, man. We sold this place out."

"But the songs? Like, there aren't actual songs… Some chords and a lot of jamming."

"Not all of them. There was a new one tonight—"

"'Almost Time.' OK, yeah, I hate to admit it. But that's a good one."

"Ronny has a good ear, man. I think you guys could, like, go off for hours and get all eggheady about writing music."

Ronny must have been hinting at this earlier when he talked about writing for a larger band with good musicians. They've all been talking about asking Calvin to join them, and Ronny must have thought having a chance to write with him and hear the songs played with the One Four Three machine would make the gig more appealing. And while it could be a cool challenge to try and use those musical talents for good instead of evil, Calvin also understands any time he spends working on songs with Ronny will be time away from

11:50 PM

working on his own songs. Zombies don't want to be friends; zombies just want to eat your brains.

He wonders if he should tell Grady about the talk with Ronny. If he does, he could talk about why he's worried about doing that, but it could also sound like his ego is out of control and like he's trying to compensate for the fact that they had asked Grady first.

"Man, Grady, I just don't — I mean, I just don't know how I could survive being in that band."

"And I don't know why you can't see how great this could be," Grady continues. "Being paid to go to California in an actual bus with actual music nerds?"

"But I'd have to learn all these songs," Calvin says, his voice coming out whinier than he wants. "For months, these songs would taking up valuable space in my head. I wouldn't have time to work on any of our songs. I'd have to be learning theirs."

"Yes, but — but can't you see it as a chance to learn? To figure out how to make a life out of playing music?"

"Playing their music?"

"Playing music in front of actual people is a good thing. It would be their music for now, yeah, but it doesn't have to be forever."

"And taking orders from Roddy?" Calvin keeps coming up with what he thinks are great closing arguments; having to take orders, to do what Roddy said, would be worse than apologizing to assholes in their BMWs for putting their chicken sandwiches in the wrong place. "Doesn't it drive you crazy, to have someone telling you what to do?"

Grady raises his eyebrows. "You realize you just described our band, right?"

"What?" All this time, Calvin has thought of Grady as the leader.

"You call the shots, man. And it's fine. Like, that's my gig, I get it. It's more fun with you, because we're friends, and because your songs are so much better. But Roddy's not that bad — and the money is great. So, if we can just suck it up and drive around in a big bus, and make some money? And, come on," Grady continues, "let's face it — if I'm out until February, what else you gonna do?"

Calvin stretches, looks around, still thinking about how Grady thinks Calvin's the one in charge. Is that really how it works? The muscles in his body feel like they are being pulled and squeezed at the same time. How long have they been out here talking in circles? He wants to check his phone for a text from Melli, but that could look to Grady like he doesn't care. "What do you mean, what else am I gonna do?"

"I'm just saying Lords of the Living is on this sort of, like, break, anyway. Why not make some money playing music with me while you wait?"

"Wait?" Calvin is growing more confused and angry with each turn of this conversation. Being up since 5:30 doesn't make him more patient, but even if he weren't exhausted, he would know this last question is ridiculous. He's supposed to sit around and wait for Grady to decide to come back and make music together again? "Why would I wait? I'm still working on new stuff."

"But you can't finish anything until I get back. So why not—"

"I can finish them."

Grady looks at Calvin but doesn't say anything.

"I mean, I have finished some," Calvin says.

"What do you mean?"

"I mean, I finished some songs. Without you."

"Who wrote the melodies?"

"I did." As frustrated as he is, Calvin feels a pang of sadness at the hurt look that flashes across Grady's face. "I couldn't just sit around and wait."

"Oh." Grady looks as if he is about to say something, then stops, shakes his head. "You don't have to, now. Come out with us, make some money. It's just for a while."

"Just for a while? The same way you were gonna be gone for four weeks? And now it's gonna be closer to a year. At least."

"But then that'll be it. And that's a lot of money the two of us could be making. Four hundred a week, man, with all expenses paid."

"How much have you saved so far?"

Grady looks surprised by the question. "What do you mean?"

"Like, how much have you actually saved?"

"Why?"

"Because maybe that would help convince me. Like, if we could figure out how much you actually save each week. And then multiply shit and figure out how much actual money we're talking about."

"I can't do math now, man," Grady says, shaking his head. "I'm tired, and I'm—"

"Stoned."

Grady raises his eyebrows. "You say it like it's not something we've done a million times, man."

"I know," Calvin says. "But it makes it hard to have a serious conversation." He wants to tell Grady that Little Dee and Roddy both mentioned the pot use, but he's afraid if he brings it up now it'll seem that he's only saying it because he's angry.

"About money? We haven't seen each other in four months and you want to bitch about money?"

"Only because you keep harping on it, trying to get me to go play with these cartoons.."

"Yeah, sorry about that," Grady says. "Just thought it might be fun to play music on stage with my best friend."

"It is. It will be again." Calvin pauses, trying to watch this all from some drone shot up in the sky. From up there, maybe he looks like the asshole and Grady is the hero. From up there, maybe it's obvious Calvin should say yes, go off and make lots of money and write songs with Ronny. But maybe it's even easier to see it could also be a trap. That years would pass, the money would be too steady to give up and suddenly all they would be doing was touring the country and working for Roddy. "Just not with this band and these songs, man. I can't do it."

Grady is staring at the ground. "How many songs?"

"What?"

He looks up at Calvin. "How many songs did you finish?"

Grady looks more bothered at the idea that he finished songs without him than Calvin had expected. His first reaction is to tell Grady there's nothing to worry about, King Cal is just a way to keep himself from going insane. As he thinks about it, though, he understands that while it may have started that way, it feels like it could turn into something else, especially if Grady is gone until February.

"Six."

"Six. And you didn't tell me?"

"I needed to do something. I was going a little crazy."

"But why not tell me? Like, let me hear them, right?" He has his phone out now, scrolling. "Did you post them? I don't see them on the Lords page."

"I couldn't call it Lords — not without you."

Grady looks up from his phone. "But you posted them, right? That's what you do when you think it's done."

Calvin nods. His best friend does know him. "SoundCloud. King Cal."

"King Cal?"

Calvin nods. He should have planned better for the moment when he has to say all this out loud to people. "I didn't think anyone would listen but I made myself do it."

Grady scrolls, then grins. "There it is. Sixty-two listens on this first one."

"I'm huge," Calvin says, trying to keep it light.

Grady looks up from his phone, no longer grinning.

"But why?"

"I needed to do something," Calvin says. "You were gone, and I need to make something."

"Maybe. Or maybe it's just what you want to do."

"I mean, write songs? Yeah. That's what I want to do."

11:50 PM

"Sure. But now I'm wondering if you really want to risk putting yourself out there in the world, to see what happens."

Even if he had thought about discussing King Cal with Grady, he wouldn't have considered this angle. "Of course I want to see what happens. That's why we moved here. But you're not here now, so for the sake of the band—"

"Which band? I'm not in King Cal." Grady shrugs.

"That's not a real band. Just something to keep me busy while you're gone. Our band is the real band."

"Is it?"

"Of course."

"But real bands play."

"We do."

"I mean, out in the world, more than just a few times a year. And practice, in loud rehearsal spaces. And go out and meet other bands and take every chance they can to try and get ahead. But you'd have to leave your room to do that." He pauses, and his voice has a harsher edge when he continues. "Maybe that's why you never say yes to any of the drummers or bass players. If you said yes, we would have to practice more, and then we could play out more, and you'd have to go to the outside world."

Calvin shakes his head as Grady talks. The conversation has become this sprawling, ugly thing he was not prepared for. "Where is this coming from, man? We've been a band for years. We've recorded a lot of music. Just because I want to hold out for a drummer who—"

"Really? I don't know. It's like you're happiest just working by yourself. Maybe you really think you don't need anyone. Even me."

"What? That's not it, at all."

"Ken warned me," Grady continues. "He told me you'd move on someday without me."

"What are you talking about?" Calvin is trying to figure out how this turned so quickly. He'd been left by Grady, but now Grady was acting like the abandoned one.

"He warned me, man. Said that you'd figure out you could do it all on your own, so I needed to make sure I, like, proved my worth. I thought I had."

"Of course you have. There's no band without you."

"Exactly. Remember: without me, you'd still be stuck in fucking Mayo, jerking off to Elliott Smith. Without me, you'd never have even met Melli, just stared at her from behind your keyboard."

Close friends always have a secret list of cruel things they silently agree to never say to each other, and Grady is reading from the list. Calvin waits to respond, hoping Grady will say something that shows he understands he went too far, but he doesn't. Calvin does not want to read something from his list about Grady, because he knows how hard that will be to recover from — that is one of the few lessons his parents passed on. "I didn't think you'd be so mad," Calvin finally says. "It's just a few songs."

"You didn't tell me. That's the shitty part. That's the part that makes me think, yeah, you've decided you don't need me." Grady pulls out his phone. "I gotta go get ready for the ride tonight. See ya."

And with that he turns and starts to walk back toward the bus. Grady has never been much of a hugger, for sure, but it is an especially sudden departure, even for him.

THURSDAY, JUNE 15
12:05 a.m.

He watches Grady disappear then texts Melli.

Where r u
Asleep in my car waiting for stupid bf
What an asshole
Tell him im up by bike store

Calvin walks over to the next entrance for the back lot; when he turns to his left, he sees her leaning against her car. He never imagined being so happy to see someone waiting for him. "Sorry, that took forever," he says, walking over to give her a kiss.

"I knew it would. I just couldn't stay in that room." She pauses, examining his face. "You look like shit, by the way."

"Thanks," he says, practicing slow breathing. The last thing he wants to do is to start crying in the parking lot. "Good to see you, too."

"So, what happened?"

"It was ridiculous." As he answers she brushes his cheek with her right hand, and that's when his eyes start to water. "He's not coming back for six months."

"Six months?"

"Oh, but wait, there's more." He holds her hand, breathes in, steadies himself.

"What?"

"They need to replace Greg."

"Who is Greg?"

"The guy in the back, playing guitar and keys."

She shrugs. "Stick them in a cowboy hat and they all look the same to me."

"Grady asked if I'd want to do it."

"Really?" Melli looks confused. "That's why you're upset? Why?"

"Because it's a ridiculous idea."

"But you'd be great, and you'd get to play with Grady again."

"Playing those crappy songs."

"And getting paid for it."

"Oh, I don't think there's enough money for that. And all that time lost to fucking One Four Three?"

"Is six months really that long?"

"It depends." He's ready to get in the car now, to get away from here, but she's still leaning against the door.

"It depends?"

"A six-month prison term is one thing. Six months in Paris is another."

"This wouldn't be as bad as prison, I don't think."

"Six months with Roddy?"

"You don't have boobs, so he should leave you alone." She smiles. "What's the pay?"

He hopes that she's just trying to play devil's advocate and to make him less angry at Grady. "Four hundred a week."

"And Grady said they get a per diem, too?"

"Yep. Twenty bucks." He is annoyed by the questions she's asking, which make it sound like she thinks this is an idea worth considering.

"And most places will feed you, so you could save some of that, too?"

"Yeah, but—"

"So, the money part, that's not awful, right? More than pushing burgers, with less daily expenses. Six months from now you'd have Step One of The Plan all by yourself, if not more. We'd be that much closer to our own place."

For the second time in less than an hour someone is trying to talk him into taking this crappy gig. He has a harder time dismissing Melli's arguments, though. The idea of making enough money to have their own apartment makes him wonder for a second if he *could* survive six months on the road with One Four Three. Could he live with those songs in his head if he was doing it for The Melli Plan? Maybe it wouldn't take as long as he was afraid it would to learn them. Maybe—

But no. He can't. His chest grows tight at the idea of enduring Roddy's tips and advice and writing sessions with Ronny that suck the energy out of him and keep him from writing his own stuff.

"I can't do it," he says. "Just, just having to learn all those songs and play them night after night. And Jesus, rehearsals with Roddy telling me what to do — I just can't."

Melli watches him closely as he talks and slowly shakes her head when he finishes. "I'm trying to understand, I am. I can see how it might be tricky, because for you the thing you want to make you money is also something you never want to feel like a job."

"Yes, yes," Calvin says, impressed with how she can put one of his biggest problems into words so clearly. "That's it."

"But. But if there was something I could do to make that much money for us? I'd do it."

"Anything? What if it was something you hated?"

"I think that knowing what I'd be getting — what *we'd* be getting — would overwhelm that."

"I just. . . I can't do it."

"But then what are you doing for our Plan? You still haven't told your parents—"

He holds his hand up. "Let's not add my parents to the discussion, please."

"Of course not," she says. "Because you don't like talking about them, either. But sometimes we have to talk about things we don't want to talk about."

"Just not now," he says. The last thing he needs now is the image of four disappointed parents and step-parents standing in the parking lot, shaking their heads at the sight of him.

"So, when? It's part of The Plan, right, which was your idea?"

"I thought you liked The Plan."

"I do. But, like, we have to actually work at it? This thing with One Four Three sounds like it would really move us forward. I mean, it's not like working at Burger Buddies is ever going to pay more."

"God, no, unless I'm willing to become a manager."

She pauses, narrows her eyes. "Wait, what?"

He never told her about Tomás hassling him to train for manager. It was a ridiculous suggestion he will never accept, so why would he ever need to mention it to Melli? The look on her face makes it clear that she wishes she had been told, though. "They offered me a chance for some management training, but, like, how could I do that? I can't work nights and weekends."

"Because of the band?"

"Of course."

"But you just said Grady will be gone at least another six months. That's six months of more pay you could have, but you said no?"

"It would be—"

"What? Hard? Sometimes stuff is hard, Calvin."

First Grady, now Melli: it's like everyone imagines he can't do anything without Grady. "Great. Grady's already pissed at me, and now you're pissed at me."

"I'm not pissed at you, Calvin. I just . . . I'm just trying to figure out what you want. Or maybe, like, trying to figure out how you think you're going to get what you want. I mean, this seems like a chance to get paid to play music, so I can't figure out why it makes you so upset. But you also don't want to take more money at Burger Buddies. Even though Grady's not here, so, like, what is it you're willing to do?"

"I'm doing stuff." He says it before he can think about how it will sound — and it comes out whiny, juvenile.

"I mean, you're working," she says. "And coming home and feeling sorry for yourself. But what else are you doing?"

"That's a little harsh." He considers playing her a King Cal song to show he has been doing something. But, his brain reminds him, she could also say the song isn't that great, certainly not worth giving up these other chances to at least make some money.

She pauses, nods, her expression softening. "OK, maybe that is a little harsh. I guess what I'm asking is: what are you doing that can't wait for a few months?"

"Six months is more than a few." He tries to calm his voice. "Six months of not working on my stuff. Six months away from you."

"Six months is long, and I'd miss you." She pauses, tilts her head. "You could still work on your own stuff, right? At least a little? And it would be a lot more money than we have now."

Hearing her say "we" is nice; it means she thinks of the two of them as a team. He thought he would do anything for that team once he was part of it, could make any sacrifice needed to help the team. But now he knows playing One Four Three songs for six months is not on that list of potential sacrifices. The effects of needing to turn off enough of his brain to play that music for six months could be permanently damaging, and he wishes there was a way to explain that. He also wishes he didn't need to explain it, that she could just understand. "It could, like, make me hate everything."

"Hate everything? That's a bit dramatic. I mean, it'd be better than Burger Buddies, wouldn't it?'

"That's the thing," he says. "As shitty as that job is, it doesn't use the music part of my brain. In fact, I can pretty much think about music all day. With One Four Three, with Roddy, and his band of dudes, and like, the work it would take to learn how to play that kind of stuff — it would be so hard that it could fuck music up for me."

She seems to slump back against the car. "OK."

"Melli. I'm sorry. I really don't want to make you mad."

"It's just, you know." She shrugs. "I'm gonna have to go out on a big limb, at some point, and tell my parents about you. At the very best, they don't speak to me for a couple of months. At the worst? I could wind up literally being disowned."

"I know," he says, wishing he could think of something smarter or more insightful to say.

"But it's all part of what we have to do, so I'm readying myself to do it, you know? And working every shift I can get, trying to save every buck I can. But you haven't told your parents about us yet and turned down two chances now to make some money." She shakes her head. "That's one thing I have to say my parents got right — I've never been afraid of doing the work that needs to be done."

"It's not that I'm afraid of doing the work."

"So, what is it, then? Is this some dumb male ego thing? Because the offer comes from Grady? Because they asked Grady first?"

As frustrating as it had been to talk with Grady, this conversation is even more exhausting. Melli should already be driving Calvin home, and instead they're stuck in this parking lot. It's an even more stressful conversation, too; do he and Melli also have a secret list of cruel things they silently agree to never say to each other, so secret he does not even know what is on his? He does not think he could bear it if she says something off her list now. But before he can think of what else he can say to make her understand, Melli pushes herself away from the car.

"Sometimes I feel like I'm the only one trying, Calvin."

She grabs the door handle. As he starts to walk to the passenger side, though, she turns, holds up the palm of her right hand. The look on her face is a combination of disappointment and anger. It's a look he's used to seeing, a look he's received from both of his parents and both of their spouses and countless teachers. He had become immune to it, but on Melli's face it's crushing.

12:05 AM

"I told my parents Diane took me to see *Les Miz*, so it's time for me to go home. You should find a way to do that, too."

"What?" He says it because he can't believe he's understanding her correctly, but it's also a general plea to this whole night: what is happening?

"I'm afraid if we get in this car, I'm gonna say stuff I shouldn't. So, call an Uber, and we'll . . . We'll talk later."

He's still trying to think of what to say as she pulls away.

12:39 a.m.

She really left without him.

 His forehead feels as if it has fully fused to the sticky spot it landed on. Calvin is not sure how long he has been sitting outside the closed coffee shop, head resting on the dirty metal table, when he feels his phone buzz. It could be Grady or Melli, so he summons the energy to pick the phone up. It's Alex again. He swipes up and sees a series of missed messages.

> *Show should be over unless these guys play 4ever*
> *How was it*
> *Are you there testing testing*
> *Click here for free money*
> *Ok now the setlist is up where the fuck are u*
> *I messaged melli too but no answer did u guys run off to get married*
> *Maybe you and melli and grady all gonna get married*
> *Wait I dont wanna know*
> *Well I need to send this before I lose nerve msg me asshole*

 The last message has an attachment. It takes a few seconds to download, because he's out of fast data for the month — please, don't let him run out of data completely tonight on top of everything else — and then it takes him a few seconds to decipher. Not because the image is confusing, but because the concept of the image is. Before today, only Calvin, and a few anonymous listeners, even knew King

Cal existed, and now he is staring at a logo: a melty-looking crown by way of Dali, with the name spelled in random capital and lowercase letters. Alex has always been an amazing artist, as far as Calvin is concerned, but he has always kept his art to himself. It's a big deal for him to show something to anyone, so making something purposefully for someone else is, well, also amazing.

When he swipes back to the messages he sees Alex has sent a new one now that Calvin has read his others.

wtf c?
Sry just catching up its fucking perfect amazing
If u hate it I can do something else or nothing at all
I luv luv it

As rare as it is for Alex to share his art, to see him respond with a heart emoji is rarer.

Thank u
No thank u been a crappy night so I needed something good

This time there's a call. "What do you mean crappy night? What happened?"

He's exhausted, and the idea of talking through it all again makes him even more so. But it's also nice to hear someone asking about what happened, so he recaps the talk with Grady and tries to explain the fight with Melli. "I mean, I can sort of see her point of view, now, sitting here. After six months I'd have some money saved and we could get our own place."

"Maybe," Alex says. "But you'd still have to pay rent where you are now? Like, where else are you gonna keep your shit?"

"True," Calvin says, a little embarrassed his younger brother is asking an obvious question he hadn't thought of. "Some of the money would have to go to that."

"And then," Alex continues, "there's the whole idea of pretending to like that crappy music. Six months of pretending to be someone else."

Alex is right again. He wouldn't just have to learn the songs, he would have to look, every night on stage, happy to be playing them.

"If Melli has any questions about how hard it is to pretend to be someone else, she can just ask me." There's a pause. "Sounds like a crappy fight, no doubt."

The way he says "pretending to be someone else" twice hits Calvin hard. How exhausting was it for Alex? "No doubt."

"Have you called her since?"

"No."

"Dude." There's a pause. "Don't be like Dad."

"Oh, that's a low blow," Calvin says.

"I'm just trying to get your attention. You both suck when you're mad — he shouts, you shut down."

Calvin sighs, rubbing his head. "It's not that I'm mad. It's just that I don't know what to say. Or, like, how I'm supposed to handle this. Give her space? Run after the car? Show up outside her house with a boombox?"

"Uh, what was that last one?"

"Don't you kids watch cheesy movies from the '80s?"

"Nah. Unless some clips show up on TikTok."

"John Cusack, boombox, 'In Your Eyes'?"

"You're slipping into Russian, old-timer."

Calvin sighs. "I'll send you a link when I get home. If I get home."

"Thing is," Alex says, "I get Melli wanting the money and everything, but it still seems weird to get so angry that you wouldn't take some crappy gig that could actually ruin music for you. Even after you told her about King Cal, she didn't get it?"

"Oh, I didn't tell her about that."

"Calvin. What the actual fuck?"

"You know," Calvin says, adopting that Older Brother tone that drives Alex crazy, "you swear entirely too much."

"Bad fucking role models is all."

"Heh. Tell me about it."

"But why not tell her about King Cal? You're doing all this cool shit, you just don't tell anyone."

"It's not ready."

"The music is great. The music is ready. Which means it's just that you're not ready."

"OK, fine," he admits. "I'm not ready."

"You're ridiculous."

"Yeah, well you're ridonkulous," he replies. "So, so. So there." There's another pause, but what's amazing, as he sits there exhausted and broke and suddenly aware of how much he needs to pee, is that talking with Alex has made him feel a little better. He switches to the screen with the JPEG of the logo. "This drawing is amazing, Alex."

"I do have superpowers, remember."

"I remember." He closes his eyes. "Now can you use those superpowers to blink me home?"

"I don't teleport on Wednesdays, sorry."

"Yeah, but now it's Thursday."

"Oh. Or Thursdays."

"Stupid teleportation union."

"There must be someone you can call," Alex says.

"You'd think," Calvin says, but he remembers Kendall, who was going to try and hover around Little Five Points for drunk One Four Three fans. Would it be weird to ask for an Uber ride he'll have to pay for later? Are they close enough friends for him to ask? Are they friends at all, for that matter? "Let me message Kendall," he says.

"Who now?"

"Kendall. I work with him at Burger Buddies, but he Ubers at night."

"You have friends besides Melli and Grady?"

"Of course," he says. "And I'm gonna hang up on you now, so I can get home."

"Let me know you made it."

"Don't you need to sleep?"

"I'll sleep in school tomorrow, don't worry."

1:05 a.m.

U still driving
Ya fuck im tired of these drunk frat boys 5 short ass rides and no $$
Big tippers at least
Fuck no I just want one more and Im done

Calvin pauses before answering. He needs to just come out and ask Kendall for a ride before he takes one. He's still trying to figure out what to type when Kendall sends another text.

Did u go watch ur boy play
Yeah
How bad was it
Pretty bad not just the show
?
Big fight with Melli
That sux
Tell me about it she drove off and left me here
Where you at
Outside variety
Hang tight there in 10
Cant pay u until next check

1:05 AM

The dots appear, then flash, then disappear, then appear again.

Its cool I know where u work
U sure
On my way just dont forget to include tip

Calvin puts his phone back in his pocket, exhales. As weird as it felt to ask Kendall for such a big favor, he can't deny it's a relief to have a way home. The only thing he needs to do more than sleep is pee.

He stretches, stands up. Since it's not your standard Uber ride, Kendall doesn't have his exact location, so Calvin waits in front of the Variety. He also doesn't know what kind of car Kendall drives. Is it weird, that after thinking of Kendall as the only co-worker he likes, he's never noticed him arriving or leaving, never mind seen him outside of work? Maybe not so weird when he realizes that for all of high school he had only one real friend.

More learned behavior. He can't remember ever seeing his mother or his father with friends outside their marriages. Alex would bring home suitably odd companions, but no one seemed to come back more than two or three times. After that they wouldn't even be mentioned again. Did that mean they were never friends? He wonders if Alex has anyone to talk to now. Does Calvin really want to ask? If the answer is no, there's one more problem he can't do anything about.

He's staring at the poster for One Four Three — Roddy's dog, of course, posed on top of an old Ford van, the words "We're Comin' for Ya" in big block letters—when a sleek-looking sedan pulls up to the curb. The passenger window rolls down, and Kendall leans out to make eye contact. "May I please take your order?"

"You really didn't have to do this," Calvin says, walking to the car and opening the door.

Kendall nods, a serious look on his face. "You're right," he says, stepping on the gas to rev the engine. "I can just jet and let you walk home."

"Fuck it, you're already here," Calvin says, getting in the front. Music he doesn't immediately recognize is playing on the stereo; it's pleasant, with a welcoming, mid-tempo vibe. Everything looks and smells clean, and after being stranded in the smells of late-night Little Five Points, it's like he's been transported to some sort of secret haven. He buckles, leans back in the comfortable seat, looks over at Kendall. He's just noticing how sharp Kendall looks in a white button-down shirt and slacks. "I didn't know this ride had a dress code," he says. "I mean, are those actual khakis? They still make those?"

"OK," Kendall says, smiling. "That's enough of that, Mr. Jeans and Hipster Band T."

"It's my casual rock dude outfit. It's perfect."

"Yeah, yeah, just keep telling yourself that." He shifts the car into drive. "And I learned that people like to pretend their Uber is a limo. If I look the part, the tips go way up." He turns to look at Calvin. "So, where we going?"

"Stone Mountain. 4630 Central Drive. And you'll charge me what you'd make off the ride, right?"

"Oh, don't you worry, I'll charge you." Kendall punches the address into his phone and whistles when the route pops up. "I thought I lived close to BB, but you're like, in the back parking lot."

"Upside is oversleeping and still being on time," Calvin says. Traveling in cars always makes him feel better. There's that sense he is escaping, leaving some place he was trapped — school, or his dad's, or his mom's, or Mayo. Headed to hunt in record stores, with Ken and Grady, or taking his mother's or father's car on some pretend errand. "Yeah, need some new socks," or, "Isn't it time to take the car for an oil change?" He'd act like he was dragging Alex along against his will, and then they'd enjoy driving around aimlessly, listening to the radio and stopping for whatever snack they could afford. Funny, how the cars were so much smaller than their homes, but they both seemed to breathe much more easily in that tighter space. "And I gotta say, this is a helluva ride."

1:05 AM

"Ubering has its downsides," Kendall says, "to be sure, but yeah, at least I get to do my driving in style."

Maybe he's feeling especially impressed with the car because half an hour ago he was worried he'd be sleeping in that chair on Euclid, but the ride is so smooth he can't even feel the potholes that make up Atlanta's roads. Remembering other car rides, it's only natural his mind settles on that first time he rode into Atlanta — Grady taking the last shift on their trip from Mayo. They'd left much later than they'd planned to and stopped several times to take pictures and document the trip for future Lords of the Living historians. What should have been a five-hour drive took almost twice that thanks to those stops and an inexplicable traffic jam they would learn was a commonplace occurrence in Atlanta. He could still remember how amazing it felt, even with the traffic and the exhaustion settling on him, to think they had actually escaped, actually begun their own lives.

He makes an exaggerated inhaling sound and smiles. "You pipe in that new-car smell or what?"

"That's just Hamilton Family Love and Magic," Kendall says. "Dig the soft seats, right?"

"It's a helluva ride."

"No doubt. And," he continues, "quite the story, too, about how we got this thing."

"Oh, I need to hear that. I could use a good story."

"When my grandpa died, my mom's dad, it turns out he had this life insurance policy no one knew about. Not even my mom. Money came in, but so did all the fights about what to do with it. My mother had ideas, for sure, and so did my father. And my grandma was still alive, is still alive, and getting ready to move in with us, so you know she had ideas. And the three of us kids, we knew, just knew that Grandpa would have wanted us to have a Playstation or two."

"Obviously."

"Like, the kitchen table was already noisy, but for a few weeks there, it was even more lively."

Calvin is trying to imagine sitting around a loud, crowded, multi-generational kitchen table. His father and stepmother had tried to get him and Alex to eat at the table with them, but they'd done their best to avoid it and succeeded in eating in their rooms more often than not.

"And then, just like that, the fighting was over."

"What happened?"

"My mother, man. Just shows up one day in this ride. Says she prayed on it, and then her dad came to her in a dream and said she'd better spend that money before we all killed each other."

"And no one got angry at her?"

Kendall laughs. "You'll meet my mom one day, man, and you will understand — no one gets mad at her."

"And she told you to keep the car clean as that first day, right?"

"You know it. 'People don't tip smelly bathrooms,' she said."

"Words of wisdom."

"Indeed."

And then silence. This is the first time he and Kendall have ever seen each other outside of Burger Buddies, and it's hard not to think about those moments he bumped into teachers in the outside world, selecting bananas or looking at cards in Walmart. The break in conversation allows more of his brain to focus on the music, which sounds mellower than he expected, almost like a '70s band he's never heard of. "You getting your Fleetwood Mac on tonight, then?"

"You mean to tell me that I get to introduce someone new to Mr. Music Geek himself?"

"Well, it's not something I've heard before." As they talk, part of his brain is trying to pick apart the sounds. Female vocal, lots of keyboards, poppy changes and twists.

"Band is called Tennis. Just two in the band, I think, sort of like you and your boy."

Calvin steers his brain to the music, which is interesting and more fun than wondering if Grady is still "his boy" after tonight. "It's

1:05 AM

not awful. Arrangements are pretty tight. How did you find them?"

"Tip from a rider, man."

"Really?"

"Yeah. Some old dude heading in from the airport."

"Gotta say, never talked to any of my Uber drivers about music."

"Wasted opportunity. I mean, I don't talk to everyone — lots of them come in here, head down, staring at a phone, looking like they're going through some shit. I leave them alone. You need to learn how to read the room. Sometimes the vibe off the passenger is more open, so I'll ask if they want me to play anything in particular."

"Who knew?" Calvin says. He's impressed not only by the idea, but at how confident he now imagines Kendall to be, moving through the world. "Sounds like real drums, too, with some programmed stuff mixed in."

"Yep. Telling you man, I know you guys are having trouble finding someone, but a real drummer makes all the difference."

"Ah, that's just you old-schoolers. Plenty of great music made with machines now."

"Sure. But even more stuff that just sits there because it can't swing."

Calvin shakes his head. "You've never had to actually work with a drummer, man. Few of them are worth it."

"I haven't worked with them, but I have listened to what happens when they get replaced. You telling me Prince records with Sheila E. don't sound better than his records with a machine? And let's not even talk about what happens to Stevie, once he stops playing drums and starts programming stuff."

"We have had this debate before," Calvin says, and they have. "And you always go straight to Sheila and Stevie, and yeah, if I could have them playing drums in my band, it'd all be worth it. They haven't returned my calls yet, though."

"Shoot for the best, right?"

"And when I get stuck with the drunk guy who dreams of being Neil Peart?"

"Neil who now?"

"Rush? Have I not filled you in on the tortured history of prog rock?" Calvin air drums a busy fill, complete with sound effects.

"Not yet, but I'm hoping that's not one of your songs. 'Cause it needs some work."

"Nah. When you program everything, you can keep the drummer from stepping out of his lane."

Kendall shakes his head. "But isn't it good, sometimes, to watch someone float into some new lane?"

"Maybe I'm just a control freak. Or maybe I'm just tired of trying to find someone who can show up sober and ready to do the job right."

"My money's on the control-freak thing. You the boss of Grady, too?"

"Boss of Grady?" Grady told him he called all the shots, and now Kendall's wondering if Calvin bosses everyone around. The idea still seems ridiculous to him. "No. Not even sure I'm the boss of myself. But I guess since they're mostly my songs, I want to shape them as much as I can."

"I can see that. Though you gotta watch out — Prince could have used a producer on some of those later records, right?"

"Right," Calvin says. He's suddenly aware of how close the ride is to ending, and as anxious as he is to sleep, he'll also be sad when he's forced out and once again has to think about Grady and Melli.

"And, speaking of bosses: Tomás spoke to me after you left."

"Yeah?"

"It was weird, man. I didn't think he even knew my name."

"Hey, I bet he just called you 'Guy,' right? So maybe he still doesn't know your name."

"OK, yeah, you got me there. But he did call me over and asked if I had any interest in moving into management."

"Look at that. The man finally did something right."

Kendall turns to him, raises his eyebrows. "Did you have anything to do with it?"

1:05 AM

"I can't tell Tomás what to do, man."

"You know what I mean."

For a moment Calvin wonders if he should lie, but he's too tired and drained to think of anything to say besides the truth. "Yeah," he says, nodding. "He came at me again about taking the job, and I made it clear I just couldn't go for it. So, I told him he should talk to you." Calvin can see Kendall's hands tensing on the wheel. "Sorry, man. I thought I was helping."

"Don't get me wrong." Kendall's hands loosen. "I mean, that was good of you and all. It's just, you know, I shouldn't need you to put a good word in with him."

"I know."

"Like, white people keep running the world, and I can't seem to escape it. Even from brown people, in Stone Mountain, running the world for white people."

Calvin has to admit he's never thought of it in those terms. He's never seen himself as being in any sort of advantaged position He never thought too much about how poor his family was, but he always knew they were, the same way he knows that when he pays rent he's going to be broke until the next paycheck. Thinking about it from Kendall's point of view, though, Calvin suddenly understands of course he's in an advantaged position, even if he's broke. "Sorry, man," he repeats. "I didn't mean to make things weird for you."

"No, no, that's not it." Kendall sighs. "Whatever. It's not your fault, right? It is what it is. It's not like either of us can change the world on our own, right? Since a word from you helps, I'm glad you gave it."

"So, you gonna do it?"

"Of course I'm gonna do it. I could wind up making enough money with one job and not have to take over Uber duty after dinner. Maybe even let Dad skip driving some days, you know?" Kendall checks the side mirror and changes lanes. "Just remember why I'm doing this if you ever hear me asking why you're six minutes late."

"For the money," Calvin says. "That's why we all do it."

"Well, yeah, but I do this crappy job for the same reason as you. We do it so that someday we won't have to."

"That's a good way of putting it," Calvin says. "Let's hope that someday comes soon."

"Heard. Heard loud and clear." They hit a red light, and Kendall turns to Calvin. "Your turn, man. How'd a nice boy like you wind up out so late without a ride?"

"It's a long story. After a long night."

"No company out there dumb enough to give you a credit card?"

"Oh, no, I have one, but we maxed it out buying gear."

"This making art shit ain't cheap, huh?"

"Not even close."

"But, c'mon, not even a secret MARTA stash?"

"What, you have a secret MARTA stash?"

"Of course. Last thing I wanna do is be stuck somewhere I don't wanna be. Didn't your mama teach you to always have a way home?"

He wants to defend himself and explain that Melli was supposed to give him a ride and it never occurred to him that she wouldn't, but he's tired of sounding whiny. And he doesn't want to think about Melli. "My mother wasn't big on, like, life lessons."

"Always have that emergency way to get home. Always respect your elders. Always remember that God loves you, no matter what."

Kendall doesn't drop God references too often, but Calvin never knows what to say, so he lets it drift by. "Well, I had parents and step-parents, and none of them were especially big with insights."

"Yeah, you know, I've picked that up, just from stuff you've said." Kendall is turning off Memorial Drive onto Hambrick. They're almost to Calvin's house. "That maybe things at home weren't that great. And I've noticed that you, like, never go home."

Calvin is surprised Kendall noticed. "Yeah. My plan is to never go back there if I can avoid it." Grady's parents had flown him home twice, for Thanksgiving one year and for Christmas one year, but no such offer had ever come from either of Calvin's parents. Spending his

1:05 AM

own money, even for gas, seemed silly, since all they would wind up doing was fighting. Getting Alex to Georgia was his only family goal.

Kendall turns left into the driveway at 4630. "Gotta say, more boring digs than I expected."

Calvin looks at the house. He and Grady had thought the same thing, pulling up to it for the first time. He never imagined it would come to feel so much like home. "Well, we just get one of the bedrooms, remember. But everyone is pretty chill."

"White Boy Central?"

"I mean, me and Grady, and the guy who's been kind of in charge of keeping the place full and paid for. But the other two are usually brown or women or both."

"Kind of nice to think Klan Central has changed colors."

"You knew about the Klan thing, too? Grady told me when we first came to check the place out."

"Of course, man. Burning cross, top of Stone Mountain. They still come out every year for something called Confederate Memorial Day, and we all get the hell out of Dodge."

"Another important life lesson," Calvin says, opening the door to get out. "Knowing when to get the hell out of Dodge." He is aware, as he unfolds his legs and moves them, so slowly, out of the car and onto the driveway, of how exhausted he is. Whatever mixture of adrenaline and nervous energy kept him moving these last few hours has disappeared. He steadies himself, leans in to say goodbye. "Thanks again," he says. "What do I owe you?"

"Friends and family discount. Let's say thirty."

"Sounds good," Calvin says, trying to keep a chill expression even as he did the math. With the generous tip he'd want to give, Friday's paycheck was suddenly forty dollars smaller than he'd been counting on. "I'm gonna go sleep, for, like three hours."

"Burger Buddies waits for no one, man. There are new friends to be made."

"Truth," Calvin says, before he shuts the door.

1:30 a.m.

Calvin stands in the driveway while Kendall backs out. For the third time tonight he's watching somebody leave him, but at least Kendall leans out and flashes a peace sign. Calvin nods, returns it and turns to stare at the house. There's a light on in the living room, but everything else looks dark. He pulls out his phone to see the time (1:32, which means he clocks back into Burger Buddies in less than four hours) and if there are any messages from Melli (no).

He starts typing a message to Melli, erases it, starts again. After deleting three longer attempts, he settles on a single word: *sorry*. Then he sends a message to Alex: *home*.

Calvin puts his phone in his pocket and bends his neck, suddenly aware of a soreness behind his head he had not noticed before. Something about the way the sky looks, the way the shadows from the living room light hit the bushes by the front window, reminds him of the night he and Grady moved in. They'd been sharing a bag of very good weed with Downy and the first set of roommates when Calvin suddenly needed to be outside. He stumbled through the front door, barefoot and stoned, and Grady followed him. They walked wobbly circles on the driveway, looking up at the stars and laughing at some-

1:30 AM

thing. "You OK?" Grady asked after a few minutes, still laughing. "Why are we out here?"

"We're out here because we can be," Calvin said. He stopped and held his arms out. "If we want to be out here, we can be out here."

"True," Grady said, still walking in uneven circles, looking up at the sky. "And here's not bad, right?"

"Right," Calvin said. "I was just in there and wanted to be out here, and realized — fuck it, no one can stop us. After waiting, like, our whole life to start our life, we did it."

At that Grady stopped. "You're right. We did it."

"We did it."

"And!" Grady held his hand up dramatically but then paused. "And?"

"And I forgot what I was gonna say. But it was also smart."

"Of course it was," Calvin said, before starting to walk down the driveway, placing one foot in front of the other, as if walking a tightrope.

Calvin now realizes he's been standing in the driveway long enough to forget how long he's been there. Probably just a few minutes, but a few minutes he will regret not sleeping when he wakes up. Why doesn't he move more quickly? Because it's easier to stand still, not moving, thinking back over everything that has happened tonight since he showed up at the Variety. Second-guessing himself has been one of his superpowers since he started talking, and he's only gotten better at it over the years. He could start now and spend his last few hours before work running down a long list of mistakes he made, but he will have plenty of time to beat himself up tomorrow. There's nothing left to do now but go inside, sleep just long enough to be even more tired and then go back to work.

But first, pee. After taking care of that, and rubbing some cold water on his face, he wanders from the bathroom to the living room, where a home remodeling show is playing silently on the TV. The show selection has to be the work of Downy, the house's

KING CAL

resident night owl, but his usual nest on the couch is empty, aside from a few crumpled-up tissues and a crushed can of La Croix. Calvin watches the perky couple on the screen walking around their enormous house, pointing out all the things they want changed. Even without the sound he can see the woman is much unhappier with everything than the man, but he has mastered the art of looking at her and nodding. On a more average night, Calvin would be rehearsing snarky lines in his head to share with Downy, but tonight his mood is so weird he feels no anger at them. In fact, he envies them. How nice it would be to show someone all the shit you want fixed and then come back thirty minutes later and find it all taken care of.

He walks into the kitchen and finds Downy, wearing a red robe and staring into the oven. "Ah, young Calvin. You have timed your return perfectly."

"I have?"

Downy opens the oven door and carefully lifts out a tray. "Only if you like brownies."

Calvin smiles. When he is an old man talking about things he misses, Downy's baked goods will be high on the list. None of the adults he grew up with enjoyed baking, but Downy does, and his skill in making sweets is only surpassed by his love of sharing them. "Turns out I do," Calvin says. He watches Downy place the pan on a wire rack. "But isn't this late for baking something? Even for you?"

"Is it ever too late for brownies, really?" Downy looks at Calvin and shrugs. "Though I do have to get up tomorrow at one of those morning hours that should not even exist."

"How early?"

"I need to look presentable by nine a.m."

"For you that's, like. . ."

"Inhuman. As it should be for everyone." He studies the pan of brownies, as if trying to decide how long he needs to wait before cutting. "And thinking about it had me so wired I could not sleep. Baking relaxes me."

1:30 AM

"Why do you have to get up so early?"

"I have an interview."

Calvin goes to the cupboard to get glasses. "Wasn't that today?"

"Indeed, it was, good sir. But it went well enough that I seem to have made it to the final round much more quickly than I had anticipated."

Calvin heads over to the fridge, hoping to find some non-spoiled milk. He must be more tired than he realized; he's not normally two or three beats behind Downy. "But the final round for what?"

"Trust me, I share your confusion. But it seems that I have made it to the final round of interviews for an actual job."

Calvin struggles to process that information. He's heard Downy talking about "needing to get some work done" before, but never often, and whatever the work is seems to combine surfing his laptop with drinking Tecate. "Um, again, no offense intended here: but what job?"

"Marketing, my friend. I have tried to keep this skill of mine hidden from friends, so as not to lose whatever little respect they may have for me."

"I had no idea." He takes out the milk, opens it up to sniff and decides it is relatively safe. "You think I would have asked what sort of work skills you had before this. Sorry."

"No need to apologize," Downy says, reaching into a drawer and pulling out a knife. "It is far more important we talk about art than commerce. It is just that now I may in fact start doing this again for some of that evil money. Capitalism always calls. And sometimes it calls so loudly and persistently that we must turn and engage."

"Downy with the secret marketing power. Nicely done. And, come to think of it," Calvin continues, snapping his fingers as he remembers, "you did make some great posters for Lords of the Living."

"And I hope to use my evil powers for good for future shows," he says, bowing, a knight offering services to his king.

Future shows with Grady seem anything but certain, so he shifts his brain to imagine what it will be like if Downy actually has a job. "It sure will be weird to have you, like, leaving the house in the morning and coming back for dinner. Will you get to wear a suit? Bring a lunchbox?"

Downy makes a first, careful slice into the brownies. "The suit may not be required, brother Calvin, but I shall have to up my wardrobe game, to be sure. Believe it or not, I do not think they are paying to see my legs."

"Crazy."

"Agreed," Downy says, twisting his right leg like a model on a runway.

"Those smell amazing, by the way," he says, watching Downy slicing the brownies into squares of admirably consistent shape, even though they still look molten and gooey. Once again, he compares Downy's homemaking skills to his parents'; did his father or mother ever make brownies for him and Alex? Never mind brownies from scratch, cut into perfect squares? Not even Dottie, who was the best at any of that stuff, pulled that off. Does this mean Downy is the best mother he's ever had?

"Thank you, kind sir. The process has calmed my mind a bit, and I am hoping a few of these — and their secret ingredient — will calm me enough for a few hours of beauty sleep." He lifts the knife out and runs his finger along the blade to gather the sticky crumbs. "Not that I need any more beauty."

Downy carries the brownies over to the kitchen table, and Calvin follows with their milk. This is the first bit of good news he's had all day: a pot brownie might be just the thing that lets him sleep even for an hour or two before work. Downy grabs them each a napkin and a brownie. They're still warm, so wonderfully fudgy as to barely be holding their shape. Calvin takes his first bite and has to resist the urge to lean over the table and kiss Downy. "This, friend, is so just what I needed."

1:30 AM

"I am glad to hear that," Downy says after his own first bite. "It is a gift to know you have given someone something they needed just as they need it." He takes another bite, smiles. "As far as leaving the house goes: as weird as it will be to go to an office every day, what will be weirdest of all is leaving this house for good, after lo these many years."

Calvin refuses to believe that Downy means what he just said. "You're gonna leave the house? As in, move?"

"That is under discussion. If I get the offer, it does seem like I will be required to reside in a new locale."

"Really?" Calvin can't imagine the house existing without Downy. "Like, move to a different part of Atlanta, or. . .?"

"Or."

"Wow. What does Tesla Man think of this?"

Downy smiles. "Tesla Man?"

"I'm sorry, I just can't remember his name. Especially when I already feel, like, buzzed, after two bites."

"Tesla Man is Tesla Dan. And he says he's always wanted to see Seattle."

"Seattle? Whoa."

"One step at a time, good sir." Downy finishes his first brownie with a flourish and reaches for the milk. "First, let us see what the good people of Google offer."

Calvin pauses and puts the last piece of brownie in his mouth, letting the warm sweetness dull his disappointment. He knows he should be happy for Downy, because a job at Google certainly seems much more lucrative than whatever he is doing now, but the house will be much sadder if Downy is not in it.

And what happens if the one name on the lease moves out? The landlord — that unseen force that actually owns his bedroom, and his recording studio — could put one of the other roommates on the lease, but he could also clean the place out and rent it to some normal family. Suddenly it seems like he's in danger of losing his place to live the same day he may have lost his band and his girlfriend.

When he looks up, he sees Downy watching him, looking worried. "Fear not. If not this fine dwelling, you will find some other home quickly."

"I wanna believe you," Calvin says. "But tonight I don't feel like I can actually do anything."

"Now that," Downy says, "is a statement I refuse to accept. I have watched you do hard things for almost three years."

"Just been a long night," he says, trying to sound more together than he feels.

"I forgot to ask. The gig." Downy gently lifts out another brownie and hands it to Calvin. "How'd it go? What was it like, watching Grady on that big-ass stage?"

Calvin pauses, staring at the warm and melty brownie. "It was weird. Kind of really hard, actually," he adds. "It felt like I was watching him go away right in front of me."

"I find it hard to believe he'd really go away," Downy says, starting his second brownie. "You guys are like brothers."

Calvin takes another bite of brownie, unable to think how to respond. Something about Downy's tone, so warm and genuine, makes him feel he's going to cry. Either the pot is really great or the night has been that weird. Or both.

"I've always been a bit jealous of you and the G-man, to be honest," Downy continues.

"Why?"

"I have an older brother," Downy says. He swallows the last of his milk.

"Really?" Calvin's never heard Downy talk about his family before, and he's never asked. It could be the pot creating what Grady calls "The Illusion of Epiphany," but it suddenly seems obvious: as with Kendall, he's never talked to Downy as much or openly as he could.

"Yep. But he's an asshole. One of those people who struggles to understand and accept their own feelings, never mind the feelings

1:30 AM

of others." Downy stares at the tray of brownies, as if debating what to do, and then slowly stands. "Grady might be a lot of things, but I don't think he's an asshole," he says, carrying the tray over to the fridge. "Even if he leaves, he won't leave, you know?"

"I'm not sure," Calvin says. He drinks the last of his milk, his mouth and throat and chest all warm from the brownies and whatever Downy put in them. "Sure seems like he's moving on."

"Perhaps. But moving on and leaving are not the same thing."

"They're not?"

Downy shakes his head. "Not at all. There are people who will be with us, even if they're not. And I think that's Grady for you. And you for him." He turns to head down the hallway that leads to the stairs. "And with that insight — which may or may not be brilliant — I must leave you."

"Good luck tomorrow," Calvin says.

"You too," Downy says, heading up the stairs with slow, heavy steps.

The kitchen is silent. Calvin wonders what the wealthy couple on the TV decided to do with that house. Then he checks his phone one more time: still no message from Melli or Grady, just one more from Alex: *dont be mad*. He really is worried about Calvin becoming like their father. And Alex is smart, so he should listen to those warnings. But *it's not that I'm mad, at Grady or Melli or anyone else*, he thinks, staring at the phone as if that will make the words type. *I'm just tired of everyone leaving.*

He's too tired to actually type the words, though, so he sends a thumbs-up emoji, their standard shorthand for "We'll finish this later." Then he pushes away from the table and stands up, surprised at how wobbly his legs are. If he goes upstairs now he can sleep for three hours or so before he goes out to help spread heart disease.

1:55 a.m.

As he climbs the stairs, Calvin feels more exhausted with each step. His body literally aches with the need to sleep, but his brain continues to pick up speed, processing what Downy leaving will mean for everyone else in the house. It had taken a long time for him and Grady to find a place to rent, but maybe it would be easier now that they have been in Atlanta for a few years. After tonight, though, Grady might not even want to live with him. Which means it could be a great time to get a place with Melli, but he just turned down a gig that would pay enough money for that.

Not to mention that it does not seem like a good time to ask her to move in together.

The darker the future looks, the faster his brain moves. If he has to move out, will he have to live alone, and how much would that cost? The idea of not being able to afford it, and having to return to Mayo — no band, no girlfriend, no money — flashes across his brain. Halfway up the stairs he stops to catch his breath. Shuts his eyes. Squeezes them shut tight for a few long seconds, then starts moving again.

He is never going back to Mayo. No matter how bad it gets in Atlanta.

1:55 AM

When he finally reaches the top of the stairs it feels like it's been hours since he left the kitchen. He panics for a moment, wondering if he is having some sort of breakdown, and then remembers the pot brownies should be kicking in right around now: time gets very weird for Calvin when he's stoned, circular and sticky, coated in thick reverb.

Relieved to just be high and not suffering a full mental crisis, he starts down the hallway, feeling as though he's watching the closing credits of a movie. A single camera follows our defeated hero as he passes the three shut doors of the other bedrooms, with nothing but silence on the soundtrack. Downy's room is closest to the stairs, already so quiet that Calvin thinks he must have instantly fallen asleep, perhaps dreaming of a new job and a new city. Daniel's room is next, the first door on the left. He must have gotten home from work just before Calvin got back and is no doubt also asleep after another ten-hour shift at Chili's. The last door he passes leads to the bedroom with the highest turnover rate; right now a middle-aged woman named Aja rents it, but she's staying with her boyfriend again. Calvin's thoughts drift backward as he walks, trying to remember as many stories as he can of all the people who have lived here. How many of them remember him?

Stepping into his room, Calvin checks his phone for messages. Nothing since that last one from Alex. Grady and Melli have officially entered radio silence. The only new information gained is the time: 1:58 a.m. If he really pushes it, he can sleep for... not quite three hours?

Bathroom. Brush teeth, because even though he is exhausted, he lives in fear of messing up his teeth and not having any insurance. Strip to boxers, fall onto bed. He hopes his brain will shut up long enough for him to fall asleep, but he's having his doubts. How'd that Neil Young song go? Just him and piano, singing about being stoned and "having his doubts." Yeah, Calvin's having his doubts about everything that happened tonight. His list of Ways Calvin Screwed Up is long:

KING CAL

1. Going to see One Four Three. Sure, if he'd made up some lame excuse and stayed home Grady would have been pissed — but he couldn't have been angrier than he was when Calvin turned down the chance to go on the road with them. And if Calvin had never gone to the show, then Melli wouldn't have gone, and she wouldn't be mad at him either.

2. Not fighting harder to keep Grady from taking the gig. Grady would have been angry, but maybe it had been some test from Grady to see if Calvin would keep him from going, and Calvin blew it. If he'd found a way to keep Grady from leaving, the two of them wouldn't have had that stupid fight about that stupid band, and if he and Grady never have a fight, then he and Melli never have a fight.

3. Maybe The Plan itself was a mistake. If he'd never thought of it, he wouldn't be in Atlanta right now, feeling like shit.

4. As long as he's going back that far, maybe saying anything when he heard Grady and his friends talking about starting a band was a mistake. If he hadn't said anything, if he'd just been happy staying invisible, there would never have been a Plan, and he wouldn't be lying here, exhausted but unable to sleep.

He wonders if he should go all the way back to teaching himself piano, wonders if that is the original sin, the thing that led to this day. That doesn't feel like a mistake, though, even in his crappy mood. Music and Melli and Grady and Alex were the only things that made sense in this world, and if he winds up losing Melli and Grady, he at least needs to keep the music.

It's hard to say whether he has been in bed beating himself up for ten minutes or an hour, and he refuses to look at the clock. He can feel The Spiral again starting to uncoil, can feel that twisting of his insides coming back. It's like he's back under the covers at his father's, unable to move, able to breathe only with great effort. Dottie helped him pull out once, and Grady was there the last time, but no one is here to help now. He'll have to find a way out on his own, before the Spiral pins him to the bed.

1:55 AM

It seems impossible, but just twenty-four hours ago he'd had trouble falling asleep not because of The Spiral, but because he was so excited. He'd written a new song he was happy with, he was going to have time with Melli and he was going to see his best friend for the first time in months. Those were much better reasons to not be sleeping.

He tries to distract his brain by remembering bits of lyrics he'd thought up during the day, still looking for some words he can use to finish the new one.

Crying in my Volvo, crying over what I can't see.

Oh, Sad Pearl Jam fan. Calvin wonders if the day got better for him. Like many first ideas — first idea of the day, first idea of a writing session — it doesn't seem as good as the stuff that came later. But you need that first weak idea so you can have stronger ones.

There's too much in my head today, too much for my words to say.

That still sounds a little too much like that Kinks song. Maybe it's better if he moves "words" closer to the top.

My head's too full of words today, words climb in and won't go away.

Closer. The rhythm is busy for the song's melody, but that just means he has to lose some syllables. As he runs the lines he can remember back through his head, trying to find the best combination, he can feel his chest start to move more easily, taking air in and pushing air out. It's like he didn't realize how desperately his chest needed more air until he began to take it in.

Or maybe it's that he has too much air and needs to push some out? Could it be both, that his chest is empty and full at the same time?

I'm so full I'm empty.

It feels like he's drowning from the weight of all the ideas in his head, but if someone asked him to say what was wrong, in clear words, he's not sure he'd be able to say anything. It's the same problem he's had for years, a head so full of thoughts he can't pick any of them out, which makes it feel like there are no thoughts at all.

The words are hiding in my head / lying down and playing dead / And now I'm so full I'm empty.

He imagines the lyrics scrolling by as his brain plays the music he wrote last night. They might actually line up, but the rhythm of the syllables isn't right. To know for sure if that could be fixed, he needs to play the music. And that's the risk of thinking about music to calm his brain enough to fall asleep; if it goes too well, he stops trying to sleep so he can play.

Which he now does. It's ridiculous, given how soon he has to go to work, but he knows he won't be able to shut off his brain until he takes some of these words from his head and tries to match them with the music. He would make less noise if he played it on the keyboard, listening with headphones, but he wrote the song on guitar and that's how he wants to hear it now. Aja's bedroom is closest, but she's not home, and Downy is dead to the world once he falls asleep. That just leaves Daniel, but he's recorded vocals late at night and Daniel's never said anything. Either it doesn't wake him up or Daniel is so quiet and polite he doesn't complain. Either way, it should be OK to play quietly for a few minutes.

He leans forward to pick up the acoustic lying next to his mattress. His hands instantly feel calmer and any doubts about this being the right thing to do fade away. After quietly checking the tuning, Calvin starts to play the opening chords. The revised lines running through his head feel like they fit the mood, but the verse needs to be sparser. He switches to the part that feels like the chorus: *I'm so full I'm empty*. That repetition of "I'm" doesn't work, though. Neither does "I'm so full and empty," but when he replaces "and" with "of," it instantly sounds right. He tries it again, whispering the line as he softly strums the chords and, in spite of how crappy the

1:55 AM

day has been, he smiles. It's always a magic moment for Calvin, when that first line slides perfectly into place. Sometimes it's the first line of the song,sometimes it's later, but wherever that first perfect lyric lands, the whole song comes alive in a new way, triggering a satisfaction so deep he is, for that moment, no matter what else is happening, happy.

Pretty quickly, he has the words for one verse and the chorus. With the melody and mood in place, he should be able to finish the lyrics for the other verses and think about a bridge or lead break when he gets off work tomorrow. He records a verse and chorus on his voice memos, in case he winds up being too stoned and tired to remember when he wakes up. He may have spent the day making one mistake after another, may have lost his best friend and his girlfriend and his band along the way, but he also created something new, something that would not have existed without him, something that may even, someday, be good.

He climbs under the blanket, hoping the chords of the new song will be louder in his head than the less pleasant sounds and thoughts fighting for space.

5:00 a.m.

There's no fragment of a dream to grab hold of when the alarm goes off, just the distant memory of falling into bed at some point and the present horror of "Moves Like Jagger." Calvin stretches, groans, forces himself to sit up, then angrily says, "Alexa, off."

When the music stops, he opens his eyes. That's when he sees her, sitting on the floor next to his mattress. How good was the pot Downy put in those brownies? Because he still feels buzzed, and he's pretty sure he's imagining Melli sitting on the floor next to his mattress. "Are you here?" he asks. His voice is just above a whisper, as if talking too loudly to a mirage will make it disappear.

"That's not the most important question," she says.

Air fills his chest. How long has he been holding his breath, waiting to see if it is really her? Calvin waits for her to continue, waits for a sign about whether he can lean over and kiss her, but she just keeps sitting there, watching him. "OK," he says. "So, what is the most important question?"

"Is that really what you use for your alarm?"

"Yes."

"Jesus. Why?"

"Because if the worst song ever written can't make me wake up

5:00 AM

enough to turn off the radio, nothing will. I don't let myself give that life-saving command until I'm sitting up."

"Impressive."

"It's the only system that keeps me from being late."

"To think I never knew this."

"Oh, we have much to learn about each other." He stretches again. "So, now I can ask — are you really here?"

"Yes. I am really here," she says.

"Well, then," he says, speaking slowly and softly, worried that any sharpness in his tone could push her away, "I have some follow-up questions."

"Fair enough."

"First: how? It's five a.m. Aren't your parents going to wonder where you are?"

"Oh, my mother is already up. She falls asleep at midnight and wakes up at four, and no, you can't tell her this is crazy."

"Does she nap?"

"She swears on her mother's rosary beads no, but no one believes her."

"That's crazy."

"Yes. Just never tell her that. Anyway," Melli continues, "I told her Diane was going out for her morning run and her cat got out. So, I needed to go over there and help find the damn thing."

"That's a good cover story."

"Right? I've been keeping it behind glass in case of emergency. Diane is in on it, ready to respond if my mother calls or texts asking how the cat is."

The word "emergency" makes him a little uneasy. Did she come over here to make sure he knew it was all over? "Which leads to the second question. Did I imagine it, or did you drive away last night and not respond to any of my texts since then?"

"Yes, that happened."

She sighs, shifts. He imagines she is about to get up and walk out, but instead, she moves close enough to touch the blanket covering his knee.

"I'm not saying I'm proud of it. But. I was mad, thinking there's something you could do to make things better for us, and you didn't want to do it."

"It's not that I don't—"

She holds her hands up to cut him off. "I was still mad when I got home. And also sad." She reaches out to lay her hand on his knee. "I guess I always knew it, in the back of my mind? But last night I realized you would choose music, always, over anything else."

Calvin has a sudden flash of the Christmas he got his first keyboard, can still remember the way everything else in the room melted away when he plugged it in and ran his fingers over the keys. Has there been any doubt, since that moment, what he would do if forced to choose between music and something else?

"Which means you'd even choose music over me, if it ever came to that."

He shakes his head, pressing his hand on top of hers to hold it against his knee. Music over anything, yes, but not Melli. "That's not true. That's not what I meant."

"So, it hurt," she continues, "thinking I was being passed over for something else."

"I'm sorry." He's not sure what else to say. It would be a terrible, impossible choice, a choice he has never imagined and hopes he never has to make. "I never thought of it like that, like I was choosing something over you."

She nods. "I know you didn't. But it still sucked. Then, this morning, I woke up and realized I was mad at you for being you. Like, the thing that made you turn down that offer is also one of the things I love about you."

For what feels like the tenth time in the past twenty-four hours he is aware of that about-to-cry sensation in the back of his throat.

5:00 AM

It's too much to bear, when she talks being hurt by him, but at the same time it's amazing to hear her use the word "love." Seeing her here in front of him, the answer is obvious: swallow his pride or ego or whatever it is and text Grady to say he's sorry. "I fucked up. I'm gonna talk to Grady, apologize for being such a dick and take the gig."

Melli smacks his knee.

"Ow," Calvin says. "Why did you do that?"

"Because the whole point is we're supposed to talk about big decisions. Just deciding on your own and doing something just because you think I want you to do it — that's not the right answer, either."

"Oh." Calvin nods. "OK." He would take the job with One Four Three, if needed to keep Melli, but it's a relief she isn't asking for that. "I guess there's a lot of stuff about being a couple I'm still figuring out."

"Me too," Melli says. "It's not like I've been in a relationship this serious before, either. That's part of what made me so mad, thinking we were screwing it up."

The word *serious* echoes in his head. It's not that it's not the right word, because after more than a year, it must be serious? He just hadn't expected to hear her use it. "So, I guess anything that involves like, a job change, or something, should be talked about?"

"Yes. So we can decide together."

He nods. "OK."

"But going away for so long is a big decision, too. I should have thought about that piece of it more," she says, edging even closer. "Like, do I really want to not see you for six months? No, I don't want that."

"That's so, so nice to hear," he says, quietly.

"I would miss you," she says. "So much. Too much."

"Me, too." He pauses, thinking that the best way to guarantee he doesn't cry would be to kiss her but also sensing it is not time for that yet.

"And besides, we need more King Cal songs."

He stares at her, not knowing what to say. He tries a joke. "I'm not sure that anyone needs to hear more from that piker."

"Calvin."

"Melli. . ." He should have known he would not be able to keep the music a secret from Alex and Grady and Melli. He also knows he didn't want to keep it a secret forever; he just hadn't planned on all three finding out on the same day. "How did you find out?"

"Alex."

Alex. Of course.

"Why didn't you let me know? Why keep it a secret? It explains so much about why it would be an especially hard time for you to leave and have to go work on someone else's songs."

Calvin shrugs. It seems silly, now that she's heard the songs and hasn't run away. But the decision made sense at the time. "I wanted to wait until the songs were ready."

"Ready?"

"Good. I wanted to wait until they were actually good."

"Calvin."

"Melli."

"The songs are good."

"They are?" He knew it would mean a lot to him, to have her say that, but he hadn't realized how much. "Thank you."

She leans over to kiss him. "Beyond good, to be honest."

"Thank you," he repeats. "I'm just realizing how worried I was."

"About what?"

"About my voice, most of all. That you wouldn't like it as much as—" He's so tired he is suddenly about to say the fear out loud, even though he knows how pathetic it will sound.

But Melli knows what he was going to say. Of course she does. "As much as Grady's voice?"

He nods.

"Because Grady is the hot one and the great voice and the moves like Jagger?"

5:00 AM

"Exactly. I'm glad that you can see my deepest, darkest fears."

Melli leans back, studying Calvin's face. "I never told you why I went for Grady first, did I?"

"Um, you didn't need to," he says. "For all the reasons you just listed."

"Silly boy. If all that was true I'd be on the tour bus with him now, having crazy sex."

He closes his eyes, shakes his head. "Hurry up and say something else, so I can stop imagining that."

"I was drawn to Grady because I just assumed he wrote the songs. He was so confident up there, so in control, singing them, I just — I figured he wrote them. And maybe it doesn't surprise you that he never exactly told me I was wrong, early on."

Calvin exhales. The idea that the songs are what attracted Melli relieves him on too many levels to even count. "Yeah, that doesn't surprise me," he says, wondering just how actively Grady pretended to be the songwriter.

"By the time I realized it was you, Grady and I were together. He was fun to be with, and I thought, you know, it wasn't ever like he actually lied — he let me think what I wanted to think."

"Early morning philosophy: 'What is a lie, and what isn't a lie?'"

"When I heard you singing, it was like all the bits I didn't realize were missing were suddenly there, if that makes sense." She closes her eyes, pauses, then opens them again. "Sometimes I think I should have broken up with Grady as soon as I realized I was wrong, you know, that not telling me the whole truth about the songs was probably a sign about who he really was. But, things seemed to be OK. So I didn't make a big deal of it. But it never really was OK."

"I watched you drive away and was afraid I'd ruined everything. But you're here now, so maybe we are OK? I hope?"

"Maybe."

It's better than the answer he gave himself before he fell asleep, but not as good as the answer he wants to hear now. "Maybe?"

"Maybe. I just — I don't think I would have gotten so hurt and angry if I didn't care so much. And I don't wanna have it happen again."

"I don't, either."

"But it might, right, so I guess we both need to know that. And if that's the risk, then, like, I want to work hard to make sure we don't blow it."

"I'm gonna try not to fuck it up," he says. "But I do fuck shit up."

"I make mistakes, too. I realized this morning, when I was trying to figure out when and how I could get here, it's gonna be hard to keep doing this, but I also realized I want to keep doing this. Which means we both need to pay more attention to things we need to talk about."

"Sure, talking," Calvin says. Last night when she drove away, he would have agreed to anything Melli asked for, to have a chance to work things out. Talking is very easy to say yes to. "I can talk, or not talk, all you want."

"But not now. Now I am tired, and you are tired." She looks at his Alexa. "What time do you need to leave for work?"

"5:26."

"OK. So we have ten minutes."

"That math seems right." He raises his eyebrows, grins. "What you got in mind?"

"Not that, Mr. Morning Glory," she says, rubbing his thigh. "We're saving that for later, when we have some time." She kisses him, leans back, points to his keyboard in the middle of the room. "I want you to play me a song."

"A song? But it's 5:16 a.m. I'm gonna sound like shit."

"Pretend we've been up all night. Then it's not too early—it's like we're closing out the club in style, and your voice'll be all sexy and raspy."

"It does sort of feel like I never actually slept."

"So play me a song."

Calvin pauses. "Everyone in the house is asleep," he says.

"So? What's better than a private concert?" She drops her voice to a whisper and raises her eyebrows, as if sharing a forbidden secret. "A quiet, private concert."

The idea of these songs going so quickly from being a secret to actually performed live is a little unnerving. It all seems too quick; when he woke up yesterday King Cal was still a secret identity, and he was still Clark Kent. At the same time, it's also kind of exciting to imagine singing these songs in front of someone — and who better to watch him step into the phone booth and change into someone else than Melli?

He stretches, shifts, moves his feet to the ground. When he stands up he's surprised at how relatively stable his legs feel, considering he couldn't have slept for more than two hours. He walks over to the keyboard and begins to set it up. It's tempting to try and play the new one for her, but it's incomplete, and he's not even sure he'd be able to move through the parts he does have smoothly.

After he plugs both headphones into the mixer he hands one set to Melli, then runs his fingers over the keyboard. "That volume OK?"

"Perfect."

"Good." He plays a quick scale, checks the time on Alexa. "Just enough time for one song. What you wanna hear?"

She smiles. "My favorite."

"Which one is that?"

"You know."

"I know?"

"Of course you know."

"What if I don't know?"

"Then you fail the test, grasshopper."

He thinks, then smiles. "Maybe I do know," he says. And of course he does. Without the guitar he will just have to start on piano — maybe playing softer at first, he thinks, then get a little louder to create a different mood for the second verse? He also knows there's just enough time to play, so he decides not to get the drum files loaded up. It'll be just him and piano, which is terrifying.

KING CAL

Night sounds
Lost and strange
She's here then gone again
Somewhere I'm someone else I'm not myself

Night turns
To swallow me
I don't know how to breathe
Something is holding me I can't get free

I close my eyes
To watch Mary sleep
I hide behind
The shadows she sees
I'm so grateful
She's there in my dreams
I am so grateful
To watch Mary sleep

So far away from me
So far away

Night falls
Lost and strange
Then lands on top of me
Sometimes I just let go and disappear

Night leaves
Goodbye for now
Safe here inside the sound
It's time to find a way to another day

I close my eyes
To watch Mary sleep
I hide behind
The shadows she sees

5:00 AM

I'm so grateful
She's there in my dreams
I am so grateful
To watch Mary sleep

He keeps his eyes closed while he plays, trying to focus on the sound of the piano in his headphones more than the sound of his voice. When he finishes, he turns to her, opens his eyes slowly, exhales. "Ladies and gentlemen, the bar is now closed."

She kisses him again, her lips lingering before she pulls away. "You pass the test. That's my favorite."

"It's the one that made me want to sing," he says. "Because I didn't want anyone else to sing it."

"It's a little stalker-y. But I don't mind."

"Stalker-y?" He shakes his head. "Alex said the same thing, but I'm not — I mean, the fictional narrator of the song — isn't really watching. Like in the room watching. He's watching in his head. He's trying to think of something that will calm him enough so he can sleep."

"I like that," she says. "But, um, who the hell is Mary?"

"Ah, well. I mean, I had to change the name, right? In case this is some huge hit and your parents figure out some greasy atheist is writing songs about you." He runs his fingers along the keyboard quietly as he talks. It feels like days since he played, and now that she is here, and she likes the song, and they are talking, and he is once again breathing, all he wants to do is sit here next to her and play and talk.

Oh, and kiss. He leans over, feeling secure enough to make the first move this time. The feel of her lips, and the way their mouths have learned to move together, is something he never tires of.

"Alas, my greasy atheist," she says after they slowly separate, rubbing his thigh, "you need to go make America safe for burgers again. In four minutes."

"Fuck burgers."

"Is that a new menu item? The fuckburger?"

"It should be," he says, reluctantly standing. "It'd sure make the job more fun, anyway." He holds out his hand and helps Melli up.

"Maybe," she says, "we can discuss the menu tonight, after I get off work."

5:27 a.m.

Five hours later than he expected to, Calvin finally gets in Melli's car for a ride. "You know, it'll be too early to get you a chicken biscuit," he says, adopting his lamest Southern accent.

"But I know the drive-thru dude," she says. "Isn't that good for something?"

"Oh, sure. That and two bucks will get you a cup of bad coffee."

She smiles. Her left hand is on the steering wheel, and her right rests gently on top of his thigh. It's a good moment, even if in three minutes he's gonna be clocked in and working. It's such a good moment he forces himself to turn down the volume on the other voices in his head, the ones reminding him how close he came to screwing things up permanently, reminding him he's on probation for a while and needs to start figuring out how to be a better sort of boyfriend. The voices tell him she is still out of his league, but here she is, driving him to his crappy job. If he keeps his eyes on the lightening sky off in the distance, it feels as if they are floating. He can float anywhere with Melli, even to Burger Buddies.

"So Downy is up for some, like, big-ass job with Google," he says quietly. There's no reason to bring this news up now, except he's aware that part of his brain has been nervously turning the idea around to study it from all angles. If he's learned anything at all in the last twenty-four hours, it's that he needs to share more of what goes on inside his brain with Melli.

"Really? Downy?"

"Downy. Seems he has some secret marketing superpowers."

"Downy with a big ass job," she says, turning left into the back entrance of the Burger Buddies parking lot. "Who would have guessed."

"Sounds like he'll have to move if he gets the job."

"Wow. Would the house keep standing, if he moved out?"

"I don't think anyone knows. Or what happens if his name goes off the lease."

Melli shrugs, slowing the car to a stop. "Could be a good thing? Maybe you wind up living closer to me." She points to the dashboard clock, which reads 5:29. "One minute early." She leans over, kisses him, her left hand gently grazing his cheek. "Needed to make sure we had time for that."

He wants to ask just how much closer to her he could wind up living, but that's not a conversation to start with only a few seconds left on the clock. He settles for kissing her again before he opens the door. "See you tonight?"

"Oh, yeah. You need to play me some more songs."

He gets out, leans down into the car one more time. "Thanks for the ride, m'lady."

"My pleasure, m'liege."

Calvin walks backwards to the door, so he can watch Melli drive off, feeling much better than the last time he watched her car disappear. When she's out of sight, he turns around and summons the energy to wave hello to Little Ron, who is waiting to let him in: Little Ron does love being in charge of the keys. Calvin makes it to the register to clock in by 5:32, close enough to being on time that no one will hassle him.

Little Ron is talking to him. He can hear the excited tone in Little Ron's voice, so he knows it has to be about baseball or Burger Buddies. Calvin nods as he walks away, trying to fake an appropriate level of enthusiasm. Annie gives him a big smile as he passes by. She's rolling

5:27 AM

out biscuit dough, humming a tune. He can never recognize the melodies she hums to herself and suspects she's just making them up. Which makes her a songwriter, he supposes, even if he never hears the same tune more than once. Does it count as songwriting if you never remember the song you wrote?

He can't tell if it's the leftover buzz from the pot brownies, or the thrill of having Melli be there when he woke up, or the relief of revealing King Cal, but it feels like a different world since the last time he clocked in. The smells are the same, the lighting gives everything the same unhealthy glow, but it all feels less — less permanent? Less real? It feels more like some temporary world he is just visiting, so he is less bothered by the fact he is here.

He wonders if Grady has listened to the King Cal songs. He must have, because Calvin would have listened to a secret musical project of Grady's. He tries not to think about what it means, that Grady has probably heard the songs but not sent him any reactions, but he can't stop his brain from running through the possibilities. Could be Grady didn't like them, so he didn't want to say anything, or it could be Grady loved them — and didn't want to say anything.

He's surprised to focus his eyes and see he's still walking past Annie. What was in those brownies? Time is clearly still very elastic. Flour on her apron, she is turning to shout something at Ron. He suddenly has a flash of them repeating these actions long after he is gone, and the image reassures him, even as it makes him feel slightly melancholic for the two of them.

The verse he finished last night starts playing in his head as he walks toward the cooler. *Words / Hide from me / Climb up into my head / And lay down / Then they won't make / another sound.* He pulls the heavy handle and smiles to himself. The escaping air feels especially cold, reminding him of walking in New York, that one time he and Grady went on Christmas break. "Who the fuck invented cold, anyway?" Grady had asked, and Calvin had said, "Phil Collins," the answer they gave whenever someone or something needed to be blamed.

After the initial shock, the cold air feels good as it washes over his cheeks. He lingers for a second in the doorway, then steps inside. He wasn't going to look at his SoundCloud account until he got home, but he can't wait any longer. Takes out his phone, opens the app, checks his library stats. Each King Cal song has increased by ten to fifteen listens since yesterday. Those can't all be Melli, so Grady must have listened. And unless he remembered the number of plays wrong — and, standing alone in a Burger Buddies cooler, before the sun is even up, he can admit he is slightly obsessive about tracking plays — Grady also seems to have listened to the songs more than once. Maybe he even told other people in One Four Three.

The idea is terrifying. But also kind of exciting.

Before he puts his phone back it buzzes with a message from Alex.

ok just tell me ur not mad she liked it rite?
Not mad, he writes back.
And she liked it?
She liked it.

He starts gathering what he'll need for the drive-thru cooler.

Yay yay. So u ok?
OK just tired
Any word from G
No
He will write soon
Maybe.

He puts the phone in his pocket and carries out the milk crate of supplies. Annie is still humming to herself, and the two Rons are watching something on the office computer. Another advantage of being at the same crappy job for a while — as long as you get your shit done, everyone else leaves you alone.

When he gets to the drive-thru he puts down the crate, opens the window and returns to the thread with Alex.

5:27 AM

Dont u have to work
I am working dont u have to sleep
I am sleeping
Go to school today
ok mummy
And thanks
?
For helping last night and for that perfect drawing

Alex sends another heart emoji, the second in six hours. The world really has changed.

He starts moving supplies from the crate to the drive-thru cooler. If he can work efficiently for ten minutes and get everything done he will have five minutes to drink some coffee before the orders start. Muscle memory in action: he pays no attention to what his arms and legs do, leaving his mind free to think about how long he'll have before needing to move (Downy would have to give some sort of notice), what it will take to get Alex to Atlanta for a visit (his parents would probably agree, but they won't help pay for a plane ticket — maybe a bus), how far down the road the bus carrying Grady has gone (halfway to their Chicago gig, probably) and what Grady thinks about the music (if he can be not angry long enough to give it an honest listen).

The chorus for the song he worked on last night plays on a loop in a far corner of his brain. *I'm so full of empty / Drowning in the air / I think I'm going to stop / But I don't know where.* He's waiting for the chorus to magically slide into a new verse; he needs at least one more, and knows that the key to each verse will be starting with a single syllable, sung in isolation, to lay out the theme. His brain throws "Hope" at him but he literally laughs out loud at that idea. Then he apologizes for laughing at his brain, because "Hope" made him think of "Home," which could work.

Once again, his brain was closer to being correct than he gave it credit for.

KING CAL

When the drive-thru is fully prepped he stretches, yawns. Little Ron is wiping down his sandwich station, whistling "Copacabana." Annie is leaning on the register, staring off into space. Big Ron is sitting back in the office, watching something on his phone. As crappy as this job is, the four of them have at least managed to carve out spaces where no one asks for anything from anyone else.

Calvin pours himself a cup of coffee and carries it over to the drive-thru window. He slides the window open, then takes his first sip, grateful he can have free coffee on a day he is so tired and so broke. Leans his head out into the morning air, inhales — it's early, so the air is still almost fresh, the grease-mixed-with-car-emissions smell not yet strong.

He reluctantly moves his head back inside, pulls out his phone: 5:58. He opens his message thread with Grady, knowing he will feel better if he sends something. *Sorry shit got weird talk later.* He hopes it's enough to show he wants to keep talking, but not so much that Grady thinks he's changed his mind.

He downs the rest of the coffee in three big swallows, an aging fighter snorting a line of coke before a bout. After he finishes, his eyes focus better, and the sounds around him are sharper. Off in the distance something has just been lowered into the fryer, which means yesterday's grease smell is now awake and starting to drift through the kitchen. He remembers he has a recording of "Full of Empty" on his phone, and having a reward waiting for his break will help make the first half of his shift bearable. There should be a phone call with Melli on break, too, something he was not sure would ever happen again just four hours ago.

Calvin stretches, looks up at the CCTV, turns on the reader board. There is always one waiting. Lights on, engine idling. It's only 5:59, but this morning he feels like offering some poor soul a small act of grace.

"WelcometoBurgerBuddiesmayItakeyourorder."

Acknowledgements

It's not often that I can document the exact date a novel was born, but I can with *King Cal*. On January 11, 2021, one of the online book groups I joined during lockdown met via Zoom to discuss *Mrs. Dalloway*. I had always been afraid of Virginia Woolf, but I loved that book, and we had a great conversation about time and memory and the way thoughts from the different parts of our life drift through our head all day long. Mrs. Dalloway certainly never had to worry about money, though, and I wondered how that would have changed her story. Twenty-four hours in the life of a struggling fast-food worker, for example, could show what it was like when worries about money were added to all those other thoughts.

Three-and-a-half years later, I finished *King Cal*. Many thanks to Nancy Gardos, Aric Green and Circe Link for the many great conversations about books and life, and for all the encouragement every time I updated my progress on Calvin's story. This novel would not have existed without them.

I need to thank my writing group: Beth Gylys, Jessica Handler, Sheri Joseph and Susan Rebecca White. They read early versions of chapters and offered great insights. Jessica gets an extra round of applause for reading multiple versions of the whole thing and for being the world's best accountability partner.

My early readers provided crucial feedback. Vivian Alvarez helped me figure out the best name for Melli as well as the backstory for her parents. Bob Fenster's thoughts on many different drafts have once again made my book much better. Mark Doyon sent along pages of detailed notes and pointed out, as he did with my last book, bodies that I had not yet found. My other beta testers included Marsha Cornelius, Pam Dittmer, Craig Dorfman, David Epstein, Richard Fulco, Kevin Glenn, Tricia Brock Madden, Roger Trott, Jason Warburg and Kim Ware. Insights from each reading brought me closer to the finish line.

When it was time for copy editing, Tess Hoffman proved perfect for the job. A good copy editor can perform the same magic for a novel a good mixer does for a recording. It's still your song, but now it sounds clearer, sharper — more like the song it is supposed to be.

Most of the original music in the story has been written and recorded. It can be heard at **kingcalsoundtrack.bandcamp.com**. Since I don't write music, I needed help from my friends. Kris Hauch produced the sounds for Calvin's songs, and there are not many people with the skill set for such a job, never mind the enthusiasm and patience to write seven songs. He also provided the voice for Grady, while Paul Melançon was just right for King Cal. Jeff Jensen wrote the music for One Four Three's songs and played acoustic guitar. I've known Jeff since we were in third grade, and the idea that we get to keep making music all these years later is beyond amazing.

We assembled a crack team of musicians to create that infamous One Four Three wall of sound, so thanks to Allen Broyles for playing keyboards, Rob Gal for bass work and Halley O'Malley, Paul and Jeff for singing backing vocals. Jonny Daly played electric guitars on those tracks and mixed them. Joel Boyea then sprinkled everything with magic mastering dust. Detailed credits as well as websites for all these talented musicians can be found on the Bandcamp page in a cool booklet.

Speaking of that cool booklet: It was designed by Michael Hunter. Sarah Marks eagerly accepted a request to create a logo for a fictional burger chain. Kristina Juzaitis designed the book's text and came up with the perfect cover for it.

Ira Robbins was kind enough to answer a random e-mail from some random writer in Georgia, which led to Calvin finding a home at Trouser Press Books. Considering all the years I read the magazine, back when I devoted more of my life to making music than writing, I was thrilled at the opportunity. Ira has been an enthusiastic supporter and a great editor; the book has become much better as a result.

Finally, none of this could have happened without the support of B, O & T. Thank you for being the perfect family for me to come home to.

Peter McDade
January 2025

About the Author

Peter McDade spent fifteen years traveling the highways of America as the drummer in the rock bands Uncle Green and 3 lb. Thrill, releasing a half-dozen albums on various major and independent labels. Raised in New Jersey, he now lives with his family in Atlanta, where he teaches at Clark Atlanta University. *King Cal* is his third novel.

Photo: Vivian Alvarez

Made in the USA
Middletown, DE
13 April 2025